LORD SEBASTIAN'S *Secret*

JANE ASHFORD

sourcebooks
casablanca

Published by Sourcebooks Casablanca, an imprint of Sourcebooks, Inc.
P.O. Box 4410, Naperville, Illinois 60567-4410
(630) 961-3900
Fax: (630) 961-2168
www.sourcebooks.com

Printed and bound in Canada.
MBP 10 9 8 7 6 5 4 3 2 1

Praise for *What the Duke Doesn't Know*

"Ashford soars to new heights of literary excellence by creating a cleverly conceived story that takes all the traditional elements readers love in Regency romances and making everything seem refreshingly new. Throw in Ashford's gift for creating intriguingly different characters and her dry sense of humor, and you have a romance worth cherishing."

—Booklist

"A unique heroine... Remarkably well-written... She is quickly becoming one of my favorite romance heroines. Every bit of *What the Duke Doesn't Know* is a joy to read, and I can't wait for the next book in this, so far, fabulous series."

—Fresh Fiction

"Enchanting...a charming romance."

—RT Book Reviews, 4 Stars

CONTENTS

THE MAJOR'S WIFE

by Merline Lovelace

To my sister, Pam,
who shared my love of books and also wore the
uniform of her country. I'll miss you so much....

> "Half a league, half a league,
> Half a league onward…"

> —The Charge of the Light Brigade
> By Alfred, Lord Tennyson

Chapter One

London
May 1856

Bright afternoon sunlight poured over Lady Marianne Trent as she devoured the *Times*. The report of the ceremonies held to mark the signing of the peace treaty that ended—finally!—the war in the Crimea held her riveted. Her fingers trembled, rattling the thin sheets of newsprint. She was sure the names of faraway places like Sebastopol, Balaklava, and Inkermann would remain forever seared on her soul.

Detailed newspaper accounts of the three-year war had both enthralled and appalled Lady Trent, as they had most of Queen Victoria's subjects. For the first time, intrepid correspondents and photographers had followed Her Majesty's troops right onto the battlefield. They'd captured in stirring prose and stark, black-and-white prints the gallantry of the British and French allies fighting to free Turkey and the Balkans from the czar's dominance. They'd captured, too, the agony of broiling summers and long, freezing winters, when incompetent leadership, hopelessly confused supply lines and the shameful lack of medical care caused twenty times more British casualties than Russian cannonballs.

One such account of the desperate medical situation had spurred Florence Nightingale to sail to the Crimea with nursing matrons she herself had recruited. Another had plunged Marianne Trent into the relief efforts here at home that had earned her such approbation from her sister-in-law and admiration from the slender young man seated across the tea table.

She lifted her gaze to him now, hope and anguish warring in her breast. "Oh, Edmond! It says here our troops should set sail for home immediately now that the treaties have been signed."

"Since the ceremony was only a formality, I

would guess some contingents are already under way." Removing his spectacles, Edmond St. Just set about polishing them with a handkerchief. "The first troop transports could dock at Portsmouth any day now...if they haven't already."

"Surely we would have heard if they had!"

"One would think so," he replied in a carefully neutral tone. "Lady Beatrix has such excellent connections at the War Office, after all."

Marianne bit her lip. After three years of marriage, the mere mention of her sister-in-law still roused sadly conflicting emotions.

As a new bride, five minutes in Lady Beatrix's company was enough to put her in a quake. She'd been so young then, so pathetically eager to please the formidable matron who'd plucked her from the dreary, tomblike silence of her great-aunt's home in Shropshire, rigged her out in silks and laces and engineered a brilliant match with her brother, Major Sir Charles Trent.

For weeks after the fashionable wedding, Marianne had trembled every time Lady Beatrix sailed into the palatial Trent town house she still considered her personal domain. If the servants had moved a side table or a flower vase as much as inch or two, the new bride could count on receiving a basilik-like stare and a glacially polite request

that the object be returned to its proper position immediately.

Yet those first whirlwind weeks of marriage had been so thrilling in every other way, Marianne hardly minded her sister-in-law's overbearing ways. When her husband wasn't off readying his troops for war, his commanding presence filled both the town house and the days with bustling activity.

And the nights… Dear Lord above, the nights! Heat rose in Marianne's cheeks just thinking about the hours spent in the major's arms.

She was under no illusions about why Charles had married her. He'd been charmingly honest with her from the start of their brief courtship. After almost forty years of peace following the defeat of the French at Waterloo, war once again loomed on the horizon. It was his duty to ensure the Trent line didn't die on some distant battlefield. In exchange for Marianne's hand in matrimony, he'd offered her his name, an escape from her dreary incarceration in Shropshire, and a secure future should anything happen to him in the far off Crimea.

Lady Beatrix had been brutally honest, as well. As she informed Marianne, her brother had buried his heart years ago with the laughing, beauteous Miss Warrington, whom he'd loved with all the

passion of his youth. Now, he sought merely to make a sensible match with a lady of good standing and good breeding.

As a result, Marianne had gone to her nuptial bed a girl determined to do her duty. Unfortunately, she'd left it a woman quite hopelessly in love. To one long starved for affection, her husband's teasing smiles, skilled kisses, and quite magnificent body had awakened in her a passion she'd never dreamed she possessed.

Then Charles had sailed for the Crimea, his wife had miscarried his heir some four months later, and Marianne's shimmering fairy-tale world had shattered.

Now…

Now she bore her sister-in-law's strictures with calm fortitude. She had her work and Edmond's friendship to sustain her. It was enough. It would have to be enough.

Still, the idea that Charles might be on his way home at this very minute made her foolish heart ache. Blindly, she stared at the newsprint and tried not to think of what might have been.

Edmond's mild voice called her back from the brink of despair. "Did you read the article about the new medal the War Office has proposed?"

Dislodging the painful lump in her throat, Marianne shook her head. "No, I didn't. Where is it?"

"On page four, I believe."

The earnest young scholar and ardent reformer slipped his spectacles back onto his nose and tucked his handkerchief into his pocket before circling the back of the settee. Leaning over his hostess's shoulder, he pointed out the tidbit of information she'd missed.

"In the Queen's honor, they intend to call it the Victoria Cross. It would constitute England's highest award for valor."

"If such a medal is approved, Charles's regiment should be among the first to receive it," the major's wife avowed fiercely. "Dunbar's Dragoons lost one in every three men at Balaklava."

To this day, Marianne couldn't recall the accounts of that brutal engagement without a shudder. According to the dispatches, the Light Brigade had been ordered to attack the Russian-held heights above the city. Six hundred and fifty mounted cavalry launched a gallant, desperate charge that took them straight through a murderous crossfire of cannon. Most had died within minutes. The survivors, Charles among them, had been forced to retreat after reinforcements failed to arrive. Maimed, injured, their faces blackened by gunpowder and eyes burning from smoke, they'd hacked and sabered their way back to the allied lines.

That the Light Brigade been showered with

praise for their magnificent charge in no way mitigated the magnitude of their losses...or the fact that they had failed to secure the heights. As Charles had sardonically noted in a letter home some months later, the Balaklava clasp on the Crimean War medal constituted the only military decoration the British government had ever awarded for ignominious defeat.

"Dunbar's Dragoon's lived up to their motto of *Truth and Valor* that day," Edmond remarked.

"Yes," Marianne murmured. "They did."

She might have known her friend would note the catch in her voice. "I'm sorry it pains you so to talk of him."

Helplessly, she looked up at him. Her ash-brown hair, styled in a knot of the corkscrew curls so fashionable at the moment, spilled over the shoulder of her glazed taffeta afternoon dress.

"I... I..."

Reaching down, he took her hand and gave her fingers a sympathetic squeeze. She was still struggling for the words to describe her wrenching emotions concerning her husband when the sound of booted footsteps rang outside the parlor door.

"I'll show myself in, Dunston."

"Yes, sir." The butler's reply was shot with unabashed happiness. "It's good to have you home at last, sir!"

"It's good to *be* home."

Marianne's heart stopped in her chest. She couldn't breathe, couldn't move. Her fingers clenched Edmond's as the parlor doors slid open. Stunned, she stared at the tall, broad-shouldered figure in scarlet-and-green regimentals who passed through them.

"Charles!"

The cry ripped straight from her heart. Thoughts of her husband might generate raw, painful doubts. Seeing him again after so many long months produced only a wild, splintering joy.

"Hello, Marianne."

The major strolled into the sunny room where he'd bid goodbye to his bride all those months ago. Keen blue eyes fringed by gold-tipped lashes flicked from her to Edmond and back again.

"I hope I'm not disturbing you," he said in his deep, rich baritone.

"Disturbing me?" Her voice rose to a squeak. "Dis*turbing* me!"

Snatching her fingers from Edmond's, Marianne sprang up. Newspapers scattered across the rose-patterned carpet as she rushed forward, hands outstretched, hooped skirts swaying.

"Oh, Charles, I don't believe it! We were just speaking of you!"

Tucking his black fur shako under his arm, the

major caught her hands in his and bent to brush a kiss across her knuckles. When he raised his head, his blue eyes smiled down at her.

"Were you?"

"Yes! Edmond and I were discussing the account of the treaty signing in the *Times* and... and..."

Her voice failed. Tears stung her eyelids, blurring the face that had haunted her dreams. He was thinner than she remembered, but every bit as handsome. No, more so! When first she'd met him, she'd thought him so big, so splendidly elegant in his regimentals. Now, with his tawny hair bleached by the sun, his skin tanned almost nut-brown, and his face honed to lean planes, he looked like the war-tested officer he was.

Or perhaps it was she who'd changed. She'd viewed him through a girl's bedazzled eyes three years ago. Adoring. Trusting. So astonished that he'd chosen a meek little country miss as his bride that she'd barely been able to stammer out two sentences in a row. She was almost as incoherent now.

"After reading about the ceremonies, I knew... I hoped... I thought you must come home soon. Now you're here," she finished breathlessly.

"Now I'm here," he echoed with one of the teasing smiles that had captured her heart. "Didn't

you get my note? I dashed one off to both you and Beatrix when our ship docked at Portsmouth."

Mutely, Marianne shook her head.

"It appears I caught you all unawares," he said lightly. Dropping another kiss on her knuckles, he released her hands and addressed the man watching them in silence. "You, I would guess, are St. Just."

"Yes, sir."

"I've heard a great deal about you from my wife's letters...and those of my sister."

Marianne's soaring joy faltered, dipped, plummeted to the earth like a wounded dove. She could imagine the scathing terms Beatrix must have used to describe the radical intellectual who, in her considered opinion, had led the new Lady Trent seriously astray.

"I've heard a great deal about you, too, sir." Squaring his shoulders, Edmond came around the settee and held out his hand. "It's an honor to meet the hero of Balaklava."

"My men are the heroes," Charles answered gravely, taking the proffered hand. "Not I."

"The dispatches indicated otherwise."

"Even eyewitness reports can become hopelessly distorted during battle. It would be a mistake to believe everything one reads in the dispatches."

"In letters, too, I would guess."

Charles leveled a quick, hard look at the younger man. Unblinking, Edmond returned his stare.

Marianne's stomach sank. Her friend was only trying to help, she knew. Attempting to blunt the acrid disapproval Lady Beatrix had no doubt relayed to her brother. Yet Edmond of all people must know Marianne would have to answer to Charles herself.

Her husband appeared to think so, too. He dismissed the younger man with the same brisk efficiency he might one of his staff officers.

"You'll excuse us, I know. My wife and I have a great deal to catch up on."

Edmond's gaze went to Marianne. She dipped her head in a small nod.

"Your servant, sir. Lady Trent."

Executing a stiff bow, he withdrew. The parlor doors slid closed behind him with a snick. Silence descended, broken only by the call of a pie seller on the street outside and the shrill of finches feasting in the mulberry trees that shaded the windows.

Nervously, Marianne wiped her hands down her wide, hooped skirts. Beneath her steel-ribbed corset, her breasts rose and fell in swift, painful little breaths. It had come. The moment she'd anticipated for so many sleepless nights. The moment she'd dreaded. Now she must unburden her soul of the secret she'd carried for too long.

She was staring at the uniform that filled her vision, trying to summon her courage, when her husband's deep voice broke the quiet.

"I'm sorry about the babe, Marianne."

"I, too," she whispered.

She wouldn't cry. She *wouldn't!*

"Beatrix wrote that you had a hard time of it."

A shudder racked her. The scarlet uniform blurred before her eyes, became a sea of blood. It had soaked her, drenched the mattresses, stained the carpet. She hadn't thought she could lose so much life fluid and survive. Nor had the surgeons Beatrix had rushed to her bedside.

Given a choice, though, Marianne would have gladly exchanged her life for the babe's. She'd wanted a child so badly, had longed to lavish on its small, warm person all the love she'd lost when her own parents had died in a carriage accident and left her consigned to her great-aunt's care. She'd longed, too, to present Charles with the heir he'd wed her for.

A knuckle curled under her chin and tipped up her head. The regret in the blue eyes gazing down at her slashed into her soul.

"I'll never forgive myself for the way I rushed you into marriage, knowing my regiment was shipping out. I'm sorry I left you alone for so many years."

Pride kept her tears at bay. Pride, and the knowledge that he couldn't possibly regret their hasty wedding any more than she now did.

"You didn't know the war would last so long. No one expected it to."

"No one ever does."

His grim reply stiffened her resolve to have it all out now, before she lost her nerve.

"I wasn't alone these past years. I made friends here in London and..." She took in a steadying breath. "And I have my work."

"Ah, yes. Your work." He traced the line of her jaw with his thumb. "You mentioned it in your letters, but very modestly. If even half of what Beatrix wrote is true, I understand you've become quite absorbed in your efforts to help the children orphaned by the war."

"Not just by the war. We've expanded our efforts a bit."

And "absorbed" hardly described her passionate activities on behalf of the urchins she and Edmond rescued from London's slums. Some had been left in the care of relatives when their fathers marched off to war, only to be lost or abandoned in the streets. Some had been stolen from their homes and sold to brothels to satisfy disgusting sexual desires. Many, like the tousle-haired imp currently residing in a cozy attic bedroom above-

stairs, were small and quick and much sought after as pickpockets and chimney sweeps.

If Marianne couldn't hold a babe of her own in her arms, she could at least help these poor, wretched children find homes. And if some of her methods for rescuing them put her outside the pale of the Royal Society for the Care of Foundlings and earned her frequent scolds from Lady Beatrix, so be it!

Thoughts of the restraints her sister-in-law had attempted to impose on her banished Marianne's incipient tears and replaced them with a militant sparkle. The face she raised to her husband was very different from the one he'd tipped up so gently a few moments ago.

His thumb stilled. Surprise showed in his blue eyes. Surprise, and a sudden spark of interest.

She should have moved away then, taken a step to the side and eased away from his strong, warm hand. Instead, she stood like a starstruck fool while his palm slid to her nape.

"I swore I wouldn't do this," he murmured, slowly pulling her forward.

She'd made the same vow. Yet she could no more stop him than she could herself. One kiss, Marianne thought desperately. Surely she was allowed one brief kiss!

She'd counted without the hunger fed by three

years of yearning. At the first brush of his lips on
hers, it leaped to life, raged through her veins,
drowned out the warnings her mind tried to shout.
With a sound halfway between a sigh and a moan,
she rose up on tiptoe and fit her mouth to his.

Hellfire and damnation!

The moment his lips covered hers, Charles realized his mistake. He'd sworn to move cautiously
during this long-delayed reunion. Had ridden up
from Portsmouth determined to sort through the
mess he'd made of things by plunging Marianne
so precipitously into matrimony.

He'd known at the time she was too young, too
sheltered. She'd barely tasted of life, buried away
all those years in that dank, echoing tomb her
great-aunt called a home. Yet she'd shown herself
so eager, so trusting. Her clear, moss-green eyes
had pulled at him, just as her cloud of toffee-
colored hair had made his fingers itch to bury
themselves in its fragrant mass. And her mouth, so
soft and full, had tempted him.

The way it did now...

Warm and eager, her lips moved under his. Despite the promises he'd made to himself during the
voyage home, despite every stricture of common
sense, Charles tossed aside his shako, wrapped his
arm around her waist, and pulled her up against
him.

Instantly his senses registered the fact that the slender bride he'd wed three years ago had matured in more than just age. Her layers of petticoats and corseting couldn't disguise the ripe curves straining against him.

This wasn't the blushing, untutored miss he'd taken to bed and gently teased and taught. Nor the young wife who'd professed herself content to curl up in a chair by the fire and listened in wide-eyed silence while he instructed her in the matters that would require her attention after he sailed for war.

This was a woman grown, with a woman's need quivering through the body pressed against his. A hunger Charles hadn't felt—hadn't expected to feel!—since the day Abigail Warrington died ripped through him.

He was no callow youth, however. He hadn't spent sixteen years in uniform and three years in the Crimea without learning how to bridle such unruly passions. Slowly, with a reluctance that staggered him, he raised his head.

His wife stared up at him, her eyes so wide and bruised with emotion that Charles damned himself all over again.

"Marianne, sweetheart, it's all right. We'll sort through…"

"We must talk."

Her ragged whisper sliced into him like a Rus-

sian saber. "We will," he said calmly. "Come and sit beside me."

"No." Tugging free of his light clasp, she retreated a step or two. "I'm so glad you've come home safely, Charles. I've prayed... I've been waiting... I must—"

"You must what?" he asked prompted gently when she stumbled to a halt.

Anguished green eyes looked straight into his. "I must ask you to divorce me."

"Theirs not to make reply,
Theirs not to reason why,
Theirs but to do or die..."

—The Charge of the Light Brigade

Chapter Two

The major stared down at his wife, stunned by her outrageous demand.

Beatrix had warned him in her letters that all was not well at home. Marianne's increasingly stilted communications had hinted at some inner perturbation. Yet Charles hadn't realized things had reached such a desperate pass that his wife would call down the stigma of divorce on her head.

She'd be an outcast, a social leper in this age where the Queen's relationship with her beloved Prince Albert allowed only one view of marriage. Husbands might seek less homey, more exotic

pleasures in the brothels that flourished in all parts of London. Wives might take a lover if they were utterly discreet and allowed no hint of scandal to get about. But divorce carried with it lifelong disgrace...particularly for women, as the law allowed only men to put aside their wives.

"Do you love him so much?" he asked, searching her heart-shaped face.

"Him?" Confusion blanked Marianne's expression, followed swiftly by a rush of red. "I see Beatrix has kept you well apprised. I presume by 'him' you refer to Edmond?"

"Yes."

"I *do* love him very much." Her chin tipped. "As a friend and trusted companion."

The major's brows snapped together. Neither his wife's letters nor those of his sister had mentioned any other possible suitor, but he could think of no other explanation for her extraordinary request.

"Is there someone else, then?"

Anger flared in her eyes, sparking a green flame her husband had never seen in them before.

"You could not know me very well if you would ask such a question!"

"It appears I do not know you at all," he said slowly.

Her chin came up another notch. "I have never dishonored you or my marriage vows."

In the few seconds it took for the echo of her ringing declaration to fade, Charles weighed her words and the brief insight he'd gained into her character. In those same few seconds, he decided she spoke the truth. He'd spent too many years in command to doubt his instincts when it came to judging character. Although the shy, stammering young girl Beatrix had brought to his attention three years ago hadn't roused in him the same wild passion as the willowy beauty he'd once loved with all his soul, he'd recognized immediately Marianne's intelligence and integrity.

Those qualities had led him to ask her to be his wife. The same qualities now shone as bright as a warning beacon in her eyes. Although logic and the dire hints in his sister's letters might dictate otherwise, he believed her. Which didn't explain her astonishing demand of a few moments ago.

"If you don't wish to be free to marry St. Just, would you care to tell me what this talk of divorce is all about?"

The fire faded from her eyes. Turning away, she moved to the windows. Sunlight burnished her hair to honey-gold and shimmered on the taffeta covering her stiff-set shoulders.

"I can't conceive any more children."

Her voice lacked all inflection, yet the message

it delivered drove into Charles like a Bengal lance. Stunned, he stared at her rigid back.

"When I lost the babe, the physicians tut-tutted and patted me on the head and assured me I could have others. All but one physician. He didn't spare me the truth."

The pain buried in her flat, colorless recital twisted his gut. Striding across the room, Charles gently turned her around.

"Why does this particular physician's opinion carry so much more weight than all the others?"

"It's not just his opinion. I know."

"How?"

A tide of red washed through her cheeks, but she refused to look away.

"A woman's body is governed by certain rules of nature. When those go awry... When she doesn't follow the moon's courses for months on end..." She lifted her clenched fist, let them drop. "She knows."

Charles swore a silent, savage curse. His conscience was already heavy with the knowledge that he'd rushed a young, inexperienced female into marriage after scant weeks of courtship. Yet the guilt that had nagged at him on intermittent occasions during their long years apart was nothing to the withering self-disgust that now seared him. He'd done his damnedest to impregnate his inno-

cent bride, then callously left her alone to suffer through the loss of a babe and the wrenching aftermath.

"I'm sorry you or Beatrix didn't write me about this. I would have arrived home better prepared to offer you comfort."

"Beatrix doesn't know," his wife said stiffly, surprising him once again. "I thought it a matter for discussion only between you and me. As is the matter of our divorce."

"Let's speak no more of divorce. We swore vows to each other, Marianne. We'll hold to them."

"No, Charles. You were truthful with me from the start, for which I'll always be grateful. There's never been any talk of love between us. Only respect and... And affection."

"Respect and affection are more than many couples bring to a marriage. You were well pleased to accept them three years ago."

"That's true, but our circumstances have changed considerably since then. You wanted an heir. I..." Her gaze wavered, turned away, came back to his. "I wanted what your name could give me."

He sensed there was more, but she plunged ahead before he could decide what.

"We struck a bargain, you and I. One I can no

longer honor. I must insist that you institute divorce proceedings."

"Well, I don't intend to do anything of the sort," he said roundly, "so you may put the idea out of your head."

"I cannot. You must see that I—"

"The subject is not one I wish to discuss further."

Any of his subordinates would have recognized his tone and retreated immediately. His wife, Charles discovered to his complete surprise, possessed a good deal more pluck than his battle-hardened staff.

"Very well," she replied after a moment of heavy silence. "We shall not speak of it further. You may confer with your solicitor and *he* can then explain to me what must be done to terminate our union under the eyes of the law. Now if you'll excuse me, I'll go instruct the servants to draw a bath. You must wish to refresh yourself before dinner."

Head high, hoops swaying, she glided out, leaving Charles torn between exasperation and amazement. He wasn't used to having his orders questioned, much less rebutted. That his slight, slender wife would dare to do so astounded him.

He shoved a hand through hair bleached by the Crimea's fierce sun. This wasn't at all the home-

coming he'd envisioned. Despite Bea's hints and warnings, he hadn't expected to walk into his home and find that twig, St. Just, mooning over his wife. Nor had he anticipated the hot, unbridled lust that had slammed into him when he'd taken Marianne in his arms.

All these months he'd thought of her only as the shy, blushing bride he'd tutored so carefully in the ways of love. That she could rouse such passion with one kiss astonished him...almost as much as the fact that she'd shrugged aside his refusal to consider her absurd demand for a divorce.

He was still pondering the unexpected turn of events when he heard the rattle of carriage wheels on cobblestone. His batman, he guessed, arriving from the ship just docked at Portsmouth with his gear. Charles strode into the hall and reached the stairs as the footman opened the door. Instead of his military aide, a matron dressed in rustling black bombazine sailed through the portal. She caught sight of him on the stairs and gave a joyous shriek.

"Charles!"

With a fond smile, he went down to greet his sister. She was twelve years his senior, fashionably stout, and, in her own words, very comfortably widowed. She was also so overbearing in her ways that her even closest friends shied away from her on occasion. But no one—Charles least of all—

could deny that she held her only sibling in the deepest affection.

"I was in Somerset! I came as soon as I returned home and read your note." She held out her hands, her face wreathed in smiles. "My dear, dear boy, how good it is to see you."

"And you, Bea."

Dodging the towering plumes on her bonnet, Charles bent to kiss her cheek. Arm in arm, they went back up the stairs to the parlor. Beatrix stopped just inside. A fierce frown knit her brow as she cast an eye around room.

"Don't tell me Marianne wasn't at home to greet you! If the dratted girl has gone haring off on another of her rescue expeditions, I shall be all out of patience with her."

"'Dratted girl'?" Charles lifted a brow. "Are you speaking of my wife, Bea?"

The cool inquiry raised a flush in his sister's cheeks. "You can't know all Marianne's been about in your absence," she began portentously.

"No, of course I can't, but I'm sure she'll tell me when we've had time to talk."

The warning wasn't lost on Beatrix. Her cheeks went from bright red to an alarming purple hue. As much as he loved her, Charles had learned as a youth how to spike her guns when necessary.

He'd never been the kind to let anyone, including his forceful sister, ride roughshod over him.

Despite the clear warning, however, Beatrix forged ahead. She was obviously laboring under strong emotion.

"As much as it pains me, I must speak to you about Marianne and Edmond St. Just."

"There's no need, I assure you. St. Just was with my wife when I arrived home."

"After I told him he shouldn't call here anymore? The insolent puppy!"

"That was my thought exactly," Charles drawled, recalling the scene he'd interrupted. He'd trained enough subalterns to recognize the signs of a lovesick swain when he saw them. Whatever St. Just's feelings for his wife, however, Marianne didn't return them in kind. That much she'd made clear.

"St. Just *is* a pup, Bea, and one who doesn't particularly concern me. Nor need he concern you."

Even the strong-minded Lady Beatrix couldn't fail to heed that steely note of command. She bit back whatever she'd intended to say and folded her lips into a tight line.

Now, Charles thought on a wry note, he'd have to teach his surprisingly strong-minded wife to heed his commands, as well.

"Marianne's upstairs," he informed his sister, smiling to take the edge from her scowl. "Come, take off your bonnet and shawl and be comfortable while I ring for Dunston to bring some sherry. You must tell me all the latest London happenings before I go up to change for dinner. You'll join us, won't you?"

Four hours later Charles acknowledged silently that he'd committed two rather serious tactical errors since returning home.

The first was sweeping Marianne into his arms when common sense and three years of separation dictated a more deliberate pace for their reunion. The second was inviting Beatrix to join them on his first evening home.

He recovered from his second blunder easily enough. After changing into black britches, a snowy linen shirt, and one of the cutaway frock coats his valet had kept under covers during his long absence, he entertained his wife and sister with a highly edited account of his years in the Crimea. Despite the obvious constraint between the two women, the meal passed tolerably well.

Correcting his first blunder took a good deal more effort, however. The lust that had slammed into Charles earlier that afternoon kicked him square in the gut again each time his glance strayed

to the woman seated opposite him at the long, polished table. Her dinner gown of emerald silk bared her shoulders and gave him a tantalizing glimpse of high, full breasts. In the glow of the oil lamps, her skin carried the luster of pearls. Her maid had dressed her brown hair into a complicated arrangement of tiny braids and long, shoulder-teasing curls that caught her husband's eye whenever she moved.

All through dinner he battled urges better suited to a barnyard than to an elegant room papered in flocked red damask and hung with portraits of long-dead ancestors. Thus it was with a feeling of decided relief that Charles escorted Beatrix downstairs to her carriage after an hour spent over sherry in the library.

"Good night, dear boy."

"Good night, Bea."

"See that you get some rest," she instructed, settling a carriage rug over her lap to ward off the April chill. "You must be exhausted after your long journey."

Rest was the last thing on his mind when Charles remounted the stairs. His body tightened painfully at the thought of the woman he'd left in the library.

What a damnable coil, he thought wryly. He'd returned home expecting to gently reintroduce his

bride to the delights of the marital bed. Now here he was, hard as the regimental flagpole and aching for a sensual, seductive wife who wished for a divorce.

He could blame no one but himself for this tangle, Charles admitted. As Marianne had so bluntly reminded him, he'd been honest about his reasons for marrying her. A puffed-up sense of his own worth had translated into a desire for a son or daughter, someone to carry on the Trent line if he didn't return from the Crimea.

Against all odds, he *had* returned. He'd survived three years of war, pestilence and disease...not to mention the suicidal charge at Balaklava. And now, for reasons he had yet to fully understand, the primitive need to propagate that had spurred him into marriage seemed to have lost its potency.

Perhaps those three brutal years had taught him the preposterousness of such human vanity, Charles thought. He'd seen so many of his comrades die. Wondered at the incomprehensible twist of fate that would cause a cannonball to sever one man completely in two while another merely knocked a second trooper from his horse, leaving him dazed but otherwise unhurt. Making a mark on posterity now seemed far less important to Charles than simply living each day as it came.

And each night.

His muscles constricted at the thought of the hours ahead. Surely he could convince Marianne to forget this absurd notion of divorce. Explain that he viewed the matter of an heir differently now than he had three years ago. His step quickening, he thrust open the library doors and strode inside.

It wasn't his wife he found curled up on the hump-backed sofa, however, but a golden-haired nymph of four or five with limpid blue eyes and a thumb stuck firmly in her mouth.

"Hello," he said, checking his stride. "Who are you?"

The thumb slid out. "My name isth Annie," she replied solemnly. "Who are you?"

"I'm Major Trent. I live here."

"No, you don't."

"I've been away," he explained, smiling, "and only just returned. Aren't you up rather late?"

"I couldn't thleep."

She must be the daughter of one of the servants. No doubt she'd slipped away from her quarters below-stairs to warm herself by the library's fire.

"Shall I ring for Dunston?" Charles inquired, certain the butler would know which parent to deliver the sprite to. "He'll take you back to your room."

She regarded him through wide, guileless eyes, then held up her arms. "I want you to take me."

Charmed, Charles bent and scooped her up. "Let's find your mama or papa, shall we? I'm sure they'd be quite worried if they knew you were gone."

He'd taken only a step or two when the sound of running footsteps thudded outside the library. A scrawny youth of eight or nine streaked into the room. When he caught sight of Charles and the girl cradled against his chest, he skidded to an abrupt halt. His jaw thrust out belligerently.

"'Ere! Wot you doin' with 'er?"

"I beg your pardon?"

"Put 'er down," the boy demanded. "Annie ain't for the loikes of you."

Charles hadn't spent his youth in London without sowing a few wild oats...or catching an occasional glimpse of the city's dark, twisted underbelly. Before he could respond to the suggestion that he harbored foul intentions toward the cherub in his arms, the thin-shanked youth bunched his fists and advanced into the library.

"Put 'er down."

"Save your gunpowder for another shot," Charles advised the bristling youth calmly. "I don't intend the girl any harm."

"So you say."

"I assure you, my word is good."

"So you say," the towheaded urchin repeated

ominously. "'Ho are you, will you answer me that?"

"I'm Major Trent," Charles explained for the second time in as many minutes.

"Wot? Be you Lady Trent's major?"

"I am," was the dry response. "And you are?"

"'Enry 'Ackett.'"

"Well, Henry Hackett, suppose you tell me why you and Annie are up so late and in my library?"

"I can answer that."

Marianne's agitated reply turned all eyes to the library door. She rustled in on a swish of taffeta to relieve Charles of his clinging burden.

"Annie, darling, you promised you'd stay abed."

"I wasn't thleepy."

"Yes, well, perhaps some warm milk will help. Henry, would you be so kind as to take Annie up to her room? I'll have one of the maids bring her…and you…some milk."

"I don't s'pose you'd make that beer?" the boy asked hopefully.

"No, I wouldn't."

"Cor, I thought as much." His thin shoulders lifted in a resigned shrug. "Com'on then, Annie."

Grasping the girl's hand, he started for the door. He took a step or two, then halted and glanced down at the angelic face of his companion.

"'Ere!'' he declared. "You'd better give the major whatever you dabbled from 'im first."

A thumb worked its way into the girl's mouth again.

"Go on, now," Henry admonished sternly. "Give it back."

With a soulful look, the girl turned and retraced her steps. She stood before Charles with wide eyes swimming in innocence. When she opened her fist, it held the diamond stickpin that had clasped his snowy neckcloth in place not two minutes ago.

Disbelieving, Charles glanced down at his stock, and then at Marianne. His wife heaved a sigh.

"I do apologize. Annie's trying. Truly, she is. But her fingers are so nimble and quick, she can't seem to resist practicing her, er, skills."

"She's one o' the best," Henry confirmed with a grin. "I couldn't do better meself if I was to try me hand at the nimble-namble, which I don't intend to, mind you. It's a shop-dodger, I am."

With that obscure comment, he ushered the girl out of the room. Charles watched their progress as far as the curving staircase before turning to his wife.

"A shop-dodger?" he inquired politely.

"I'm not exactly sure *all* the term encompasses. I'm told it involves snatching wares from merchants' shelves and making off with them."

"I see." Thoughtfully, Charles reinserted the stickpin. "You will explain, won't you, why a pickpocket and a street thief are at present making their home here?"

Flushing, his wife pleated her skirts. "I intend to send them down to the home farm to join the others. Edmond...Mr. St. Just...is making the necessary arrangements."

"I see," he said again.

So this was the work she'd taken up, the cause she'd written him about. The obsession Beatrix had railed against. He wondered how these city bred children would take to life on the farm that supported the Trent country estate, but kept the thought to himself.

"Just out of curiosity, how many 'others' have you sent down to the home farm?"

Her forehead creased. "I believe the last count was seventy-three."

"Seventy-three!"

"It may only be seventy-two," she amended hastily. "Henry has made the trip several times. Unfortunately he has a tendency to run away. He claims he can only squeeze milk from a goat for so long before he gets a hankering for city soot."

"I don't doubt it," Charles drawled, his earlier question answered.

Her flush deepened at his sardonic tone. Lifting her chin, she answered with a bite of her own.

"You needn't think that I have allowed the children to run wild and harass your crofters. Nor have I squandered your estate to provide for them, as Beatrix so often suggests. I've found homes for most, and pay for the upkeep of the rest with the very generous allowance you arranged for me before you left."

"Neither the crofters nor the financial arrangements concern me," Charles protested.

"Something obviously does. May I inquire what?"

"You, Marianne."

Crossing the room, he curled a knuckle under her chin and tipped her face to his. She'd changed so much. A stranger gazed back at him. Mature, self-possessed, and so damnably attractive that Charles felt his lower extremities go tight once more.

"You just gave me a hint of what you suffered after you lost the babe," he said. "Do you have the strength for this kind of crusade?"

"Yes," she answered quietly. "I do. I'm not the girl you left three years ago. Nor the wretched, despairing woman who sobbed for weeks after she lost her babe. I've found a purpose. One that will sustain me after our divorce."

Charles gritted his teeth. In a tone of absolute finality, he spoke his last word on the subject.

"There will be *no* divorce."

> "Cannon to the right of them,
>   Cannon to the left of them,
>   Cannon in front of them
>   Volleyed and thunder'd…"

—The Charge of the Light Brigade

Chapter Three

"Thank you, Hardwick." With a smile, Charles dismissed the valet who had served him since boyhood. "I'll finish undressing."

The venerable Hardwick folded his lips in disapproval of the free and easy ways Charles had adopted during his years abroad. He might even have forgotten himself so far as to protest if the third party in the bedroom hadn't advanced across the Brussels carpet, bristling with indignation.

"Here, where are you going with the major's boots?"

The short, barrel-chested trooper who had served Charles as batman in the Crimea glared at his rival. Not ten minutes after Dragoon Sergeant O'Donnelly's arrival with the major's baggage, the two loyal servants had taken one look at each other, fired a few opening salvos, and promptly declared all-out war.

"I'm taking the boots to polish them," Hardwick replied in his loftiest manner, "as I do every night Sir Charles is in residence."

Sergeant O'Donnelly squared his shoulders. "Well, you kin just take yer mits off them leathers. I've been shining 'em these past three years. I ain't about to let no civilian ruint 'em by rubbin' on some bluidy mixture of cork soot and champagne."

"Champagne is for those who know no better," Hardwick sniffed in disdain. "I use a blacking of my own recipe."

"D'ya now?" Still pugnacious, the banty-legged sergeant followed the valet through the door. "And what's in this here recipe, boyo?"

"That, my good man, is no concern of yours."

Charles paid little attention to the exchange of fire as he tugged off his neckcloth and tossed it aside. When a blessed silence filled the spacious, high-ceilinged chamber, his gaze went to the door that connected his bedroom with his wife's.

The panel was made of stout English oak, intricately carved and polished to a gleaming luster. It should have muffled all sound, but Charles had developed the acute hearing of a man who'd spent the past several years sleeping with one ear tuned for the distant booms that signaled an imminent barrage. Despite the thick panel, he picked up the murmur of Marianne's maid counting out brush strokes.

In his mind's eye, he saw his wife's long, shining sweep of honey-brown hair. Saw, too, the sloping curve of her shoulders above a lacy nightdress. His groin tightened as memories of the few nights they'd shared a bed crowded into his head.

He'd handled her so gently, soothing her maidenly fears, taking great care to not bruise her creamy flesh. She'd been an apt pupil, but when Charles had thought of his young bride during his long years in the Crimea, it was with a sort of affectionate regard.

There was nothing affectionate in the heat that raced through him now. And it wasn't his young bride he craved with an urgent, growing desire, but the woman Marianne had become.

"Good night, ma'am."

"Sleep well, Judith."

The indistinct murmurs drew him toward the closed door. He'd tell Marianne about his change

of heart, he decided, his pulse quickening. Explain how siring an heir had lost its significance in the senseless carnage of war.

They were wed. They would hold to their vows. Maintain a household. Share their lives. Share a bed, too, if Charles could convince her to pick up where that gut-wrenching kiss had left off this afternoon.

Wrapped up in the remembered heat of that kiss, he almost missed the snick of her bedroom door opening again. A plaintive cry stopped him with his hand on the brass doorknob.

"I had a bad dweam."

Annie. A grin tugged at his mouth. He'd have to watch his pockets until Henry Hackett and the little girl departed for the home farm that supported the Trent country estate.

"Oh, poor darling," his wife murmured. "Here, climb under the covers. You can sleep beside me."

The major's grin slipped. He stood with one hand on the knob, his body tight and aching. The sound of scampering feet made him slowly, reluctantly retreat.

That Marianne would share her bed with a street urchin added another surprising dimension to the woman he'd married. That she *wasn't* sharing it with her husband kept Charles awake long after the rest of the household had settled into slumber.

Somewhere in the dark hours of the night he realized that his slender, stubborn wife had completely erased the memory of the vibrant beauty he'd once loved to distraction. It was Marianne's piquant face that filled his mind. Marianne's emergence from her chrysalis that fed his curiosity as much as his desire.

After several sleepless hours, Charles concluded that he'd have to do what he hadn't had time to do during his hurried courtship. He'd have to woo his wife.

Like the well-trained cavalry officer he was, he clasped his hands under his head and began to lay out a campaign. He'd take matters slowly, he determined. Learn her likes and dislikes. Gift her with flowers and pearls and other trinkets to wear at the parades and balls that would commence to celebrate the victory in the Crimea once the full contingent of troops returned home. In the process, he'd convince her to lay aside her absurd idea of a divorce once and for all.

Unfortunately, his military duties precluded immediate implementation of his campaign to win his wife. Charles spent the next week attending to the thousands of tasks incumbent on an army's return from war.

Dunbar's Dragoons, founded when Lord Dunbar

raised mounted levies for service in 1685, boasted a long and distinguished record of service. They'd fought in the American Colonial Wars from 1776 to 1779. Had won honors at Talavera and Salamanca before participating in Napoleon's final defeat at Waterloo in 1815. Had faced formidable artillery at Allwal in 1848, during the Second Shikh Wars. But the regiment had suffered some of its most grievous losses in the Crimea.

The troop transports arriving each day at Portsmouth disgorged hundreds of wounded and ill men who required immediate care. Their mounts demanded similar attention. Supplies and equipment had to be inventoried and marked for repair or replacement. Troops recruited specifically for service in the recent war grumbled constantly in the way of all soldiers while they awaited demobilization.

Charles left the house early each morning and returned late each night, when his duties allowed him to return at all. Whatever hour he arrived home, he found a cozy fire and a collation of cold pheasant or chicken breast, rare roast beef, fruit tarts, and cheeses waiting for him in the library. Even more welcome was the selection of ale, wine, and prime French brandy.

He assumed his ever-efficient butler had arranged the late-night feasts until he strolled into the library a little before midnight the second week

after his homecoming. He found Marianne standing by the tray. Busy with her thoughts she didn't
glance around.

"Perhaps we should include one or two of the
beef and kidney pies Cook made for Henry, Dunston. They're not quite as good cold, but perhaps
the major will like them."

"If Cook made them, I'm sure I will."

Startled, she spun around. A quick flush stained
her cheeks. That she'd mistaken his approach for
that of the butler was obvious. What wasn't as obvious was the reason for that intriguing blush.

Tossing his hat aside, Charles unbelted his
sword. It landed on a chair with a clatter that echoed loudly in the late-night quiet.

"I thought you were Dunston," she said, recovering her composure, although a delicate rose hue
still tinted her cheeks. "I sent him to instruct Cook
to cut into a fresh wheel of Stilton. This wedge has
dried a bit."

The mere thought of the creamy, blue-veined
cheese produced at dairies in Derbyshire and
Leicestershire had been enough to make Charles
salivate during the worst months of deprivation at
the front.

"Lord, I missed the bite of the blue," he confessed, reaching past her to crumble off a morsel.
"Stilton's always been my favorite."

"Yes, I know."

He paused with the tantalizing bit halfway to his mouth. "How could you know that?"

"From your letters." Her lips curved. "You made mention of it rather frequently."

The small, surprisingly sweet smile started a quiver in his stomach, but the fact that she'd gleaned such an accurate understanding of his tastes from his hurried letters humbled Charles. Just a few nights ago he'd decided to resort to a formal campaign to get to know his wife. Marianne, apparently, hadn't required any such elaborate plan.

"I tried to send you a wheel of Stilton, you know."

"No," he replied, hitching a brow, "I didn't."

"I sent a number of boxes packed with foodstuffs and warm stockings and other items, as a matter of fact. I guessed they never reached you when you didn't remark on them in your letters."

"The re-supply lines to the front became somewhat tangled."

With that magnificent understatement, Charles dismissed the nightmare of incompetence that had stockpiled ton after ton of desperately needed food and equipment at Balaklava harbor, while British troops just six miles away starved and stole out in the dark of night to retrieve spent cannonballs.

"I read about the supply problems in the dispatches in the *Times*," Marianne said, shaking her head. "However did we win the war, when the foodstuffs we shipped in rotted right there at the harbor or were stolen by dockhands and sold to the very Russians you were sent to fight?"

As impressed by her detailed understanding of the situation as by the fierce light that sprang into her eyes, Charles grinned.

"Perhaps you should come along the next time we go on the march," he teased. "Several of the officers' wives follow the drum and very ably manage their husbands' mess."

Popping the bit of cheese into his mouth, he bent to examine the rest of the tray's contents and missed the look of longing that swept over his wife's face.

He wasn't serious, Marianne knew, but she couldn't imagine anything more thrilling than accompanying her husband on the march. The long years spent catering to her cantankerous old great-aunt had subdued her spirit, but hadn't destroyed it by any means. She allowed herself a few, magical moments to imagine stepping ashore beside her husband in some faraway port, filled with exotic sights and scents, before reality crashed down on her. By the time the major sailed off with his

regiment again, Marianne would no longer be his wife.

Ignoring the pain that lanced into her breast, she forced a smile. "You've yet to recover from the last campaign. I sincerely hope you don't embark on a new one anytime soon."

A small smile played at the corners of his mouth. "Do you?"

Wondering at the odd look he gave her, she dipped her head and bid him good-night. "It's late, and I know you must be fatigued as well as hungry. I'll leave you to enjoy your supper."

"Won't you join me? If you're not too tired?"

"Well…"

"I should enjoy the company…and the chance to hear of Henry Hackett's latest exploits," Charles added casually. "From your remarks a moment ago, I take it the boy hasn't yet left for the home farm? Or has he been and already made his way back?"

"No, he hasn't left yet." A sigh escaped her. "Nor has Annie. They both profess a rather decided preference for the city instead of the country. Poor Dunston has been kept busy returning various pocket watches and coin purses to the staff these past days, I can tell you."

Laughing, Charles tucked a hand under Marianne's arm and led her to the sofa. She felt his

touch right through the sleeve of her gown. The flush that had warmed her when he'd strolled into the library unannounced surged through her again, even hotter than before.

"Here, sit down and tell me how you found these orphans of yours."

"Edmond...Mr. St. Just...knows someone in the city. This gentleman, er, refers the children to us."

Actually, the bearded, haggle-toothed ruffian Edmond dealt with did more than just "refer" the waifs he handed over. He demanded extortionate amounts for them. Marianne would have denounced the villain to the Royal Society for the Care of Foundlings months ago if her previous experiences with that august body hadn't proved the futility of such reports. The directors of the well-intentioned society were overwhelmed with the needs of the children already in their care and hadn't the time or the funds to deal with those Marianne rescued.

"I must admit," Charles said with a lift of one brow, "the magnitude of your involvement with this cause surprised me..."

She stiffened, bracing herself for the stinging rebuke that always followed his sister's stilted words of praise for her work.

"And makes me quite proud," he finished calmly. "Would you care for a plum?"

Marianne's mouth opened, closed, opened again. Her husband evidently took that as assent, for he lifted a section of the succulent fruit he'd just peeled and placed it between her lips.

Still stunned, she nibbled at the sweet pulp, then pulled back with a flush of mortification when juice dribbled along her lower lip.

"How clumsy of me," Charles muttered, his gaze fixed on her mouth. "Here, take my napkin. Or better yet..."

His voice trailed off. Mesmerized by the shimmering ripeness of her lips, he slowly bent his head.

Pull up! his mind shouted. *Retreat!* This wasn't part of his campaign strategy. He was supposed to ride slowly over this rough ground. Get to know his wife in bits and pieces. Woo her with jewels and picnics in Hyde Park and slow, sensuous waltzes, as he should have done three years ago.

Like any good tactician, however, he'd been trained to adjust to unexpected variances in circumstance. Without a qualm, he modified his plan of attack to take advantage of the situation that presented itself.

Marianne's heart slammed against her ribs as her husband traced the trickle of juice with his tongue.

She sat as if turned to stone, unable to move, unable to think while sensation after sensation bombarded her.

His scent filled her nostrils, rich and redolent of wool, leather and horse. The late-evening bristle on his cheek scraped against her chin. Through a loud buzzing in her ears, she heard his breathing go ragged. Without knowing quite how it happened, the plate he'd been holding landed on the carpet and she was in his arms.

With a hoarse cry, she tore her mouth from his. "No, Charles! I cannot... The divorce..."

"Damn this talk of divorce!" He took her chin and brought her face to his with something less than his usual gentleness. "Listen to me, Marianne. I've had time to think since I returned. You were right. I won't deny it. I married you with the intent of fathering children and leaving my mark on posterity."

The blunt admission stilled the wild clamoring in her blood. Her heart aching, she tried once more to turn away. He held her still, forcing her to meet his gaze as well as to listen to his words.

"Such human vanities lose their importance when one charges through a barrage of cannonballs."

"Wh-what do you mean?"

"The Crimea taught me many lessons. Not the

least of which was to live the hours God gifts us with and not worry about the weeks and months to follow."

"You say that now." Despair welled up from deep inside her. "But when the thunder of the cannons has faded from your memory, you'll think differently."

"Will I?"

"Yes! You must! Don't you see, Charles? You're just experiencing the euphoria of having survived against all odds. You charged straight into the jaws of hell and battled your way out again. Now... Now you must get on with the everyday mundane business of living."

Much to her consternation, her impassioned attempt to make him see reason produced an unexpected reaction. A rakish grin tilted his lips.

"What I have in mind at the moment, my dear wife, can scarcely be described as mundane."

She pushed out of his arms and scooted to her end of the sofa, too wrought-up to let his laughing charm sway her this time. "You'll view things differently a year from now."

The teasing light left his eyes. "Then we shall have to wait a year and see, shall we not?"

"I beg your pardon?"

Setting his own jaw in lines every bit as stub-

born and determined as hers, he rose and held out
a hand to help her to her feet.

"If you wish to wait twelve months to resume
our marital intimacies, we shall wait twelve
months."

"You cannot be serious!"

"Indeed, I am."

She stared at him in openmouthed confusion before fleeing the field in disorderly retreat. Charles
was left to retrieve his dropped plate and contemplate twelve months of celibacy.

Thoroughly disgruntled, he stabbed at the Stilton
and muttered a string of oaths entirely unsuited to
an officer and a gentleman.

"Stormed at with shot and shell,
  Boldly they rode and well,
  Into the jaw of Death,
  Into the mouth of Hell..."

—The Charge of the Light Brigade

Chapter Four

Had he taken leave of his senses? Had a cannon-ball grazed his skull and left him prey to deliriums? Did Charles really intend for them to maintain a facade of marriage for another year? Could she bear it if he did?

The questions tumbled through Marianne's whirling mind in the days that followed. One repeated itself with ever-increasing urgency.

Had Charles been speaking the truth when he said he'd changed his views on posterity, or was he merely attempting to make the best of his wife's failings?

The Queen's frequent accouchements and very pointed views on matrimony set the standard of the times. Rather conveniently ignoring her own regal status, Victoria made it clear that women had a single, overriding purpose in life, and that was to fulfill the destiny of their womanhood. The knowledge that she couldn't bear a child cut Marianne to her heart. More to the point, the certainty she couldn't bear *Charles* a son or daughter left her swinging between resignation and despair.

The fact that her heart pounded every time she heard the door slam and his boot heels ring on the oak stairs didn't matter in the least. Nor did the ridiculous leap in her pulse when she heard him moving about in the bedchamber adjoining hers long after they both should have been asleep.

Her only refuge, her only check on her wild emotions, was her work. And her first order of business, she decided after returning the undergardener's watch to the wooden-faced butler one afternoon, was to find homes for Annie and Henry Hackett. The two had become quite inseparable, which added another challenge to her task.

"If you don't wish to live in the country," Marianne said firmly after the city-bred Henry balked yet again at making the trip to the home farm, "you must tell me what trade you wish to learn.

Perhaps I can apprentice you with a good, kind master.''

"Cor, that's easy,'' the boy replied, brightening. "I've always 'ad a 'ankering to jiggle the bits.''

"'Jiggle the bits'?''

"You know, slap the 'indquarters.''

Faintly alarmed at the image that evoked in her mind, Marianne looked to Annie.

The girl slipped her thumb from her mouth. "He wants to drive carriage horthes.''

"Oh. Yes, of course.'' She eyed the boy doubtfully. "Do you have any experience handling horses?''

"I knows just how to 'andle 'em,'' he bragged, puffing out his thin chest. "I once jumped on coal seller's 'ack what was kickin' up the traces. Give 'im a good thump atween the ears with an ax pole, I did. Dropped 'im in his tracks.''

Somehow, Marianne didn't think that particular technique for quieting a fractious equine would impress a stable master.

When she said as much to Charles during the late-night supper that had somehow become a routine for them both, he laughed.

"Actually,'' he confessed ruefully, stretching out his long legs, "that's pretty much the technique we resort to with the mules hitched to our ammu-

nition wagons and artillery caissons. Quite often they require a good thump to make them move forward during a barrage.''

"I should require more than a good thump," Marianne responded with a shudder. She could only imagine the courage it took to hold the line amid a hail of cannonballs, or worse, draw sabers and charge straight for artillery pieces spewing smoke and death.

Resolutely, she banished all thoughts of war. They didn't belong here, in the peaceful quiet of the night. It was late, well after midnight. Silence blanketed the house beyond the library, a comfortable companionship reigned within.

Always a light eater, Marianne rarely indulged in heavy cheeses or sweets at meals or tea. Yet during the past week she'd developed a surprising partiality for the rich, pungent Stilton and iced cakes. She was quite content to nibble at both while the major lounged beside her and satisfied his much heartier appetite.

"Why don't I take Henry to regimental barracks with me tomorrow?" her husband suggested casually. "I'll show him about a bit, then Dragoon Sergeant O'Donnelly can take him down to the sheds where the mules are stabled."

"Oh, Charles, *would* you?"

Grinning at the note of desperation in her voice,

he nodded. "Perhaps one of the stable sergeants and his wife might be convinced to give the boy a home."

"They'd have to take both Henry and Annie," she warned. "The two have become quite attached."

Her husband lifted a brow, but forebear to comment on the potential difficulties of finding a home for a child who couldn't seem to comprehend the impropriety of nipping off with every pretty bauble that caught her eye.

"I'll see what I can do."

Marianne could only wonder at the difference between brother and sister. She'd endured so many strictures from Beatrix about her work, particularly after she lost the babe. Attending to these street urchins was not a task suited to a lady of her station, Beatrix had announced. It would drain her energy as well as her resources, and interfere with her duties as Lady Trent. Consequently, Marianne had learned to withhold details from her sister-in-law, and had made only the briefest mention of it in letters to her husband.

That Charles not only supported her efforts, but was prepared to take an active role, warmed her from head to toe. The glowing look she cast his way came straight from her heart.

"Thank you."

Her husband's sun-bleached brows snapped together. To her surprise, he deposited his plate on the tea tray with something of a snap.

"Don't look at me like that."

She blinked, taken aback by his gruff command. "I was merely trying to express my gratitude."

"I don't want your gratitude."

"Do you not? I beg your pardon, then." Stung, she rose and dusted down the front of her skirts. "I'll leave you to finish your supper. Good night, Charles."

With a muttered oath, he surged to his feet and detained her with a hand on her elbow. "Wait. Please. That was badly said of me."

She arched a brow.

"Badly said, but true," he admitted slowly. "Gratitude is the last thing I want from you."

Pardonably annoyed and just a little hurt that he would reject her heartfelt thanks, she cocked her head. "Then perhaps you'll tell me what it is you *do* want from me?"

He hesitated for so long that she began to think he wouldn't answer.

"I wish you would tell me," she pleaded, quite serious now. "You refuse to divorce me. You…you say it no longer matters whether a child comes of our union. Tell me, Charles, what is it you want of this marriage? Of me?"

A rueful light came into his eyes. "I thought I'd made my desires in this matter of our marriage quite clear."

"Not to me!"

"Then let me speak more plainly. I want you in my arms and in my bed, Marianne."

Her jaw sagged. Her heart thumped so loudly the echoes thundered in her ears.

"I want to trail kisses from your mouth to the hollow of your throat," he said outrageously, following the proposed path with his gaze, "to your breasts."

Little pinpricks of fire stabbed into her skin everywhere his glance lingered. Her nipples hardened and pushed against her corset stays with painful insistence.

He lifted her hand, brushed a kiss across her knuckles. Lamplight glinted on the gold threaded through his tawny hair. When he raised his head, the look in his blue eyes melted her bones.

"I want to slide into your welcoming warmth, Marianne. Lose myself in your heat."

She stood stock-still, her hand in his. He cocked a brow, awaiting her answer.

"That..." she gasped when she could breathe again. "That is plain speaking, indeed."

Charles went to bed quite satisfied with the progress he'd made toward achieving his objective.

It wouldn't take a year. The dazed look in Marianne's eyes when he kissed her good-night at her bedroom door gave him hope that he'd storm her defenses well before twelve months had passed.

The next morning dawned cold and drizzly, but Charles rose with a general feeling of optimism. Even the rather daunting results of Henry Hackett's introduction to the regimental stables failed to dim his good spirits.

The stable master set the boy to work mucking out the stalls of the mules, generally considered by cavalry troops as misbegotten, contrary and ill-mannered animals in no way comparable to their noble cousins, the horse. Nimbly dodging yellowed teeth and lashing hooves, Henry cheerfully answered each attempt to remove a piece of his anatomy with a solid whack of his shovel.

Unfortunately, he wasn't as adept at dodging the disapproval of other stable hands.

"He swears like a Russian," one corporal reported when the major stopped by to check on the boy. Since Dunbar's Dragoons weren't particularly known for their gentle speech, such censure was severe indeed.

"He don't take orders well, neither," another chimed in, casting a dark look at the unrepentant newcomer.

"I don't take no notice of empty-'eaded crows

what flap their beaks is what 'e means,'' Henry replied, bristling. "I asks you, Major, what sense do it make to shovel droppins from the stalls, dump 'em in a pile, then shovel the 'hole mess into a 'oneywagon? Dump the 'orse apples in the wagon first off, I says!''

Charles agreed, but he couldn't take this raw recruit's side in the matter of mule droppings over that of his corporals. "I would prefer you learn the army's ways of doing things before you decide to how best to change them.''

"But..."

"Yes?"

The icily polite query quelled Henry on the spot. Muttering, he went back to his shovel.

"It'll take a few knocks up aside the head to get that one into shape,'' the stable sergeant predicted.

"No knocks,'' Charles ordered sternly. He suspected Marianne wouldn't appreciate an application of rough-and-ready army discipline. "Just keep him busy and out of mischief.''

The stable sergeant took him at his word. As a consequence, the boy who accompanied Charles back through the streets of London later that evening wore a weary and thoroughly disgruntled expression. He also carried a scent so ripe that the major's first instruction to his long-suffering butler

was to see that a bath was drawn immediately for Master Hackett.

"'Ere!" Henry protested, thoroughly alarmed. "That weren't no part of the bargain!"

"I beg your pardon?"

The boy flushed, but held his ground. "Lady Trent promised I'd only have to dunk me spuds once a week!"

"Did she?"

Quite sure Marianne had never couched any promise in those particular terms, Charles nevertheless gave him the benefit of the doubt.

"Then we'll have to refer the matter to Lady Trent. Let's go upstairs and find her, shall we?"

The butler cleared his throat. "Begging pardon, sir. Lady Trent's not at home. She left nearly an hour ago, as a matter of fact. And..." He cast a speaking look at his employer. "Lady Beatrix has called. She's waiting in the upstairs parlor."

"Blimey!"

Evidently more alarmed at the prospect of coming face-to-face with the major's sister than dunking his spuds, Henry promised he'd set himself all right and tight and skipped down the hall toward the kitchens.

Charles mounted the stairs, wondering where Marianne might have gone. As she'd told him upon his return, she'd made a good number of friends

in London. Invitations to dinners and musicales had poured in once word of the major's arrival spread, but his duties precluded acceptance of such invitations until all troop transports had docked and his men were cared for. Marianne refused to attend, as well, insisting that she didn't wish to establish a public facade until private matters were settled between them.

Perhaps she'd changed her mind, he thought, or had gone to visit a particular friend.

In that, he was correct. As an indignant Beatrix informed him when he joined her in the parlor, his wife had indeed paid a visit to a *very* particular friend.

"I couldn't believe my eyes when I saw her, Charles. There she was, as bold as brass, climbing out of a hackney coach. A hackney coach!"

The fact that Marianne had chosen to hire a vehicle rather than take one of the Trent town carriages seemed to offend Beatrix almost as much as her sister-in-law's destination.

"She wasn't even wearing a veil," the widow fumed. "She climbed out, crossed the cobbles, and knocked on St. Just's door without so much as a peacock feather to hide her face."

"Perhaps she feels there's no need to hide her face," Charles said coolly.

"When she calls at a bachelor's lodgings?

Come, come, my dear brother! You must know what a scandal it would cause if word of such doings got about."

"Then you shall have to see it doesn't get about."

At the unmistakable warning, his sister's already high color deepened. "You may snap my head off if you wish to, Charles, but the fact remains that I saw your wife pass through Edmond St. Just's door more than an hour ago and she has not yet returned home. I *knew* there was more to their association than these scruffy orphans they rescue from the streets!"

"Bea..."

"Just what do you intend to do about the matter?"

"I intend to take off my uniform, get out of these boots, and enjoy a comfortable supper," he replied with a look that warned his sister she was treading a fine line. "You're welcome to join me...if you can refrain from casting what we both know is only a friendship in a light that isn't worthy of either you or my wife."

"Well!"

With a huff, she declined his invitation.

Despite his dismissal of his sister's suspicions, Charles found himself watching the clock with increasing impatience as the evening wore on.

The drizzle outside turned to a dark, pelting rain. Inside, the cheerful little fire in the library did nothing to lighten the major's mood.

Hellfire and damnation!

Had he frightened Marianne with his talk of wanting her in his bed? Or worse, driven her in desperation right to the arms of that young twig, St. Just? Was she so determined to end their marriage that she'd sacrifice her honor, her reputation?

No! Whatever else his wife might do, she wouldn't dishonor her vows. Charles knew her well enough by now to believe that with a deep, unshakable confidence.

So why the devil hadn't the confounded woman returned home? What were she and St. Just up to?

The answer arrived just after ten o'clock, delivered by a rain-drenched, snaggle-toothed individual of indeterminate age and gin-laden breath. When he rattled the knocker on the front door of the town house, the footman refused him entry. The ruffian's repeated pounding and vociferous protestations brought Dunston hurrying to the scene.

After a heated exchange, during which the individual identified himself as Cecil Bloodworth and reiterated his demands to see Major Trent, the butler delivered a crumpled note to the library. Dunstan's face was folded into lines of grim dis-

approval when he returned to escort Bloodworth upstairs.

Charles stood ramrod straight beside his desk. The greasy, hand-scribbled note lay on the blotter.

"Where is my wife?"

The man's avid glance roamed the rich tapestries, the leather-bound volumes, the crystal decanters shimmering in the firelight.

"Aren't you going to offer a bloke a nip o'coffin varnish to warm his innards afore gettin' down to business?"

"Where is my wife?"

"At what, er, you might call a gentlemen's club in the Rookery."

The mere mention of the district bounded by Bainbridge, George, and High streets made the major's blood run cold. The triangular area was honey-combed with garbage-strewn courts and blind alleys, inhabited by the poorest of the poor and the degenerates who preyed on them. With only one way in or out, the Rookery was a retreat for thieves and criminals in hiding from the police. It was also a favorite haunt of men seeking the perverse and often dangerous thrills found within its reeking, malodorous confines.

Even before Charles had left for the Crimea, the newspapers had been trumpeting the need to erase this blight on London's good name. That Marianne

was now being held in a brothel located on one of those dark, teeming streets started a cold sweat at the base of the major's spine.

"Walked right in, she did," Bloodworth related, shaking his head in mingled disgust and disbelief. "Her and this young idiot with her, comin' to rescue one o' the girls from the clutches of evil, if you kin believe it."

Charles could.

"We hustled her into a private room. Her and the gentleman what come with her."

"How much?"

With another regretful glance at the crystal decanters, Bloodworth commenced serious negotiations.

"Two hundred pounds."

"Fifty," Charles countered coldly.

"Fifty!"

"Twenty-five when you escort me to this club, another twenty-five when we return safely."

"You don't think much of yer wife!"

"On the contrary. It's you I don't think much of."

Thoroughly disgruntled, Bloodworth caught the bills Charles tossed his way.

"Yer wife would fetch more 'n this in just one night on her back at the club," he muttered, wetting a filthy thumb to count the banknotes. "A prime little piece like that would— Awwwk!"

With a strangled screech, he dropped the money and grabbed frantically at the hands wrapped around his throat.

"Let's be clear on one thing." With a flex of his biceps, Charles lifted the man right off his feet. "If my wife has suffered any harm—*any* harm, you understand—you won't live to see sunrise."

> "Flashed all their sabres bare,
>   Flashed as they turned in air,
>   Sab'ring the gunners there,
>   Charging an army, while
>   All the world wondered..."

> —Charge of the Light Brigade

Chapter Five

"**M**ajor!"

With a clatter of boots on the polished wood of the hall, Henry dashed from the kitchen regions to intercept Charles on his way out the door.

"I needs to talk to you."

"Not now, Henry."

"But..." The boy skidded to a halt, his eyes rounding when he spotted the individual at the major's side. "'Ere! Wot you doin' in the West End, Bloodworth?"

"Do you know this man?" Charles asked sharply.

"'A course. He's the bloke what sold me 'n Annie to yer missus." Aggrieved, Henry glowered at the gap-toothed ruffian. "Fetched a good sum, too, 'e did, and didn't even slip me so much as a tuppence on the deal! Wot are ya doin' here?"

A sudden look of enlightenment crossed the boy's face.

"You gots 'er!" he exclaimed, his fists bunching. "You gots Annie, don't you? Now you're tryin' to sell 'er back to the missus."

Charles shot him a hard glance. "Annie's missing?"

"That's wot I come to tell you. Cook says she was a snifflin' over being scolded for liftin' another watch. Took 'er doll and the straw bonnet the missus bought 'er and slipped out the garden gate this afternoon, she did."

Two pairs of accusing eyes swung to Bloodworth. He spread his palms wide.

"Is it my fault the girl ran away? Or that yer lady is so anxious to buy 'er back?"

Cursing, Charles hustled his visitor to the door. Henry scrambled after them.

"Stay here," the major ordered.

"You can't trust this one to get you in an' out of the Rookery!" the boy protested. "He'd sell 'is

own mother fer a nip of gin. I knows the place like the back of me 'and. I'll get you where you needs to go.''

Charles hesitated for less than a heartbeat. As he'd learned only too well in the Crimea, charging headlong at the enemy without proper reconnaissance or reinforcements was as dangerous as it was stupid. He'd tucked a pistol into the waistband of his trousers before leaving the library and ordered Dragoon Sergeant O'Donnelly and an armed footman to augment the driver of the carriage he'd ordered brought around. Still, Henry's knowledge of the enemy's terrain might provide an added advantage.

''Alright. Let's go.''

Signalling Bloodworth to proceed him, Charles stepped out into the dark, foggy night. Pools of light from the gas lamps glowed blurry and dim. Rain drizzled through a thick, enshrouding fog. Grimly, he gave the driver and his small troop a few terse instructions, then climbed into the carriage.

The distance from the affluent West End to the Rookery might be measured in a few miles, but to those who inhabited its rabbit-like warrens, the teeming district was another world entirely. To the woman who paced the narrow, stuffy upstairs bed-

room of a house located on a street with no apparent name, that world was strange and rather sinister.

The tang of spilled gin and a sickly sweet odor Marianne suspected was opium rose from the faded carpet. Shutters nailed tight over the windows trapped the odors inside. Frayed tapestries decorated the walls. An odd-shaped mirror reflected the light from a tarnished, if once elegant, chandelier.

Strange thumps and an occasional shrill of high-pitched laughter came through the papered walls. What sounded very much like the bleat of a sheep produced a long series of giggles, followed by a muffled groan. Frowning, Marianne cast a glance at the child on the bed. Annie slept the sleep of the innocent, her thumb tucked firmly in her mouth.

Across the room, Edmond St. Just sat dejectedly in the room's only chair. A bloodstained strip of linen torn from Marianne's petticoat was wrapped around his head. His spectacles rode at a drunken angle on his nose. One lens was cracked and webbed as though spun by a spider. Fingering the lump under his bandage, he heaved a morose sigh.

"I shouldn't have allowed you to come with me."

"Really, Edmond, you must stop berating your-

self. You didn't 'allow' me to accompany you. The decision was mine.''

"Your husband won't see it that way. Not only did I lead you into this—'' he threw a look of loathing around the garish room ''—this den of iniquity, I let that villain downstairs get the jump on me.''

Marianne suspected the fact that the young scholar had dropped like a stone after being hit from behind bothered him more than anything else.

"Well,'' she declared bracingly, ''Annie is safe and that's all that matters.''

"If you think any of us is safe, you don't know all that goes on in places like this.''

"And you do?''

"No, of course not,'' he replied, coloring, ''but I've heard rumors.''

"So have I, and I prefer not to dwell on—''

She broke off, her brows lifting as another long *baaa* came through the walls. "What*ever* is that farm animal doing in an upstairs bedroom?''

The red in Edmond's cheeks turned to brick. He was still fumbling for an answer when a deep voice sounded just outside the door.

"Which room, damn you?''

With a glad cry, Marianne rushed across the room. "Charles! We're in here.''

"Open the door,'' the major commanded to

whoever accompanied him. A silence ensued, followed by a startled oath.

"I've lost the key!"

"No tricks, Bloodworth. You'll open this door within the next five seconds or I'll use you as a battering ram and knock it down."

"I don't have the key, I tell you! It was right here in my pocket and now it's gone."

"'E's stalling," a youthful voice pronounced in disgust. "'E just wants more money. Give 'im five in the chops, Major, and 'e'll find the key right enough."

With a disgusted command to step aside, the major shouted a similar warning through the stout panel. "Stand clear, Marianne."

Hastily, she scrambled back. A moment later something heavy slammed against the panel. There was a second thud, then a third. The wood around the lock splintered.

The door flew open and crashed against the wall. The noise startled another bleat from the unseen sheep and woke Annie. Blinking, the girl scrambled upright on the bed just as Charles charged in.

Marianne flung herself at her husband's chest. "You can't imagine how happy I am to see you!"

"Yes," he replied grimly, "I can."

Grasping her arms, he held her away from him.

She'd never seen him look so angry...or so dangerous.

"Whatever possessed you to venture into the Rookery?" he demanded furiously. "I credited you with more sense."

"I *told* her she shouldn't come with me," Edmond put in, holding a hand to his brow.

Stung by this attack from both her friend and her rescuer, Marianne pushed out of his hold—or tried to. Charles kept a firm grip on her upper arm as he advanced into the room. Henry followed on his heels, as did the villainous Bloodworth. The bandy-legged dragoon sergeant who served as the major's batman hovered in the doorway, his pistol cocked.

Henry looked about with unabashed interest. "'Cor, I never been upstairs in this place. I 'eard about these rooms, though. They sets 'em up special for the toffs what like whips and peep'oles and a bit o' the—"

"Enough!"

The curt command silenced the boy. It didn't, however, silence Annie. Sliding her thumb out of her mouth, she regarded the major solemnly.

"You bwoke the door."

"It was locked," he explained, his tone softening, "and I didn't have the key."

The sudden guilty look that crossed the girl's

face had Henry slapping his knee in delight. "Annie, you little bugger! You nipped the key from ole Turd-face 'ere, didn't you?"

With another guilty glance in Marianne's direction, the golden-haired nymph nodded. Slowly, she reached into the pocket of her pinafore and produced a length of rusted iron.

"I don't believe it!" Marianne exclaimed. "We've sat here and stewed for hours, and all the time you had the key in your pocket?"

"I didn't want anyone to come in and hurt you," she explained with a simple, heart-breaking wisdom that went well beyond her years.

Utterly, completely humbled that the child she'd rushed to rescue had in turn tried to protect *her*, Marianne felt tears sting her eyes. She swept Annie into her arms and buried her face in her golden curls.

"Oh, my darling girl."

A hopeful note crept into the child's voice. "You're not going to scold me for nipping the key?"

"No, Annie, I'll never scold you again."

While the two females sniffled, Charles cast a critical look over St. Just. "Can you walk unaided?"

"Yes."

"All right, then. Annie, hold tight to Lady

Trent's hand. Marianne, stay behind St. Just. Henry and Sergeant O'Donnelly will bring up the rear." Pulling an evil-looking pistol from the waistband of his trousers, Charles gestured to Bloodworth. "You, I want you in front."

With a firm grasp on Annie's small hand, Marianne walked down the dimly lighted hall. A stocky footman stood guard at the top of the stairs, holding off the crowd of scantily clothed women and rough-looking men gathered at the bottom. She picked out the big, loutish brute who'd bludgeoned Edmond instantly. He stood half a head taller than the others.

"Watch that one," Henry warned the major. "'E's the one what snatches the little girls like Annie from their prams and brings 'em to Bloodworth to sell. Meaner 'n any mule in the regimental stables, Nicklesby is."

Evidently Charles had taken his own measure of the man. The unmistakable snick of the major's pistol being cocked raised the hairs on the back of Marianne's neck. Women shrieked and fled the scene. The men, including the brutish Nicklesby, melted into the shadows.

Step by step, the small cavalcade descended the stairs. Another dozen steps brought them to the front door. The sight of a carriage waiting in the eerie, swirling fog flooded Marianne with relief.

Relief melted into dismay, however, when her husband handed her inside the carriage and lifted Annie into her arms, then turned to head back toward the house.

"Charles! Where are you going?"

"I have some business to finish with our friend inside. St. Just, if I'm not out in ten minutes, you will see that Lady Trent gets home safely."

"The hell I will," Edmond retorted. "I've a bit of business to finish, too."

With a terse order to Sergeant O'Donnelly to stand guard, the major strode back through the door. Edmond followed, as did the incorrigible Henry, who ignored all instructions to get in the carriage at once. Bloodworth must have sensed what was about to happen. Prudently, he remained outside.

They found Nicklesby in a rank, odorous back room, berating the rouged hag who'd allowed the major entry the first time. His big fist smashed into the woman's face at the same instant Charles kicked open the door.

Startled, Nickelsby released his grip on her soiled dress and let her fall to the floor. Sobbing and spurting bright red blood from her nose, she scuttled away.

"Ferget something?" Nicklesby sneered, unfazed by the pistol in the major's hand.

"As a matter of fact," Charles returned coolly, "I remembered something."

"And what be that, toff?"

"I don't like men who steal little girls from their prams."

The words fell into a sudden, deadly silence. Nicklesby's eyes narrowed to black slits.

"You talk big with a pistol in yer hand."

"I talk the same without a pistol in my hand."

Thrusting the weapon at St. Just, Charles advanced on the hulking rogue. He'd taken only a step before Nicklesby whipped an arm behind his back.

"Watch 'im, Major! 'E totes a pig-sticker!"

Charles didn't need Henry's warning to feint to one side as a long, wicked blade sliced through the cloth of his coat.

Nicklesby lunged in the direction of the feint. His momentum carried him right past the major, who calmly stepped back a pace, allowed him to stagger by, then rammed his bent elbow down on the back of the bull-like neck.

Bone cracked. A surprised grunt split the malodorous air. Nicklesby dropped like a stone.

"'Cor!" Henry hopped from foot to foot in delight. "I niver knew the army taught a man to fight dirty like that! Maybe'll I'll take the colors, after all."

Not until Charles bent to roll the hulking brute did he and the others discover that Nickelsby had landed on his own knife. The blade was buried deep in his gut. A gurgling sound bubbled from his throat, then he was quiet.

Perched on the edge of the seat, Marianne rocked Annie in her arms. Her heart thumped more and more painfully with each passing moment. She was all ready to order Sergeant O'Donnelly and the footman back inside when the wide-shouldered form of her husband appeared in the open doorway.

"Your services are no longer needed," he told Bloodworth. "Henry will show us the way out."

Digging into his pocket, Charles dragged out some banknotes and flung them at the man while Henry and Edmond climbed into the coach. Beneath his bandage, St. Just's face wore a look of intense satisfaction.

"What happened?" Marianne demanded.

A gleeful Henry answered. "Ole Nicklesby won't be snatchin' any more little girls. The major made sure of that!"

Hours later Marianne knocked lightly on the door between her rooms and those of her husband. Annie was tucked into her bed above-stairs.

Henry had celebrated their victory with a foaming glass of suds, compliments of the major, then gone to his own bed. Edmond had departed shortly afterward. With the entire staff abuzz about the night's events, it had taken some time for the town house to quiet.

It had taken even longer for Marianne to gather the courage to knock on the connecting door. If she hadn't heard what sounded like the chink of a pitcher against a washbowl, she might not have ventured from her bed.

"Charles?" she called softly. "Are you still awake?"

The door clicked open. He was definitely awake, she saw on a swift, in-drawn breath, and very nearly naked. His broad chest filled her vision, smooth muscled and lightly fuzzed with gold. White knit underbreeches rode low on his hips.

"I'm sorry," he said. "Did my moving about disturb you?"

Gulping, she raised her eyes from his lean, muscled flanks. "Yes. No. That is, I heard you and..." Her glance caught on a crusted cut on his left shoulder blade. "You're hurt!"

"It's only a nick. I was just going to wash it and dust it with basilicum powder."

"I'll do it."

"There's no need, Marianne. I've doctored far worse cuts than this in the field."

"You're not in the field now. Sit down and let me tend to it."

Smiling at the brisk way she ordered him about, Charles made himself comfortable on the side of the bed. His smile disappeared the instant Marianne moved into the light cast by the flickering oil lamp and wrung out the cloth he'd left in the washbowl. Her fine muslin nightdress might have been spun from frosted glass. He could see the outline of her figure quite clearly. See, too, the darker aureoles tipping her breasts when she turned to him, cloth in hand.

"Lean forward."

Swallowing, Charles obeyed. Taking her lower lip between her teeth, she daubed at the cut. He spread his legs to accommodate her, then cursed his blunder when she pressed closer.

The cool cloth did nothing to quench the heat she raised under his skin with each featherlight touch. Folding his hands into fists, he suffered an agony much, much worse than the one he'd endured at the hands of the regimental surgeons. They'd had no laudanum to dull the pain when they stitched up the saber slash to his thigh after Sevastopol, but iron will had held Charles immobile under the surgeon's needle.

It held him immobile now. Gritting his teeth, he willed himself to not flinch at her light touch, to not breathe in her scent or nuzzle the soft skin of her neck.

His every effort at control proved futile, however, when Marianne set the cloth aside and blew on the cut to dry it before applying the basilicum powder. Charles gave a little grunt. Blood rushed straight into his groin. His shaft leaped to life under the knit drawers and stabbed into his wife's thigh.

Marianne went suddenly, rigidly still. Eyes wide, lips pursed, she stared into the face mere inches from her own.

He wanted her. In his arms and in his bed!

The echo of his words thundered in her head. The feel of him hard and rampart against her thigh sent the blood coursing through her veins.

He wanted to trail kisses from her mouth to her throat to her breasts.

Her nipples tightened, pushed against her linen nightdress.

He wanted to slide into her welcoming warmth and lose himself in her heat.

Want gushed damp and slick between her legs. Her belly clenched on waves of desire.

The tall, dashing major had infatuated Marianne from the first moment he'd turned one of his teasing smiles her way. Despite her pain when she'd

lost their child, her heart had thrilled with pride for the hero of Balaklava. After watching him stride back into that horrible place tonight and to give Annie's kidnapper his just deserts, Marianne knew she loved him with every breath she took. She could no more hold back at that moment than she could turn the tide or snatch a star from the sky. With a moan, she bent and brought her mouth to his.

Like the experienced cavalry officer he was, Charles immediately swooped in to take full advantage of the breach in her defenses. Wrapping an arm around his wife's waist, he pulled her hard against him. His mouth held hers while his deft fingers tugged at the neckstrings of her nightdress. Within moments, the soft linen had pooled at her feet. Moments more, and she was stretched out on the embroidered coverlet, her body flushed and eager and straining under his.

Setting his jaw against the hunger that clawed at him like a savage beast, Charles slowed his stroke, gentled his touch, dragged out each mating of their lips and tongues and teeth. Every tendon and muscle in his body screamed with need when he wedged a knee between hers and made sure she was ready for him. Even then, he couldn't bring himself to savor his victory without making sure she understood the terms of her surrender.

Burying his hands in her tangled hair, he tipped her face to his. "This changes all."

"Wh...?" She slicked her tongue along her lower lip. "What do you mean?"

"After tonight, we share a bed as well as a house."

She pulled in a sharp breath. Mossy green and dilated with desire, her eyes held his.

"I won't let you go," he told her roughly. "Ever."

Her heart hammered against his ribs. Charles could feel its wild fluttering, see the pulse that throbbed in the small blue vein of her neck. He didn't realize his own heart had suspended its beat until her soft, ripe lips trembled into a smile.

"I don't want you to let me go. Ever."

"When can their glory fade?
Oh, the wild charge they made!
All the world wondered.
Honor the charge they made!
Honor the Light Brigade..."

The Charge of the Light Brigade

Epilogue

London
June 1857

June! It was June already! A year and a month since Charles had returned from the Crimea.

Marianne could only marvel at the swift passage of time as the Trent carriage inched into its reserved space among the hundreds of others that crowded Hyde Park this bright, sunny morning. A smile played about her lips when she remembered

her fervent declaration that Charles would feel differently about the matter of posterity after his memories of war faded…and *his* fervent declaration that they would maintain a facade of marriage for twelve months to see if her prediction held true.

So much had happened in the past year, she could barely remember that heated argument. Charles had received a posting to the staff of Field Marshall Viscount Combermere, commander of the Queen's own guards. Marianne, with her husband's encouragement and Edmond St. Just's dedicated support, had organized the Institute for the Apprenticeship of Foundlings. Charles had attached only one stipulation to the financial backing he provided the foundation. Marianne had to swear that she would never again venture into the Rookery or similar environs without her husband's knowledge and a fully armed escort.

The months had been so busy, so tumultuous, that she could scarcely recall a time when she and Charles hadn't filled their private hours with lively discussion of the day's events, or a night when they hadn't shared each other's warmth.

And now…

Now they had come full circle.

Her smile turned inward, filling her with a glow that suffused her whole being. Today Charles and some sixty other men of all ranks would receive

from the Queen's own hand the honor they'd earned more than a year ago. And tonight Marianne would…

"Look, Lady Beatwix!" Bouncing up and down on the velvet seat, Annie pointed excitedly to rows of cavalry drawn up between the infantry and horse artillery. "There's the major's regiment! Dunbar's Dwagoons."

"Yes, I see them. I do wish you would sit still."

The stern command failed to quell the girl's spirits. Beaming a beatific smile, Annie slipped her small fingers into the widow's lace-mittened hand.

"I can't," the girl said simply.

Lady Beatrix heaved with a long-suffering sigh. "No, I suppose you can't."

Despite her grumbling, Marianne noted that the widow didn't extricate her sausage-like fingers from Annie's. The girl had stolen the older woman's heart over the past year…along with several diamond clips and gold brooches, which she'd returned with a melting look from her innocent eyes. Annie and her diminutive champion, Henry, were now permanent fixtures in the Trent household.

Marianne's fond glance fell on the boy seated beside her. Resplendent in snowy linens and a new frock coat tailored for this grand occasion, Henry was every bit as excited as Annie. Awestruck, he

craned his neck to survey the troops massed in a long line of contiguous columns.

"'Cor!'" he muttered. "Just look at them bayonets aglintin'."

Marianne followed his gaze, her own breath catching at the brave sight. Row after row of officers and men awaited the Queen's arrival. Cavalry. Infantry. Horse artillery and field batteries. A company of the Royal Engineers. Even a squadron of sailors, drawn from the ships that had participated in the siege and the final storming of the Redan.

Gilt-handled swords gleamed. Curiasses sparkled. Polished helmets flashed in the bright sun, their long-tailed plumes fluttering in the breeze. And there, in the center of the mounted cavalry, were Dunbar's Dragoons, their regimental colors flying.

The men to be decorated had been drawn up in a line at the center of the formation. Sixty-three of them, the first to receive the newly minted Victoria Cross, England's highest award for valor. Marianne had no difficulty picking out her husband's tall, broad-shouldered form among the group of honorees.

Her heart swelled at the sight of his gleaming black boots, scarlet regimentals with their green facings, the tall black shako with its shining brass

plaque and gold ropes. If ever a man was born to command, it was Charles.

The first three years of her marriage had taught her to bury her terror for her husband and show only a smiling, patriotic face while war raged in a distant corner of the world. This past year, she'd learned a great deal more about the duties and responsibilities incumbent on an officer's wife. But never, ever, had she felt the pride that shot through her when the horse artillery unlimbered their guns and fired a warning salute.

"Oooooh!" Squealing, Annie snatched her fingers free to cover her ears.

"'Ere she comes!" Henry jumped up. His thin body quivered from head to toe. "The Queen's comin'!"

Warned by the initial shot, coachmen sent footmen scurrying to hold their horses' bridles. Soon volley after volley boomed through the park. Smoke wreathed the trees and momentarily blocked the view of Serpentine Lake sparkling in the distance. The last echoes were still rolling across the grassy fields when the crowd picked up the stirring beat of pipes and drums. Moments later, the royal cortege entered the park.

The music swelled. Shoulders squared. Sabres rattled as six hundred troops snapped to attention.

Attended by her officers of state and an escort of her household guard, the Queen trooped the line.

"Blimey!" Henry's eyes popped at his first glimpse of the woman who ruled one-fourth of the world.

Mounted sidesaddle on a roan charger, Victoria wore a dark blue riding skirt, a scarlet tunic of military cut with a gold sash over one shoulder, and a black hat topped by jaunty red and white feathers. The Prince Consort rode beside her, attired in the glittering uniform of a Field Marshall. The Prince of Wales and Prince Alfred sported Highland dress and trotted behind their parents on frisky ponies.

Once the Queen finished trooping the line, the ceremony itself took a surprisingly short time. As their name was called, each of the honorees stepped forward. Victoria spoke a few words to each before stooping to pin the cross bearing her name to their uniforms.

Once all had been honored, the men stood at rigid attention while the combined regimental bands broke into a flourishing march. Unit after unit, the troops marched past, saluting their queen and their comrades who'd distinguished themselves by undaunted bravery under fire. Marianne's throat closed. She'd never seen such a stirring sight, and knew she never would again.

She was daubing away her tears when the last of the troops marched past the Queen. The artillery boomed a final salute and the royal cortege departed. Shouted orders echoed across the fields. Dismissed, the troops broke ranks to join their families and friends who'd turned out to witness the spectacle.

It took quite some time for Charles to make his way through the crowd of well-wishers. Fellow officers came up to congratulate him. His particular friends added hearty pummels on the back and ribald advice for the next time he decided to charge straight into an artillery barrage. Enlisted personnel offered salutes and gruff words of praise.

Beatrix, when her brother handed her down from the carriage, beamed with pride. Her wide smile quickly gave way to alarm, however, when Charles lifted Annie out. Snug in his arms, the little girl fixed her gaze on the gold cross dangling from its ribbon.

"That's prwetty."

"Annie!" Lady Beatrix exclaimed. "Do not *dare* steal that medal! Sir Charles must wear it on his uniform."

Laughing, her brother set the girl on her feet. "Only on my dress uniform, Bea." His gaze went to his wife. "Do you feel well enough to walk with me a bit?"

His sister swung to face Marianne, her brows beetling. "Are you ill?"

"No, not at all." A blush started under the netting of her gown and worked its way up her throat. "Merely a bit...tired."

"And no wonder! Really, Charles, can't you convince your wife spend fewer hours at the Institute? She quite wears herself out."

"I expect she'll carry less of a load now that you've taken over as director of contributions, Bea."

"Yes, well, that's as may be," his sister said obscurely.

Beatrix still didn't completely approve of Marianne's day-to-day involvement with the Institute, but, at her brother's quiet urging, she'd thrown the full force of her personality behind the fund-raising necessary to sustain operations. Few of her acquaintances and even fewer of her particular cronies had escaped her vigilance. As a result of her amazing efforts, the Institute was already fiscally sound and flourishing.

Beatrix harrumphed when Marianne tried to say as much and shooed her off to walk with her husband. Arm-in-arm, they strolled down one of the paths that wound toward the lake. Trees heavy with summer green rustled overhead. Gradually, the sounds of voices faded.

"You'll have to tell them soon, you know."

She glanced up, her heart thumping at the smile in his eyes. Charles had guessed weeks ago, long before she had begun to suspect the reason for her uncharacteristic lethargy.

"I will," she replied, wonder threading through her voice. She still couldn't quite believe that a child quickened in her womb. "When I've convinced myself it's not a dream."

They fell silent, each lost in their thoughts.

"If it's a boy," she murmured after a moment, "I hope he chooses to wear the colors like his father."

"If it's a girl, I hope she chooses a dragoon for her husband and not some crab-footed infantryman," her husband replied feelingly.

Laughing, Marianne gazed up at him. "Have I told you how proud I am of you?"

"Several times."

Reaching out, she fingered the shining decoration. "Oh, Charles, how wonderful that you were among the first to receive the Victoria Cross."

Names drifted through his head. Of distant battlefields. Of officers who led charges. Men who stormed redoubts in the face of overwhelmingly superior forces. Generals like Wellington, and colonels like the first Lord Dunbar.

"The ranks are full of brave men," Charles said quietly. "I accepted this for all of them."

The major's wife slid her lace-gloved hands up to frame his cheeks. The love she felt for her tall, brave soldier brimmed in her voice.

"The ranks may be full of brave men, but you're my own particular hero. You will always be."

"You say that now," he warned, grinning as he threw her own words of a year ago back at her. "You might view things differently twelve months from now, when you've got a babe in your arms, another on the way, and we receive a posting to India or China or the wilds of Canada."

"I can't imagine anything more thrilling than a posting to the wilds of Canada," Marianne breathed, her eyes shining at the thought of such adventures, "as long as I'm with you."

"I thought I made myself plain on that matter." Slipping an arm around her waist, Charles pulled her against him. "You're an officer's bride, my darling. Wherever the regiment goes, whatever the future holds, we'll face it together."

Dear Reader,

Did you have to memorize poems in grammar and high school? I did, and can still recite many of them. Among my favorites is Alfred, Lord Tennyson's "Charge of the Light Brigade."

The poem gained a personal significance for me when I went to Vietnam as a young lieutenant. Like Major Sir Charles Trent in "The Major's Wife," I "rode into the valley of death" and returned with a profound respect for my comrades in arms. And like the major, I was surprised at the changes that occurred on the home front while I was away. I had fun showing how Charles must adapt to those startling changes, and hope you enjoy reading "The Major's Wife" as much as I did writing it.

I hope, too, you'll watch for my next historical, *The Gunfighter,* coming from MIRA Books in January 2002. Set in the Dakotas during the rip roarin' days of Wild Bill Hickok and the Deadwood Stage, it features a hard-as-nails gunslinger and the woman who challenges him to a passionate showdown at high noon!

THE COMPANION

by Deborah Simmons

For my dear friend Renee Rebman

Chapter One

Christopher Armstrong, late of the Twentieth Cavalry, stood at the tall windows, looking out over the brilliant colors of Yorkshire in autumn, the thickets of oaks, beeches and limes ablaze upon well-tended lawns stretching out into the most picturesque of landscapes, all belonging to him. And he felt absolutely nothing.

"Well, Hawthorne?" The sound of his grandmother's shrill voice broke the silence, and Christopher winced at the misnomer.

"My name is Kit," he said, without turning from his view.

"Nonsense!" his grandmother replied. "You're the Earl of Hawthorne now, not some ragtag boy trailing after your brother's lead! And you have responsibilities to this family!"

Kit didn't move. He had heard it all before, re-

peatedly, ever since he had returned home. There had been no mention of his military career, not one word about the shocking loss of his brother, nothing, in fact, except this constant harping upon his duty. In a way, it was like being back in the army, for he felt as though he were simply a body to be used in a pinch, for the greater good.

In this case, instead of giving his all for his country, he was to sacrifice himself for the illustrious position of the family, at least his grandmother's version of it. And though he had once charged into battle with the most honorable of intentions, Kit felt no such loyalty to the dubious trappings of political power, wealth and privilege. Nor could he muster up the slightest interest in the continuation of a so-called dynasty that had dwindled to one battle-weary man and a fierce old woman.

"Do you hear me?" she screeched, thumping her cane loudly, just in case he didn't.

Kit's lips curled in bittersweet remembrance. There was a time when just the sound of that cane had struck fear into the hearts of his brother and himself during their otherwise bucolic days of childhood. How everyone, even his own father, had bowed before the famous dowager! But now Kit saw his grandmother for what she was: an old

woman railing against the fates, with no real power to change them.

She had always sought to run the lives of those around her, while Kit long had balked at her demands. He had even bought his commission partly to thwart her, though he had ended up hurting himself far worse than he ever could his grandmother. She seemed to be made of stone. Indeed, if she were grieving now for Garrett, Kit couldn't tell. Although she wore the required black, she seemed wholly unaffected, while he could not take a breath without counting the loss, not only of his brother, but of all those men who had served under him, all those who had died in the bloody carnage of Waterloo, all those who had gone off to war never to return.

And here he was, not only alive, but supposedly thriving as the fifth earl of Hawthorne. The irony had not escaped him. He had charged off into battle time and time again only to escape death, while Garrett, who had stayed safely here at home, had lost his life. They said he cut himself on the agricultural equipment that had always fascinated him, dying within the week.

It was so stupid, so senseless, so untenable. Kit couldn't count the number of times he had been slashed by a blade or even a sword. At Waterloo, he had taken a bullet and had been crushed beneath

his horse, leaving him with broken ribs, numerous contusions and a leg that had been proclaimed useless. Yet Kit had made them set it and had forced himself up and onto it until he had but a limp to show for his suffering.

Now he could only wonder why he had expended the effort. He had been mending in Brussels when Garrett died. And although his grandmother claimed to have sent a messenger, there was so much confusion after Waterloo that no one had ever reached him. So when at last he returned home, it was to find the house in mourning, the funeral long over and his grandmother determined to remake him into his brother. Perhaps if he had never joined the army or never been to battle, he might have been able to take Garrett's place. But now he just hadn't the stomach for it. He couldn't muster interest in anything, least of all the business of being Hawthorne.

"You must assume control of the estates!" his grandmother was saying, as if reading his mind. "The bailiff tells me that he has tried to meet with you, but you refuse to grant him an audience, and Mr. Sawyer in London says you won't respond to his letters. They need direction, and you must provide it!"

She punctuated her point with another thump of her cane, but somehow the question of whether or

not to sell his shares in some manufacturing venture hardly seemed earth-shattering to Kit, not after what he had seen. And he could never take the place of Garrett, who had been trained since birth to be the earl, who had a natural aptitude for increasing the family coffers, who should have been here, alive, while Kit should have been killed. Surely, there was some kind of mistake, or was it simply a great cosmic joke?

"Are you listening?" his grandmother demanded.

"No," Kit answered without hesitation. And before she could protest further, he stalked from the room, away from her harping, away from his so-called responsibilities, away from himself if he could have managed it.

Her mouth tightened into a thin line, the dowager countess of Hawthorne watched him go, cursing both his stubbornness and her failure. Welcoming him home with pomp, she had organized a small gathering in celebration of his return, but he had never shown his face, a disaster that she was still living down. She had mustered friends, his as well as her own, trying to coax him into some kind of society, but he disdained any company. She had tried to tempt him with travel, with a seat in the Lords, with running the vast Hawthorne estates, but to no avail.

Desperate, she had paraded the cream of the season's new crop of eligible females in front of him, only to watch him cut them dead. Now she wasn't sure if even the promise of the title and its vast wealth could convince any sane young woman to consider him.

The dowager's shoulders sagged. She was running out of options, and she knew it. She was feeling her age, too, but she hadn't lived this long, surviving hardship and death, simply to see the Hawthorne line wither and die. And she wasn't going to let her grandson be the cause of its demise, either.

The sound of a noise at the door made her sit up straight, for she refused to show the world any weakness. And if it was her grandson, she intended to give him a piece of her mind. But it was only the butler with the post. The dowager was tempted to ignore it, for she knew what the letters would contain: expressions of sympathy from old friends, while those less dear would claim concern even as they riddled their prose with snide insinuations about the fate of the earldom.

Turning her head away, as if loathe to look at them, the dowager hesitated for a moment, then took a deep breath and squared her shoulders. "Bring me my desk," she snapped. She had never shied away from a difficult task, and she wasn't

about to start now. Not only did she proceed to read every piece of correspondence, but she answered most of them. To those who bespoke sincerity, she responded in a light, reassuring tone, and to the others, she replied with a caustic politesse that promised retribution for each slight.

The dowager did not particularly enjoy the exercise, as she once had, but there was one missive, from her insipid cousin Theodosia, that caught her interest. Theodosia was far too good-hearted for gibes and not clever enough besides, yet the woman had written something that made the dowager sit up and take notice. It was a plea concerning Miss Chloe Gibbons, lately of Suffolk.

I would ask, my dear cousin, if you know of a decent position for this young woman as a governess or companion, for she has been left nearly destitute by the passing of her father, Baron Tindale. You may remember him as William's eldest. He was not blessed with any sons of his own, so the barony is passing to a young nephew who, sadly, has no use for the girl.

It was a common enough occurrence, of course, and one that the dowager usually did not stir herself about, but now she paused. She recalled the

young woman in question as a studious creature who had never moved in society's circles. She was possessed of a quiet, nurturing nature that her father had used to his advantage, reveling in her cosseting when he should have been finding her a husband.

Now it was too late for that, but perhaps the girl could ply her skills elsewhere. The dowager felt the beginnings of an idea form, dismissed it firmly, then returned to consider it once more. It was a wild notion, certainly, but she had exhausted all other possibilities, and for the first time that day a smile curved her lips.

Dipping her quill in the ink, she began to compose a response to Theodosia.

Chloe Gibbons took one look at the elegant country house before her and nearly turned back around. Hawthorne Park was a vast estate, as she had seen from the coach, with great green lawns rolling into the distance toward tall trees, beautiful grottos and picturesque ponds. Neat gravel walks, mown turf, and an endless variety of plants and shrubs were all artfully arranged.

That had been intimidating enough, but the house itself was a huge structure in the French style boasting rows upon rows of windows in burnished stone. How was she to ever get on here?

Suddenly longing for her old, cozy cottage, Chloe swallowed hard. But the cottage was not hers, and its occupants had no place for her. Nor could she afford her own household. Long accustomed to occupying that middle ground between the lower gentry and the noblemen beyond her reach, Chloe had always felt out of place, but now she was well and truly adrift, with nowhere to go until the message from the dowager had arrived.

To Chloe's less regal relatives, the dowager countess of Hawthorne was spoken of in awe as a well-bred woman of no great family who had married above herself into wealth and privilege. Chloe, who had met the countess only once, held a more jaundiced view. She remembered a haughty old woman who ordered everyone about, made outrageous demands and possessed the manners of a goat.

Naturally, she had been less than thrilled at the chance to serve as paid companion to the lady. But what choice did she have? Her other relations had proclaimed the offer a godsend, and so here she was, determined to make the best of what surely could only be a miserable position.

Taking a deep breath, Chloe tried to put a good face on it. The place couldn't really be as big as it looked, and even if it was, that meant that she could put some distance between herself and her

employer. Hopefully. She released a sigh, still unsure exactly why the dowager would be at all interested in her company. She had servants aplenty
to order about and wait upon her. What did she
need with Chloe?

Great-aunt Theodosia had claimed that Chloe's
reputation for aiding the infirm had gone before
her, but she found it hard to believe that the dowager was in any way ailing, despite her cane. And
although Chloe had often been proclaimed a saint
for her care of her father, it had been no great task.
Papa had been undemanding and grateful for her
help, especially after his gout became so painful
he could not move from his chair, and Chloe had
not resented giving what had been second nature
to her. Some said she should have had a season,
but there had never been much money, and who
would have taken care of Papa? Anyway, she was
not one for fancy dresses and entertainment, preferring the quiet of home and hearth and garden.

With a sigh, Chloe noted the irony of that, for
nothing could be farther from the small world she
had cherished than the historic seat of the Hawthorne earldom. Its very splendor bespoke a heritage of wealth and power and privilege far beyond
her scope. And although the surrounding lands de-
noted bucolic beauty and quietude, Chloe was not

so naive as to expect any peace with the dowager countess as her employer.

Still, Chloe managed to be shown to her rooms simply enough by a chattering young maid who seemed glad to have someone new in the house. And Chloe could not deny that the elegant furnishings of the huge bedroom, sitting room and dressing room were pleasant indeed. She even reveled in the luxury of a bath after the long trip and the assistance of another maid in dressing for dinner. All in all, her arrival went quite smoothly. It was dinner, and her first contact with the dowager countess, that Chloe dreaded.

But she lifted her chin and the black skirts of her mourning gown and walked down the steep, curving stairway to the marbled foyer below, determined to make the best of this first interview. Trying not to gawk at the plaster cherubs above her, Chloe had nearly reached the bottom when she heard the sound of steps and the unmistakable click of a cane. Tempted to return to her rooms, she nonetheless continued downward. It was always better to begin how you meant to go on, and she would do well to hold her own with the imperious noblewoman.

So Chloe followed the stairs, her eyes fixed upon the space below, only to suddenly halt in amazement, for the cane she had heard definitely did not

proclaim the arrival of the dowager countess. It belonged to a man, and not just any man, but surely the most perfect specimen ever to grace the earth.

Tall and broad-shouldered, he possessed a lean yet undeniably strong physique that made her insides flutter. His hair was blond, though the word hardly did justice to the tousled, sun-kissed locks that caused her breath to catch. And when he lifted his head to look at her, Chloe saw that his eyes were no ordinary color, but a deep, mysterious green that seemed to pierce her very heart.

His face was beautiful, so much so that on another it might have appeared effeminate. Yet there was some cast over his features, perhaps the hard set of the jaw or a shadow of pain, that rendered it wholly masculine. And Chloe, who had never before found herself captivated by a handsome visage, stood rooted to the spot, unable to do more than stare as the unknown man's brows lowered and his expression darkened.

She was rescued by a most unlikely savior, the dowager herself, who called Chloe's attention with the sound of a second cane. Walking to a halt behind the elegantly attired gentleman, the dowager was now peering up at Chloe, as well.

"Ah! So here you are, gel!" she said. Giving Chloe a close scrutiny, she turned to the man, who

was looking rather fierce. "Hawthorne, I want you to meet Miss Chloe Gibbons," she said.

"Kit, my name is Kit," he said, his green eyes narrowing.

The dowager countess made a reproving sound before swinging back to face Chloe. "My grandson, Hawthorne, who has a distaste for ceremony. You may call him Kit then, since you are family, though distant, to be sure. Chloe is related to Cousin Theodosia and will be staying with us."

Kit, whom Chloe realized was the earl, appeared to be less than enthused by that news. "In what capacity?" he drawled in a rather insulting manner.

"Never you mind. She's here, that's all," the dowager snapped.

"Ah, but I do mind. I thought we had agreed that you were going to quit trying to run my life and most especially that you were to cease parading eligible young women under my nose, though I might question your judgment in this case," he added, giving Chloe a long, insolent perusal that made her stiffen.

Suddenly she was all too aware of the picture she must make: a green girl dressed in an outmoded gown dyed black for mourning, gaping at what some would call her betters. Although the maid had insisted on dressing her hair, Chloe re-

alized that she must appear woefully out of place in the earl's luxurious home.

"What would you have me do, turn the gel out?" his grandmother asked. "She's nowhere else to go. Her father's estate was entailed and went to some rascally nephew, so she's practically destitute! Shall I send her to the workhouse?"

Chloe flushed scarlet. Although well aware of her reduced circumstances, she did not care to be reminded of them and so publicly. "If there is some problem with my employment here, I can seek another position elsewhere," she said, her head unbowed.

The dowager snorted, while Kit shot her a sharp glance he had no doubt learned from his grandmother. Obviously, it was intended to scare away all comers, including the enemy. Although Chloe did not flinch, the thought brought to mind what she knew of the current earl: that he was a hero, as were any who had fought in the long war, and that he suffered for it, as was evidenced by his cane. Her gaze dropped to his leg and softened.

"If you're angling for a position as countess, let me assure you that I am not in the market for a wife," he said, abruptly forestalling her sympathy.

"Wife? Who said anything about a wife? She's a companion!" the dowager exclaimed.

For a moment Chloe forgot her own discomfort

to watch the lady and her grandson in a struggle of wills presumably of long standing. She could easily envision the two of them dueling with their canes, perhaps, as the weapon of choice, and she could only shake her head. It appeared that now she was to have two sharp tongues with which to contend, and ignoring both, Chloe swept past them in what she hoped was the direction of the dining room.

Unfortunately, she chose wrongly.

"This way!" Two heads snapped around to issue the harsh directive, and Chloe dutifully turned to follow them, anticipating a flogging with one of their canes if she did not. However, she had taken but a few steps before the dowager's preemptive voice rang out once more.

"Hawthorne, you may take Chloe in to dinner," the lady ordered. The earl, who was making surprising headway away from her despite his limp, checked and turned, a scowl on his handsome features. For a moment Chloe thought he was going to protest, and she considered demurring herself. She might be only a baron's daughter, but she knew that etiquette decreed the earl should escort the dowager. Yet she had no wish to argue so soon with her employer and over so mundane a matter, so she simply waited as he stuck out his arm for her to take.

Although Chloe avoided glancing at his handsome face, his nearness affected her in most peculiar and unexpected ways. When she touched him, it was as if she felt their connection right down to her toes. Heat and a curious sort of languor engulfed her, making her both anxious to flee and loathe to break away.

Their progress was slow because of the cane, and Chloe regretted that she was an added burden. But her sympathy soon dissipated when he seemed all too happy to be rid of her. With little more than a grunt, he saw her seated, then moved on to his place at the head of the long table set with exquisite plate. Hero or no, he appeared to be the typical nobleman, too high in the instep to acknowledge her, Chloe noted, which made dinner an interminable, awkward affair.

Although the food was delicious, more varied and sophisticated than any she had ever tasted, the conversation was stilted. The dowager brayed like a donkey, the earl was sunk in silence, and Chloe was at a loss as to what to do. It soon became apparent that Kit and his grandmother were at odds that stretched far beyond their places at opposite ends of the table.

For a moment Chloe wasted her time wishing for her own less laden board but far more gentle company, and she pined for her father, who had

engaged her in all sorts of discussions, both lively and pleasant. However, she swiftly banished such melancholy, deciding that if she had no liking for the situation here, she must do her best to change it.

And so she did. She spoke at first of her journey, trying not to wince when the dowager broke in with some dispute over her words, then she turned to her new home. "I could not help but admire the Yorkshire countryside," she said truthfully.

"Bah! Perhaps if you are a farmer or dairy-maid," the dowager said, but Kit seemed to perk up a little, if only in counterpoint to his grand-mother's disdain.

"I have seen much in my travels, but nothing to rival these lands, especially in the autumn," he said.

Chloe nodded. "I am eager to explore further," she admitted, even as she wondered if her duties would allow her any such free time. She could not imagine the dowager taking long, leisurely treks over the hills and dales. "Yet there must be many beautiful walks close at hand, for Hawthorne Park is a magnificent landscape," she added.

"It was done by Capability Brown himself and cost a pretty penny, too, I fancy," the dowager said. Although she snorted, Chloe detected a hint of pride in the older woman's voice. "Of course,

in those days people liked an elegant, clean sweep of garden, not the cluttered wilderness that is popular today!''

"Perhaps tastes have changed, but there is no denying that the Park was Brown's best work,'' Kit said, and Chloe glanced at him in surprise. Although he spoke casually, she sensed the same pride of place underlying his words. Perhaps the dowager and her grandson were not so different, after all.

"Well, if you're all that enamored of it, then why don't you take Chloe on a walk after dinner?'' the dowager suggested tartly, causing Chloe some dismay. Although her acquaintance with the earl was brief, she knew immediately that he would not agree.

"It's too dark to see anything now,'' he said, confirming her belief and withdrawing from the conversation so completely that Chloe blinked in surprise. Stepping in, she demurred, as well, but her protests were loudly overridden by the dowager.

"You may give her a tour tomorrow, then, when it is light enough for you,'' the noblewoman said, glaring at both her grandson and Chloe, as if her plans were settled between them. But one look at Kit's grim expression and set shoulders showed Chloe he held quite a different opinion.

Indeed, she guessed he would disappear rather than show her any hospitality. His attitude was so apparent as to be amusing, yet Chloe felt a sting of hurt at his rejection, which she put down to her own loneliness. It was only natural that she would seek out a friend here, but better that she eliminate Kit as a possibility. The last thing she needed was to waste her time on the sullen and sharp-tongued earl.

As if to prove her right, Kit made his escape from the table as gracelessly as possible, dismissing his grandmother's orders to join them in the grand salon and ignoring his guest entirely, so much so that Chloe was hard pressed to excuse his manners. She knew of those who had come back from the war with far worse injuries, men who had returned to nothing and still retained their civility, while here was a handsome, privileged, wealthy man who was not faced with hardship or starvation, yet could not possess the merest of manners in his own home.

Chloe was beginning to think that she didn't like Kit Armstrong, the Earl of Hawthorne, or whatever he cared to call himself, at all.

"Go on! Go after him," the dowager said, disrupting her thoughts. When Chloe turned to her in question, the noblewoman inclined her head toward Kit's departing figure. "He's probably off to

tramp about outside. Isn't that what you wanted, gel?''

Was this some kind of set-down? Chloe wondered. If so, she would have none of it. She lifted her chin and calmly added sugar to her tea, as if the conversation were of little consequence. "I believe his lordship made it quite clear that he does not care for my company," she said.

"Bah! The boy don't know what he wants!" the dowager retorted, thumping her cane for emphasis. "You were hired as a companion. Now go on to it!"

Chloe's hand stilled at the dowager's words. Surely, she could not have understood the lady correctly! Very carefully, she set aside her spoon and gazed expectantly at her employer.

"I am here to serve as *your* companion," Chloe said. Indeed, that task was unpleasant enough without these added undercurrents between the dowager and her grandson.

"I hired you to serve as a companion, but not necessarily mine. What do I need with some motherly miss simpering at me? I want you to keep an eye on my grandson, to distract him from the damned brooding he's been doing since he returned home," the dowager said grudgingly.

Chloe felt a trickle of unease run up her spine, but she decided to give the noblewoman the benefit

of the doubt. After all, the dowager was getting on
in years, and perhaps worry for her grandson had
clouded her thinking. "I'm sure that a man would
serve you better in such a capacity," Chloe suggested gently.

The dowager thumped her cane again. "Don't
you think I've tried that, gel? He won't see his old
friends, or even the rabble from his army days! He
won't take an interest in anyone or anything!"

"I am sorry to hear that," Chloe said truthfully.
She regretted that the earl should continue to suffer
for his part in the war, but how could she possibly
help? "However, I fail to see what you expect me
to do. He shuns me, as well."

"Ah, but you're a female," the dowager said
rather slyly, and Chloe stiffened, her entire body
rejecting the older woman's speech.

There were whispers, of course, of the ill for-
tunes awaiting young women who came upon hard
times, but she had never expected herself to be one
of them. Nor could she conceive of the dowager
countess of Hawthorne as the one responsible for
her fall from grace. Still, she was no fool.

And although Chloe thought of herself as a spinster, she was not wholly ignorant of what went on
between men and women. She was, after all, well
read, and the sudden thought of engaging in some
sort of illicit activity with the earl of Hawthorne

was both horrifying and vaguely titillating. Remembering the touch of his hand upon her arm, Chloe shivered, only to set her shoulders in firm resolve.

"I am afraid there has been a misunderstanding," she said. "I was perfectly willing to serve as your companion, but you cannot expect me to accept the same position for a male member of the household."

"Bah! I'm not asking you to bed him," the dowager snapped, as if fully aware of her thoughts. "Just cheer him up a bit."

Chloe exhaled slowly with some measure of relief. Although the situation was not quite as bad as she had suspected, she still could not consent. "Nevertheless it is wholly inappropriate," she answered.

"Pah! Inappropriate to aid your kinsman? The boy can't cast you out as he has the others, for you have nowhere else to go. You're here because of family duty, young woman, and you would be wise to see to it!"

Chloe frowned, unmoved by the dowager's bullying. Obviously the noblewoman thought she was being crafty by hiring a destitute relative, but Chloe still didn't see how she was going to be of any help. The earl was not infirm as her father had been, at least not physically, she thought, a blush

rising upon her cheeks at the memory of his vital form. And having no memory of his personality before his injury, how could she be expected to return him to a healthy demeanor? The man was so grim that Chloe knew it would take more than a smile and a few encouraging words to affect him, especially from someone whose presence he decried.

On the other hand, she felt a genuine sympathy for his plight. It was a rare man or woman who did not know someone who had been killed or wounded in the long war, and Chloe knew she should do whatever she could for those heroes, yet she had little inkling of what they must have suffered in battle. "It's natural that he should feel deeply, for no doubt he has seen horrors that we cannot even imagine," she murmured.

"As have other men! War is war! He must put it behind him and shoulder his responsibilities," the dowager said, as if her very demand would make it so.

Chloe could easily see why the woman was at odds with her grandson, and with compassion like that tendered toward him, no wonder he was not better. She recalled that he had assumed the title after the death of his brother, and not long ago, either. Had he even been allowed a proper period of mourning? Chloe knew that she still missed her

father with a painful ache. "He has suffered other losses," she said softly.

"He's had a few setbacks, a few reverses," the dowager admitted tartly, "that idiot girl he was so infatuated with, for one. Mind you, I told him she was nothing but a spoiled little ninny, daughter of a duke or no, but he had to have her. Proposed to her before he left, and when he returned, she found she didn't care for the new cut of his cloth!"

Chloe looked up, startled. "He was engaged?"

"Pah! If you can call it that. A youthful mistake is what I call it, and well done with!"

Somehow, Chloe found this news particularly disturbing. Of course, a handsome man like Kit would have his pick of beautiful, elegant ladies of the best lineage. In Chloe's limited experience, she knew them as pampered, snobbish and heartless, but to think that even one of those idle creatures would be so cruel, so unseeing, as to reject a war hero because he had a limp! She could not countenance it. And, against her better judgment, she found herself wondering if he had loved her. *Was he suffering from a broken heart?*

"She did him a favor taking off," the dowager said, dismissing Chloe's concerns with a wave of her bejeweled fingers. "But he can't see that now.

He's sunk too deep in the dismals. Too deep,'' she muttered.

Something in her low tone brought Chloe out of her own musings, and she eyed the dowager more closely, but the noblewoman looked away from her discerning gaze. And suddenly the lady's strength seemed to melt away, leaving only a tired old woman, thin and brittle enough to break.

"My own husband was a bit of a…brooder,'' she said slowly. "Although my son didn't inherit any of that tendency to melancholy, I can see it in Christopher, and I won't have it taking mastery over him.'' She thumped her cane for emphasis, but Chloe could see her helplessness now, as well as her frustration with it.

And, while the lady's ranting and bullying had little affect, this glimpse at the real person behind the fierce facade moved Chloe to consider her proposal. Taking in a heavy breath, she tried to make sense of the dowager's admission. Had Kit's fiancée sent him careening into darkness, or did he have a predisposition to feel more than others might? What exactly was his grandmother trying to tell her? How deep in the dismals was he sunk?

Abruptly, Chloe felt chilled to the bone as she struggled to put her new concern into words. "You don't imagine that he might…kill himself?'' she asked in hushed tones.

As if the question brought her back to herself, the dowager thumped her cane upon the floor with renewed vigor. "Of course not," she said. "I expect you, gel, to see that he doesn't."

Chapter Two

Kit didn't risk the main rooms, but took a back stair down to the kitchens, ignoring the startled looks of the servants as he exited the house. Although the morning was yet young, he had no intention of being pressed into service as an escort for Miss Chloe Gibbons, destitute relative. *If his grandmother was to be believed.* Knowing the dowager could not be trusted, Kit wondered about the young woman's circumstances, but from the look of her clothes, she did not come from wealth. Indeed, at first glance, he had questioned his grandmother's judgment, for their new guest obviously was in mourning, in a poorly dyed older gown, if he guessed aright.

What was the dowager up to? Kit knew better than to accept her explanation at face value. She was not in the habit of generously taking in stray

relatives, not without a powerful ulterior motive. Reaching the edge of the path, Kit forged ahead across the grass, feeling his stiff leg react to the moist chill in the air. He winced, gritted his teeth and went on, away from the house.

Perhaps his grandmother was simply tendering a new and different bait, he mused, for upon closer scrutiny, he had to admit that the recent arrival was rather attractive. The dowager had already been through the more obvious beauties, the toasts of the past season, with their near-perfect features, their flawless manners and hungry eyes. He knew full well that most would have laughed at a proposal from Captain Kit Armstrong, but marriage to the Earl of Hawthorne, no matter his failings, would bring them the position and wealth they craved. The lust for power was bred into their bones, and Kit could easily imagine life with one of them as, after a suitable period, she danced off to London and a string of lovers, leaving her crippled husband behind.

He had cut them all, much to his grandmother's fury, when they were paraded before him like so much prize breeding stock. And that's exactly what they were, he had decided soon enough. For whenever the dowager ceased harping about his duties to the estates, she went on about his so-called responsibility to get an heir. Kit didn't think it nec-

essary to inform her that even if he should buy himself a wife, he could not be counted upon to produce the required progeny. He wasn't entirely sure if all was in working order in that area, and, in truth, he hardly cared.

At first he had been too busy struggling for survival, to walk and return home, but upon his arrival whatever hopes he had harbored of returning to a normal existence had been dashed, not only by Garrett's death, but by Julia's reception. The daughter of a duke, she had no need for an earldom, but had taken a fancy to the dashing officer he had once been. However, she had been none too pleased by the changes in him the war had wrought. Not only had he lost the carefree recklessness of youth, but full use of one of his limbs, as well.

Kit would never forget her words as she stood before him in the grand salon, cool and untouchable. *I want a whole man, Christopher,* she had said, thereby breaking off their engagement and destroying what little desire he had for the female sex. That part of life, like so much else, left him cold, and he had begun to suspect that with all his injuries, something down there had been affected. Permanently.

But his eyesight was working perfectly, and Kit could not deny that Miss Chloe Gibbons was a

fetching thing. Perhaps his taste had matured, or maybe the near loss of his life had knocked some sense into him. Whatever the reason, he no longer cared for the sort of chilly blondes epitomized by his former fiancée. Nor could he stomach constant chatter or simpering chits barely out of the schoolroom or the overtures of bolder females.

In short, his once healthy interest in women had ceased. Yet this Chloe, with her simple clothes and her calm manner, was somehow appealing. Comforting. Steady. Not exactly the type of female he had once pursued, Kit thought with a bitter laugh.

But he reminded himself that she was here at the bidding of his grandmother, for some hidden purpose. *Or perhaps not quite so hidden,* he mused as he caught sight of the object of his thoughts exiting the house. While Kit watched, she hurried toward him, heedless of the effect of the damp grass upon the hem of her skirt. *Definitely not a typical female,* he thought. Still, he had no patience for her. Indeed, he had half a mind to keep going, but his limp slowed him down so much that she would be sure to catch up with him. A flush of humiliation crept up his cheeks, and he fixed her with a hard stare.

She seemed oblivious to the lack of welcome, however, and smiled brightly when at last she reached him. ''Oh, hello!'' she said a bit breath-

lessly. She was dressed in plain black again, a shawl thrown hastily over her shoulders, and Kit wondered if he was supposed to be moved by the poor state of her wardrobe. Moved to what? What was his grandmother's objective? Even Kit could not believe she intended him to marry this cast-off relative in mourning. But if not matrimony, then what?

Eyes narrowed, he studied her. She wasn't beautiful, really, though her face held no flaws. Her skin was clear and her eyes under elegant brows were a rich, dark brown, veiled by thick lashes. Her hair was of the same shade, lustrous and long, not cut into curls as was the fashion of the London ladies. She dressed it simply, but he wondered how it would look falling free over her breasts. When his gaze traveled downward to those gentle curves, he glanced away abruptly. Was that what they intended? Angry at the two women and himself, he turned on his heel.

"Wait! I was hoping that you might show me about," she said, reaching out to touch his sleeve.

There. Kit felt it again, that sizzle of awareness that had struck him last evening when he had been forced to escort her into dinner. He had convinced himself that the reaction was an imagined one, but denial was futile now. It was like a spark of warmth to his coldness and, as such, wholly un-

welcome, so he jerked his arm from her grasp. Without a word, he strode away, but she followed.

"Where are we going?" she asked with a calmness that irritated him. Either she was a witless, unaware creature, or she possessed no manners at all. Was she even a relative, or was she some wretch his grandmother had hired off the streets? Although her speech bespoke a gentle upbringing, he could be wrong, or she could have strayed from her heritage easily enough. Kit swung 'round to face her, determined to be as blunt as possible.

"*I* am going to my rooms. Alone," he said, pausing to give her a hard look. "Unless you plan on following me there, too?"

"M-my lord, really!" She sputtered at his question, as if unsure how to reply, and Kit's eyes narrowed once more. He had a sudden, dark suspicion that he knew just why Miss Chloe Gibbons was here, though the notion was strangely disappointing.

"I thought we established that my name is Kit," he said in a silky voice he hadn't used in years. "After all, we *are* relatives, *aren't we?*"

She appeared flustered. "Certainly, uh, Kit," she said. She licked her lips in what appeared to be an innocent gesture, but Kit wasn't fooled. He stepped forward slowly, stalking her as leisurely as was possible with his limp, until he was too close.

Although her dark eyes widened perceptibly, she held her ground, which only confirmed his suspicions. Leaving one hand on his cane, he lifted the other to the tree behind her head and leaned forward, caging her in.

"Very nicely done," he said as he bent over her, his face a hairbreadth from her own. Apparently his grandmother was sinking to new depths, while he must adjust his opinion of Miss Chloe Gibbons. But why the mourning? Was it all part of the masquerade? Kit realized his curiosity was whetted, and he frowned. He did not care to have his interest piqued by this woman or anyone. *Or anything.*

"Why don't you save us both a waste of time and let me know what you want?" Kit urged in a seductive tone long honed but little used anymore.

"Uh, a walk about the grounds would be nice," she answered in a low voice that fairly reeked of seduction.

Kit made a soft sound of disapproval. "Perhaps I should rephrase the question. Why don't you simply share with me the nature of your duties, Chloe?" He lifted his brows in question and was rewarded with a chary look that was all too telling.

"I see," Kit drawled. "And just how far are you willing to go as a *companion,* Chloe? To my rooms? *To my bed?* Or need we even bother with such amenities? Why not just lift your skirts, and

we'll have at it right here?'' He paused to marvel that she could still blush, but when the heat from her cheeks seemed to rise to touch him, Kit pushed away from the trunk with a cold glare.

"If you were hired by my grandmother to service me, then I'm afraid I have to disappoint you," he said coolly. She blinked at him then, with such a semblance of shock that he wondered whether she was an actress. "Well? Run and tell the dowager that you've failed to get a rise out of me," he advised.

She appeared to not understand his play on words, but her color heightened until she resembled a ripe apple, a scarlet stain covering skin that had gone nearly white. "Surely, you don't think I'm a—" She hesitated as though unable to finish, and Kit had to admire her technique. Perhaps she was one of those who played the outraged virgin to all and sundry clients. Although she was getting a bit long in tooth for that, he knew the so-called gentlemen of the ton would pay for anything.

She was still sputtering. "That your own grandmother would hire a woman of questionable morals to—" Again, she broke off, as if uncertain just what he had in mind.

"Why not?" Kit said with a bitter shrug. "She's so eager for an heir that I can only suppose she no

longer cares what side of the blanket the child is born on.''

Crack! For someone trained to war, Kit was taken completely off guard by the smart slap. Perhaps his reflexes had slowed, or, more likely, he didn't care anymore. He certainly had not expected such a response. Gingerly, he lifted a hand to his stinging cheek while he watched her march away in a high dudgeon that no amount of acting skill could feign.

Hmm. It appeared that he had made a mistake, and he wondered if his grandmother had, as well. Whatever the young woman was here for, she was far too willful to stand still for the dowager's machinations. Staring after her, Kit felt his curiosity stir again before he dismissed it.

But there, in the chill of the early morning, he spared a moment's fleeting regret for the fact that he had just driven away the first person to interest him in long, dead days beyond count.

Chloe hurried back to the house, determined to leave at once. Without even calling for the maid, she hauled her now-empty trunk out of the dressing room and began to pack all that had been removed from it just yesterday. Nothing, not any amount of money or even the threat of imminent homelessness, could force her to endure another moment of

that man's company. Companion, indeed! Chloe could think of other names entirely for the sort of association he was seeking!

She tried to not consider the reaction of her relatives when she returned to them. No one had room for her, but surely she could find another position. She did not shirk at the idea of more difficult toil in a smaller household, less luxurious, yet more respectable. Indeed, she was prepared to brave the threat of poverty rather than listen to one more insult from the lips of the earl of Hawthorne, no matter how attractive those lips might be!

The fact that Chloe had nearly melted into a puddle at his feet had nothing to do with her dismay, she told herself. She was unused to the ways of worldly, handsome, titled men, so she could forgive herself for acting like a mindless ninny as he bent far too close, dazzling her with his golden hair and white teeth and eyes greener than the deepest forest. Chloe made a soft sound of annoyance. Forgive herself she might, but she was old enough to know a man like that wouldn't be wooing her! And yet she had blinked up at him in a sort of dazed languor, while his insinuations grew more preposterous.

Chloe shook her head at such folly. She forced herself to breathe deeply, to dispel her outrage and concentrate upon the neat folding of her few

gowns, but she had barely begun returning her personal belongings to the trunk when the door opened, without a knock or hail. Chloe whirled, half expecting to see the earl standing there, prepared to exact *whatever it was* that he had hinted at outside.

But it was the dowager who stood on the threshold, a fierce scowl upon her wrinkled face. "So you're running already, eh?" she asked. "I thought you had more backbone, gel!"

Although Chloe did not invite her in, the dowager swept over the threshold to stand nearby with a huff of disapproval. Without even inquiring about Chloe's encounter with her grandson, the noblewoman simply continued to chastise her.

"I don't pretend to know exactly what went on, but I imagine that he trod upon your delicate sensibilities!" the noblewoman said with a snort. "Lud, I thought you country girls were made of sterner stuff than those London fripperies who swoon at the merest slight. Of course, he was rude and callous! He treats everyone that way!"

Privately, Chloe suspected he had learned such behavior at his grandmother's knee, but she said nothing.

"That's how he chases them away. Didn't I tell you he has sent all his acquaintances packing?"

the dowager demanded, banging her cane for emphasis.

Chloe, used to the sound by now, did not jump, but turned to face her employer. "Yes, you did," she acknowledge calmly. *But you didn't warn about the heat that emanated from him, the yearning that he can effortlessly rouse even in a spinster such as myself, or the scalding embarrassment of his dismissal!* Chloe held the noblewoman's gaze, though said nothing further, and with a huff, the dowager turned to go.

But not without issuing a challenge. "You are my last hope, gel," she said. "Don't fail me."

Had the old woman's voice cracked? Chloe glanced swiftly toward the door only to see her retreating figure. Again she realized that the dowager was not as unfeeling as she appeared. Nor was she as different from her grandson as she liked to pretend. The haughty noblewoman would never reveal herself. Would the earl?

Sinking down upon the edge of the bed, Chloe considered the question even as she told herself that she couldn't care less if Kit hid himself and his pain, lashing out at anyone who approached like a cornered beast. But she did care. Any human being with an ounce of compassion would, as had she before this morning's incident. Why, then, was she fleeing? Certainly she had been caught off

guard by the strength and aim of Kit's venom, but she had known he would not welcome her. With a frown, Chloe realized that it was her own weakness that had sent her running to her room and toward the comfort of her old life.

She had spent long years cozily ensconced in Suffolk, content in her own little world and unthreatened by anything except a dwindling purse. Now she was dismayed to discover a heretofore unknown vulnerability for a pair of green eyes and a tall, handsome form that wasn't marred one bit by the addition of an elegant cane.

Chloe frowned. It was not like her to be swayed by a man. She had gently dissuaded several potential swains over the years until she found herself firmly on the shelf, and none of them, not even Tommy Roe, a sweet-natured fellow as ever lived, had caused her to melt at his feet! Sadly, she must be a shallow creature indeed to be affected by looks and station rather than kindness and intelligence.

But was the earl as horrible as he pretended? Chloe could think of nothing more cruel than the way he had beguiled with his silken voice and soft words transforming her into a breathless creature of heat and yearning, only to turn upon her, tendering the very worst of insults. And yet, in that instant when he had leaned close, Chloe thought

she had seen something in his eyes, a stark hopelessness that had made her want to aid him, however she might be able. To what lengths she might have gone to do so, Chloe did not care to speculate.

She thought long and hard about her choices, but, in the end, it was that brief memory that stayed her hand. Rising to her feet, Chloe emptied her trunk once more. She still wasn't sure if she was doing the right thing, but she told herself that she was doing it for the earl, not for his martinet grandmother, and certainly not because she desperately needed a paying position. She was, instead, making an effort to give back something to one of those men who had given so much for their country and had received little enough in return.

If her concern went beyond that generalization to the specific character of one Kit Armstrong, surely the most handsome and intriguing of men, then Chloe knew she had better guard her heart. The last thing she needed was to develop some tendre for an earl when she was a mere baron's daughter, and penniless, besides! And, as if that weren't enough, to succumb to the lure of a man such as this one, tormented by guilt and suffering and heaven only knew what else, would surely be the worst folly she could ever commit.

Having lectured herself sternly and taken heed of the warning, Chloe turned her mind away from

herself. It was time to think of her task ahead serving as companion to Kit. He had suffered enough, and it was her duty to help him as well as she could.

Kit walked until he could not bear to take another step upon his aching leg. Then, at last, he returned to the house, seeking his rooms. He considered taking dinner there, as well, but that smacked of a cowardice too distasteful to allow. Let his grandmother rant! He was well used to it, though he was not accustomed to the twinge of shame he felt over his treatment of her guest. Indeed, for the first time in months, Kit had to wonder at what he had become.

Ever since his return, he had been confused about why he fared better than so many other, worthy men, including his brother. He had questioned the meaning of life itself, complex ethical and spiritual matters that theologians, philosophers and intellectuals had debated for centuries. Yet, despite all his former arrogance, Kit had found no answers, only more questions that fed his growing anxiety.

Yes, the reckless confidence of his youth had been replaced by doubts, about himself, his family and the society in which he had once moved so effortlessly. He had tried to talk about such things with other survivors of Waterloo while recuperat-

ing, only to find that his probing was unwelcome. Most men seemed content to return home to wives and families, retreating from the horror of the war.

As for his former friends, they wanted no part of such conversation as they single-mindedly pursued the inane frivolity of the ton without a thought to any larger issues. Kit had felt increasingly isolated by both his grief and his guilt, and his grandmother only worsened the situation by insisting that he take up Garrett's life as his own when he wasn't entitled to any of it. Kit gladly would have changed places with his brother, if only he could raise Garrett from the dead in exchange for his own life, but that was a useless, helpless wish that left him frustrated and bleak.

Sunk in these familiar, morose thoughts, Kit headed absently for the dining hall, but the sight of his unwanted guest jolted him from his dismal musings. He had fully expected to find her already gone, his rudeness having sent her fleeing, as it had all the other hopeful females. And, yet, there she was standing in the grand salon, as unruffled as usual, he noted with some surprise.

Obviously this one was made of sterner stuff. It was apparent in the set of her shoulders and in the calm, clear gaze that bespoke a steady temperament. *Good in battle,* he thought, though the only threat to her here came from himself.

Somehow the sight of her heartened him, and he paused to study her. She really was lovely in a homelike sort of way, with her great brown eyes and shining hair. The black looked dreadful on her, Kit mused, and he wondered what she normally wore, deep burgundy perhaps or rich blues and greens. Odd speculations, he realized. Odder still that he should be staring. He stepped forward and tendered his arm.

For a moment he thought she might refuse him, but she accepted with a slight nod. "Your rooms must have much to occupy you," she commented without even glancing up at him, and Kit blinked. So accustomed was he to the fawning of others that her barb startled, especially coming, as it did, from a woman whom he had insulted beyond all reason.

Yet she had not fled from his beastly behavior, nor did she appear to hold a grudge against him for it. The realization eased something inside of him, relaxing his stiff limbs, and his lips curved slightly, as if of their own will. "Not quite as interesting as I might have hoped," Kit heard himself say, though even as the words left his mouth, he wondered what had possessed him.

He was rewarded with the sudden, assessing glance of his companion, who tried to pull away. And although he would do better to rid himself of her, Kit held her fast. "I apologize for my earlier

assumptions," he said. "Perhaps, if you knew my grandmother as well as I, you might better understand my confusion."

Kit saw her mouth, rich and full, twitch before she smiled. "Oh, I think I know her well enough already," she said. Kit couldn't help but give her a grin in return, though it was crooked and stiff from disuse. And he found himself leading her into dinner with a lighter step than he had known in a long time. He had been right in deciding that Chloe was not in the dowager's pocket, and he wondered if perhaps the old woman's interfering would go awry.

As he escorted her to her seat, Kit was struck with the curious sensation that he had found an ally. And, indeed, Chloe proved herself to be so, for whenever the dowager started ranting, the younger woman seemed to divert her to something else. For once, Kit found himself actually listening to the conversation. He realized, as Chloe spoke, that he had buried himself so deeply here in the country that he was hardly aware of what had been happening in the world at large, and he drank in her news like a thirsty man.

It was startling, this sudden curiosity, as if someone had roused him from a heavy sleep. And although he had foresworn company, Kit found himself drawn to Chloe's speech. Well-read, intelligent, fierce in her opinions yet gentle in her manner, she

seemed like a beacon of warmth in his cold, cheerless existence.

She had a wonderful smile, not one of those showy ones, trotted out only when appropriate and to her best advantage, but a *real* smile. Slow to form, it blossomed like a flower to reveal a set of lovely white teeth with one small imperfection. One of her front teeth tipped a little to the side, and Kit was fascinated by it. When he found himself contemplating what that tiny edge would feel like under his tongue, he blinked in astonishment.

If he had met her a few years ago, or perhaps even a year ago, Kit would have done his best to make that smile appear often. Then again, in his vanity, maybe he never would have noticed her. More the fool, he. In any case, now it was too late. He might watch and admire, but he was a dead man, if not in the literal sense, then far too cold and lifeless for any woman to rouse.

Chloe was a diversion, nothing more, a momentary respite from his heretofore unrelenting guilt and grief. She might prove a help in his battle against his grandmother's shrill demands, but that was all she could be.

If he weren't so far lost to the world, he might wonder whether brave little Chloe might aid him against far darker demons. But Kit had stopped believing in miracles long ago and, as for hope, he had none.

Chapter Three

When Chloe excused herself from the table, Kit's gaze followed her, resting on her straight back and her dark coil of hair, and for a moment he very nearly *felt* something. The sensation was so strange that he blinked in surprise before he decided it was only an adverse reaction to his dinner. Although he had grown too gaunt for his tall frame, he usually had little appetite, yet this evening he had eaten more, perhaps because Chloe's speech distracted him from his grandmother's ranting.

As if on cue, the dowager, who had been blessedly silent for some time, spoke up. "Pretty little thing, isn't she, in a simple sort of way?" she asked with a nod toward Chloe.

Kit's eyes narrowed at her observation. There was nothing simple about Chloe, and his grandmother was failing if she thought so, but he was

not about to argue the merits of their guest, being too wary of his grandmother's motives. Instead he shrugged carelessly, as if the matter was of no interest, while he picked at what little was left upon his plate.

"Of course, she's not in your usual style," the dowager added in a sly tone.

The comment brought his head up. "And what exactly does that mean? How could that possibly be germane to her work here?" Kit asked. When his grandmother did not answer, he frowned as a certain dark conjecture took root. "Unless you want me to seduce the chit?"

The dowager sniffed. "Well, I'd like to see you take an interest in anything, even a bit of muslin."

Kit turned, impaling his grandmother with a cold look. "She is not a bit of muslin."

"No, of course not," the dowager conceded, but it was too late. Kit's suspicions were aroused, as well as his long-inactive sensibilities. He had already judged Chloe to be guiltless, but what of the dowager?

"Did you hire her to seduce me?" he demanded as a new, potent sensation filled him, painful yet different from his usual tormented grief.

"No!" his grandmother snapped, but Kit caught a telltale glint in the old woman's eyes before she quickly glanced away.

He seized upon it. "Then just why is she here? Certainly not as a companion to you. Did you lure her here with the promise of a position, intending to dangle her before me as some kind of bait? To what purpose? You cannot want such a nobody as countess, so what use do you have for her? Answer me!" he demanded in a cold, hard voice that, for once, left his grandmother speechless.

Or maybe her own guilt kept her silent. Kit made a low sound of disgust as he rose to his feet. "For all your fine title and grandiose airs, you are nothing more than a procuress! And as to your opinion of me, it doesn't even bear comment," he muttered before turning on his heel.

Kit stalked from the room, some kind of heat giving strength to his tired limbs. He was outraged to discover not only that his original suspicions about his grandmother were correct, but that she had duped an unwitting innocent with her scheme. It was unconscionable! She had deliberately put a lovely female in his way, hoping to rouse his dormant interest to the point that he acted upon it. Worse yet, she had involved Chloe. Kit's mind reeled, and even his jaded senses balked at the thought of so coarsely using a decent young woman, and she a relative, as well!

Rarely did he bestir himself to action these days, but Kit could not let this intrigue continue. Of

course, he had no intention of dallying with Chloe or any other, but neither could he allow her to be so misused by his grandmother. The dowager had gone too far this time. He was used to her tricks, but no gently bred baron's daughter should be put in such a position. The old woman ought be horse-whipped, Kit thought as anger, hot and righteous, surged through him.

It was such a strange sensation that he halted in confusion. He felt oddly off balance, as though muscles long unused were being employed. Glancing down at his injured leg, Kit sought to blame his wounds, but the low, dull ache there had nothing to do with this sudden warmth. Abruptly, he realized that he hadn't felt this way since returning home. Indeed, he had felt nothing at all except his twin companions of grief and guilt, and the fierceness of his rage caught him off guard.

He was staring stupidly ahead, startled at the revelation, when Chloe returned. She was going to brush past him, but he made some noise, effectively halting her. "I need to speak with you," he said a bit stiffly.

When she looked up in surprise, Kit turned his head back toward the dining room. "Not here. Come with me," he said, reaching out to take her arm. But the touch only brought more heat and awareness, and he dropped his hand in surprise.

For a long moment he stared dumbly at his fingers, puzzled by his reaction, then, recovering himself, he motioned for her to join him out of earshot of both his grandmother and the servants who spied for her. "Let us go outside," he said.

Although Chloe looked a bit wary of his invitation, she lifted her chin and walked beside him through the French doors of the grand salon into the gathering darkness. Closing the tall portals behind him, Kit stepped out onto the stone terrace, enclosed by curved railings leading down to the manicured lawns below. Beside him, he heard the gentle rustle of skirts as his companion moved past to stand by the balustrade.

"It's beautiful here, isn't it?" she asked in that sultry voice of hers, and Kit had to tear his gaze away from her gleaming hair to their surroundings.

He had been here evenings beyond count, of course, especially since his return, for the beauty of Hawthorne Park and the Yorkshire countryside seemed the only thing that gave him a moment's peace. And yet, tonight it all looked different, the stars shining brighter in the night sky, the moonlight glittering freshly on the fading grass below. Odd, but Kit felt almost...human again.

Out loud, he said, "It is quite picturesque, yes. But that is not why I brought you here. Again, I apologize for my behavior this morning, but I fear

that my suspicions were not totally groundless.'' When she turned to look at him, her dark eyes wide, Kit had to concentrate on what he had been about to say. He took a deep breath. ''I'm afraid you have been brought here under false pretenses,'' he said, deliberately focusing his gaze on the distant beeches.

When she didn't answer, Kit glanced at her again only to be caught once more in that dark gaze. Deep. Tranquil. Soothing. He blinked. ''My grandmother does not need or want a companion, nor does she care in the slightest for the misfortunes of distant relatives. Despite her title, she is no better than the meanest sort of female. In short, Miss Gibbons, she lured you here in the hope that I might be enticed to bed you. Though her logic escapes me, as is usually the case, I can only conjecture that once returned to manly vigor, she thinks I will assume all the duties she has laid upon my head without protest, thanks to your virgin sacrifice.''

Kit expected another slap, a shocked gasp, at least, but not the long, low laugh that rippled through him like a fine wine, heady and delicious. He swung his head around to stare at her, and she immediately put a hand up to cover that wonderful smile of hers, tipped tooth and all.

"I'm sorry, but the idea is just so ludicrous!" she said.

Well, yes, Kit had to admit that his grandmother was reaching on this one, if she expected him to despoil a relative without the slightest prompting of a conscience. Perhaps she thought the army had effectively eliminated all ethical codes except for kill or be killed. Or maybe she mistakenly thought him as bereft of morality as herself.

"I mean, why on earth would you be tempted by a penniless spinster who has moved on naught by the very fringes of society?" Chloe asked. Then she chuckled, as if she had not insulted both herself and his taste in one fell swoop. Obviously she was looking at the whole thing from a skewed perspective.

"And what makes you think I wouldn't be attracted to you?" Kit asked, genuinely curious. "Society bores me to death, and I have no need of money, so your wealth or position hardly matter." Indeed, he was more interested in her throaty laugh, in the dark promise of solace in her eyes, in the gentle curves of her woman's body. *That is, if he were interested in anything, which he most definitely wasn't.*

"I beg your pardon, but I am hardly the sort to catch the eye of someone like yourself, let alone drive you to uncontrollable lust!" Chloe protested.

Kit frowned at both her plain-speaking and her words. There were far too many so-called gentlemen of the *ton* with uncontrolled passions who would be only too happy to take advantage of a hired governess or companion, with or without their grandmother's sanction. Kit suddenly saw the darkly beautiful Chloe as unprotected, and he felt a raw surge of possessiveness, to claim his own...strictly in his role as a relative, of course.

"Someone like me? What does that mean?" he asked. Did she refer to his admitted lack in that area necessary to act upon lustful urges? Eyeing her carefully, Kit thought he saw a faint blush tinge her cheeks in the darkness, and he felt a heavy regret at his previous honesty.

She looked down at her hands. "I mean, someone young, handsome, charming..."

The weight lifted, making him light of heart. "Formerly young, formerly handsome," Kit muttered, brandishing his cane. "And formerly charming, most certainly," he added with a rueful smile.

Chloe laughed again. "Oh, I wouldn't underestimate your charms," she said.

"And I wouldn't underestimate yours," Kit said, his smile fading. He held her gaze, and the heat that sparked when they touched seemed to gather in the stillness like a thread between them, growing and strengthening...

Chloe dropped her gaze. "You flatter me, my lord. Kit," she amended. "And I appreciate your concern for me, though I still think it misplaced."

"You don't know my grandmother and her machinations," Kit muttered.

"Oh, but I'm learning quickly, and I believe she feels that her schemes and deceptions are justified, if the results meet her ends."

Kit opened his mouth to comment, but Chloe stayed him with a hand that rendered him speechless, soft and pale and so warm before she pulled it away. "And I know you two are constantly at odds, but she did not hire me to entice you, merely to watch you, as a companion of sorts, out of her concern for you," Chloe said.

"What?" Kit asked. Truly bewildered, he tried to marshal the thoughts that seemed to scatter at a mere touch from this young woman. Had his grandmother spun some Banbury Tale to ensure her cooperation?

For a long moment Chloe said nothing, then she lifted her dark gaze to his, serious and intent. "The dowager is afraid that you might do yourself in," she whispered.

Kit sucked in a harsh breath, unable to believe what he heard, then released it in a rush, along with several colorful curses. "I'm more likely to murder her, the interfering old harridan!"

Instead of being offended by his words, Chloe laughed, and for an instant, Kit forgot his outrage as he basked in the rich peal of it. Low and sultry, the sound made him think of long nights of love-making, and he decided that a laugh like that should not belong to the sensible spinster Chloe thought herself. Indeed, no guardian or governess or lady's companion ought to possess a voice like hers, warm and deep and sensual.

Kit blinked. No matter how attractive or pleasing or even desirable this woman might be, he had no intention of allowing her to remain here, especially as some kind of nursemaid to him! Obviously his grandmother had gone mad, or even worse, she thought *him* insane. Yes, he had often wished to trade places with Garrett, but suicide would not bring back his brother, and he would not dishonor his fallen comrades in such a fashion.

Kit swung toward the young woman who stood so calmly before him, as though she had spoken of nothing earth-shattering or soul-searing. If she truly were destitute, he could hardly turn her out. The crafty dowager had counted on that, but he need not spend any time with her.

"I'll make you a deal," he said. "You leave me alone, and I'll leave you alone."

To his utter astonishment, she shook her head. "I'm afraid I cannot," she answered.

"Why the devil not?" Kit demanded.

"Because I have been employed to complete a task, and I'm not leaving until I see it through."

Kit stared at her, stunned. Surely she did not intend to shadow him about, testing his drink for poison and removing all sharp objects from his care? A flush of humiliation stained his cheeks at the thought, and he laughed bitterly. Had he really such an intention, no slender young woman could stop him. Nor could she play at being his companion of sorts, should he refuse her. All he had to do was walk away.

"Good luck to you, then!" he said, turning on his heel and stalking back inside, leaving Miss Chloe Gibbons out in the cold. For good.

Kit slipped out while dawn was still streaking the horizon. Sleep no longer came easily to him, so it was no hardship to arise at a time when he once would have been seeking his bed after a long night spent at elegant balls or gambling dens, the favored pursuits of the ton. Now he kept the hours of a country farmer, caring naught for his old habits. It was struggle enough for him to get through his day, and, this morning, to outwit his so-called companion.

With a wicked curve of his lips, Kit headed for the stables. He might not be able to outpace her

on foot, but horseback was a different matter, and in a few moments he was mounted on Raja, looking forward to a long, solitary ride through woods bright with autumn colors. Although the horse was restive, Kit was in no hurry. He knew the stallion could outpace anything in the stables. So he went slowly, climbing the long, gentle slope that led to the oaks clustered on the hills ahead. Smugly, he told himself that Chloe was probably still in bed, but that brought to mind images of her flushed from sleep, her thick hair tousled, and he quickly turned his attention to the path ahead.

He had no use for a nursemaid, a companion, or anyone else. Why couldn't his grandmother accept that and leave him be? No one understood him, so he preferred to be alone with his own tortured thoughts. He wondered, not for the first time, if he ought not to leave Hawthorne Park, abandoning his grandmother, his heritage and the earldom in a single swoop. But something deep inside him clung to this last connection to his former life.

The Yorkshire dales were in his blood. Kit took a deep breath of air scented with grass and leaves and faint hints of lingering flowers, and he felt the tension inside himself ease some small measure. Here was the only place he could find any surcease, so why should he let the dowager take that

away from him? He ought to send her packing instead!

Kit had not gone much farther when he heard
the sound of another rider behind him. *It couldn't
be,* he thought. Chloe was surely still asleep and,
if not, she could never have followed him so
quickly. Yet, even as Kit told himself otherwise,
he felt a curious elation at the thought of her pur-
suit. Like one meeting a dangerous challenge, Kit
turned slowly only to stare in horror at the sight
of his companion atop Pegasus, a high-stepping
thoroughbred that required the firm hand of a sea-
soned rider and was known to dislike members of
its own sex. True to form, the filly was dancing
about and tossing its head, while Chloe clung, in-
effectually, to the reins.

It took Kit but one frantic moment to reach her
side, and without thought, he simply seized her
from the saddle. As he pulled her onto his lap, she
gasped in surprise and clutched at his coat, as if
fearing he would toss her onto the ground. But he
gripped her about the waist, so tightly in fact, that
Kit realized she was shaking. Or was it his own
hands that quaked, while his heart pounded as
fiercely as in battle?

"What the devil were you doing on Pegasus?"
he demanded.

At least she had the good grace to look cha-

grined. "I told your groom that I wanted a mount that would be able to catch yours," she said, her brows tilting up in a rueful expression. "But that is only because I knew you would ride ahead, rather than wait for me."

Kit cursed fluently. "Have you no sense at all? You could have been killed, and for what?" *For me,* he thought grimly. "I will not have another death laid at my door!" he swore through gritted teeth.

"I'm all right, Kit," she said softly.

Chloe's low, steady voice seemed to sweep away the red haze of anger and grief until he could see clearly, and *she* filled his vision. She was like a beacon, a point of light in his dark world. Beneath his fingers, her slender body was solid and anchoring. Her dark hair, hastily arranged, fell in great, silky locks here and there, and thick lashes lifted over eyes that drew him with some imagined promise of peace and comfort and…passion.

Of all his bizarre musings, it was that last stray thought that arrested him. Suddenly, Kit found himself looking at her mouth, wide and luscious, and a torrid heat exploded around him. He wanted to sink into that mouth, to take his refuge and pleasure there, to abandon his grief and guilt in exchange for life and love. *And it scared him to*

death. Sucking a deep breath, he jerked his gaze away and nudged Raja back toward the stables.

Kit kept his eyes focused on the low building until he slowed the stallion to a halt near the somber groom, who helped Chloe to the ground. He gave the man a look that evinced his displeasure, then he made the mistake of glancing once more down at Chloe, who was watching him with those wide, calm eyes, just as if nothing untoward had happened. And instead of racing off into the hills, putting the greatest distance possible between him and the threat presented by Miss Chloe Gibbons, Kit found himself telling the groom to find her a more suitable mount. And before he knew what he was about, they were both moving toward the oaks on the hill.

They rode in silence, and Kit relaxed once more as whatever delusions he had harbored receded into the reality of one innocent young relative perched upon a nearby gelding. What danger could she possibly pose to him? Perhaps he had imagined his response; surely he had exaggerated the depth of it. It had been a long while since he had held a woman on his lap, so it was only natural that he would be stirred in some manner even though his body could no longer function as it once had.

Taking in a deep breath, Kit banished such thoughts and let the peace of the morning wash

over him. He could no longer stand the racket of idle chatter, the sound of people who just wanted to hear themselves talk. That was one of the reasons he sought the countryside, the open spaces and still oaks, where the only noise was the call of the birds, the rustle of the leaves and the occasional movement of some small animal.

Under the branches of the sheltering trees, Kit felt his usual ease, but with a different aspect. Today, his was not the solitude of the solitary. Instead he was filled with a warmth that came with sharing the beauty of the forest paths with another. Despite his vow to the contrary, he and Chloe had settled into a comfortable companionship, and when at last she spoke, he found he was eager for her voice.

"What is that foul smell?" she asked, wrinkling her nose, and Kit laughed, surprising himself with the odd, rusty sound.

"That's our very own medicinal spring," he said. They had reached the glade where the hot waters rose up from the ground into a small pool, bubbling and foaming against the rocks. "It pops up at various points all over the Park," he said.

"How wonderful!" Chloe exclaimed, startling him with her enthusiasm. She halted her gelding and dismounted to gaze with rapt admiration at the site that he had long ignored. "Why, it is a natural

bath! Have you made use of it? I am sure it would help your leg."

Kit was lowering himself to the ground when her words brought him up short, injecting a chill into the warmth of the day. "What do you mean?" he asked, fixing her with a hard glare.

"When it is aching, bothering you especially, you ought to come out here and—"

Kit cut her off. "And how do you know it bothers me?" he demanded.

Chloe did not seem the least disturbed by his vehemence or his fierce expression. "I can tell by the set of your jaw. Oh, I see that it is well this morning, but when you've been walking a lot, I suspect it aggravates you," she answered easily.

Kit didn't know what to say. He felt naked, caught out somehow, so he frowned silently.

Chloe didn't appear to notice. "I think your spring would do wonders for it," she said. "My father always used to feel better after a trip to one of the spas, especially Bath! He suffered so from the gout." She sighed softly, seeming lost in memory, and Kit realized that it was her father she was mourning. He felt a stab of fresh guilt for his churlish behavior, for being so sunk in his own sorrow that he had failed to recognize that she, too, was hurting.

"You probably think I'm a selfish bastard," he

muttered. Forcing himself to face her, Kit fully expected the sort of disapprobation that he would likely receive from his grandmother. But Chloe only smiled, that slow, blossoming flash of white that revealed her crooked tooth, and something eased within his chest.

"No," she said, eyeing him calmly. "I see a man racked by pain and grief…and something else. What is it, Kit?"

Her perception startled him, and he moved away, his throat suddenly thick. He had no intention of telling her, of course, and yet somehow the words came out in a stark mutter. "I'm alive and they are all dead, including Garrett. It's not right."

"Perhaps," Chloe answered, following behind him to stand at his back, not too close and not too far. "But who are you to say? Had you done anything differently, could you have changed the course of Waterloo? Could you have prevented the enormous British losses? If you had been here at home, could you have saved your brother?" She paused, but Kit said nothing. "I think when your mind is clear, you know the answer," she added gently.

Kit swallowed against a sudden pressure. "But why me?" he whispered, echoing the question that had haunted him for months, that no one, least of all himself, had deigned to answer.

But answer him, Chloe did. "Perhaps because you are worthy in your own right," she said. Startled, Kit turned to find her so close that he could reach out and touch her, if he dared. But he stood still, waiting, and she lifted those great brown eyes to his. Wisdom and mercy and something else shone there, drawing him to her...

"Mourn your comrades and your brother, as I do my father, but do not squander your precious moments in senseless regret," she said. "You are an intelligent man, still young and vital, with much to offer the world. Do not waste the life that was spared!"

Her words sliced through him, abrading his open wounds so painfully that Kit nearly cried out in protest. Automatically he moved to protect them, and without a word he swung up on Raja and headed back through the woods, toward home, his unwanted companion following.

Chapter Four

Despite his initial dismissal of her words, Kit thought long and hard about Chloe's admonition, and after much consideration, his brain acknowledged she was right. However, the rest of him was not as quick to forgive himself for being alive when so many were not. Although Kit had never considered himself a creature of emotion, it seemed as though his feelings overcame his mind with a vengeance, urging him to lash out at Chloe, as well. How dare she advise him? She didn't have any idea what he had been through. He wanted nothing more than to drive her away, as he had everyone else, and sink back into his pool of misery, logic be damned.

But Chloe wouldn't leave him alone. Silence that would have sent the most greedy and ardent of potential countesses fleeing had no effect what-

soever upon her. Indeed, though Kit had not spoken at all on the ride back to the stables, she hadn't appeared to notice. Every once in a while, she commented on the weather or the countryside or the horses, seemingly oblivious to his lack of response.

At dinner Kit tried to ignore her, but she consistently managed to gain his attention and draw him out. He told himself that he was desperate for conversation after hearing his grandmother's one-sided rants, but he knew that there was more involved. He liked listening to her speech, the low, sultry sound of it, the comforting cadence, and to the words, as well, for Chloe held opinions on most everything and they were intelligent and well thought out.

When Kit found himself watching her a bit too avidly, searching for a glimpse of that one front tooth as she spoke, he knew he was in trouble. That vague sense of danger came over him again, but instead of meeting it, he slunk back to his rooms, feeling suspiciously like a coward. He had faced Napoleon's hordes without flinching, yet one slender female had him hiding away!

Even safely ensconced behind locked doors, Kit half expected the preternaturally calm Chloe to come knocking at his private apartments with innocent yet bold intent. Perhaps he secretly even

craved such a visit, so conflicted were his feelings about her, but the hours passed without any interruption.

Kit ought to have been well pleased. However, the spacious rooms that had contented him since he had left the nursery seemed stifling, and he paced incessantly. He blamed his unusual restlessness on the lack of his evening walk, which often tired him to the point where he could at last get some rest. Now, he did not even attempt to sleep, and finally, when the whole house was abed and the moon high, he slipped out into the garden.

Moonlight gave luster to the fading grass and the beds of late-blooming flowers as he made his way to the Grecian folly that stood amid a backdrop of tall oaks. It was little more than a roof and columns where his parents had once set summer chairs, but now it seemed bleak and empty, a fitting setting for his melancholy.

Leaning his left shoulder against the cold stone, Kit looked out over the well-tended lawns and sought the semblance of peace that came from the natural world, but this night it eluded him. He considered walking, yet a new unease seemed to have settled over him, and he found himself scanning the countryside as if in search of something.

And then he found it: a small dark figure hurried up the slope towards him, black cloak flying be-

hind her. *It couldn't be,* he told himself, and yet his heart lurched in his chest as he recognized Chloe running to meet him. But his momentary elation was soon displaced by other feelings, darker and more disturbing, and when she reached the small enclosure, Kit rounded upon her.

"What the devil are you doing here?" he demanded, genuinely shocked by her appearance. Plainly, she had donned her clothing in haste, for one shoulder dipped, revealing a patch of silken skin where the cloak had fallen back. She hadn't even attempted to dress her hair, and the thick mass fell over her shoulders like rich satin.

Kit took in her dishevelment, and something erupted inside him. He felt cornered, angry at being followed, at being hovered over and watched, at being treated like a pathetic suicidal wretch instead of a man.

"I need no nursemaid, no wet nurse!" he snapped.

"Good, because I don't see how we'll find one at this hour," Chloe answered with that maddening calm that was beginning to infuriate him. It wasn't the cool distance of Julia and her ilk, just a deceptively simple reasonableness. Except there was nothing reasonable about her being out here in the night with him.

"Have you no sense of propriety?" he snarled,

furious not only at her continual presence, but at her total disregard for her reputation, indeed, for her own skin. Or did she trust to his malfunctioning body to keep him a gentleman? Rage, irrational and consuming, welled up in him, seeking an outlet. "Or is it that despite your pose as a staid spinster, you crave a little danger to spice your dull days?" he taunted.

Stepping forward, Kit stalked her until she backed up against a wide Grecian pillar, and he placed his left hand beside her head to box her in. Leaning slightly, he looked down into her upturned face, gilded by moonlight, and he paused, arrested by at the intensity of her beauty. "Or perhaps you crave something else entirely?" he whispered.

She licked her lips, an innocent gesture, he was certain this time, yet the sight of her dainty tongue against that generous mouth set the spark between them alight. "I—" she began, but Kit didn't let her finish. He bent his head and took her mouth with his own. Perhaps he couldn't perform, but he could very well give her a kiss that might make her think twice about chasing after a man in the darkness of a deserted garden.

Kit heard her low sound of surprise or protest, but he ignored it. Seizing the opportunity presented by her parted lips, he swept his tongue inside, running it over the tilt of her front tooth, and the sweet

sensuality set his head to spinning. He deepened the contact, plundering her mouth even as he closed the space between them, pressing his body against hers.

He expected another slap, some form of resistance at least from his sensible companion, but instead she met his ardor with her own, her untutored response more erotic than the most decadent courtesan's. Kit's heart slammed against his ribs, and he brought his hand to the column of her throat, groaning at the satin texture of her skin beneath his questing fingers, the brush of her silken hair against his knuckles.

Her arms slipped around him, beneath his coat, and he wished that he had left off his waistcoat, his shirt, *everything,* so that she might truly touch him. She ran her hands up and down his back, and Kit felt as if he had come home at last. Here, finally, was the haven he had been searching for, where he could forget everything except the precious wonder of life he had let slip away from him. This was where he belonged, in the arms of this woman, against her, inside her...

"Chloe." Kit whispered her name in rapt adoration, his fingers sliding down her bodice to cup one round breast. She was so soft yet so real, so alive, that he wanted to weep for the pure joy of her. His lips followed the path of his hand as he

pressed kisses to her throat. Her head fell back, and she made a low, husky sound so stirring that Kit nearly lost his balance. He gripped his cane in a white-knuckled clasp as he murmured his pleasure against the tender skin above her gown.

He lifted her breast, encased in black crepe, to his mouth, wetting the material with his tongue even as he wanted to bare it to his gaze, his breath, his lips. She made that sultry sound again, arching her back, and one long, silky lock fell across his face. He kissed it, as well. Voracious hunger shot through him, unbridled and fiery, and without thinking, he lifted his right hand to pull her closer to his insistent body.

His cane dropped to the ground, clattering loudly upon the stone, and the passionate woman in his arms stiffened suddenly. Gazing up at him with those wide dark eyes, still clouded with desire, she pulled away from him, wrapping her cloak about her with a shiver. In the heat of the moment, Kit had forgotten the chill in the evening air. Though the trees at their back provided some shelter from the wind, there was nothing before them except the long expanse of lawn lined with the remnants of the season's flowers and shrubs.

The sight made Kit flinch, for he realized that he had taken outrageous liberties here where anyone could see them, and he cursed the reckless

frenzy that had seized him. Leaning one hand against the pillar, he bowed his head as he tried to catch his breath and gather his thoughts, but Chloe was already moving away, hurrying from the folly before he could reach for her.

It was only when he bent to retrieve his cane, still panting and shaken, that Kit discovered he had been wrong about one thing, at least. Everything was in working order and painfully eager to prove it.

Kit lay awake most of the night, alternately cursing the abrupt return of his bodily functions and applauding it, hoping that at last he had managed to drive Chloe away and wishing that he had not. And all the while, he wondered what she would do. Certainly she had good reason to leave after his behavior, for she was an innocent. That much was evident from the freshness of her kiss, the low hum of wonder in her voice, the tentative touch of her soft hands...

With a groan, Kit turned over, suddenly uncomfortable at the memory. The sooner he forgot about what had happened in the folly the better, for if Chloe remained here, he could not take advantage of her again or he would be living down to his grandmother's expectations. And that was something he would never do.

Nor would he purposely seduce any dependent, especially a relative, even one as misguided as Chloe seemed to be, at least where he was concerned. Kit wasn't going to kill himself, so she was wasting her time. She would do better by everyone if she went away, he decided grimly, before drifting off to sleep at last.

It wasn't until morning that Kit realized that for once his thoughts had been consumed with something other than his grief and guilt and his dreams filled with something a deal more pleasant than war and death. His state of mind being what it was, Kit wasn't sure whether to celebrate or decry the change. And although he hurried down to breakfast, he told himself it was only because his appetite seemed to have returned.

Yet as he made his way to the dining room, Kit held his breath, uncertain, only to release it at the sight of Chloe's still figure seated rather primly at the table. He felt a curious elation along with a sort of smug satisfaction. *Prim, indeed.* Although she looked the very picture of a quiet companion, Kit knew that he had the power to turn her from the staid spinster she pretended into a passionate woman. The knowledge affected him in a rather untimely manner, and he took his seat with necessary haste.

She glanced up, and Kit thought he saw a faint

blush steal across her cheeks, but she greeted him with her usual calm, steady gaze. In keeping with his current duality, he was both annoyed and grateful at her pretense that nothing was changed between them. He could prove to her that something had happened. Indeed, he could make it happen again, but *no*. Better to forget such things. She was remaining, and he must behave as the gentleman he once had been.

So Kit said nothing of the incident and neither did Chloe during the leisurely meal or afterward, when she coaxed him into showing her the grounds. Kit knew he ought to retreat, that their association was pointless, but he wanted to take advantage of the fine weather that might end at any time. And he was not about to hide away in his apartments again or flee like a coward.

Outside, they moved forward in silence, settling easily into step. But no matter how they might act as if all was the same between them, Kit, at least, felt a subtle difference, a certain warmth in the very air around them, manifest of the intimacy they had shared. And that was not all. The sight of a stray lock of Chloe's dark hair reminded him of its silky feel. A chance sigh all too easily brought to mind the low sound of her delight at his touch. And the subtle scent of her, borne by a gentle breeze, roused the memory of how she had filled

his senses. Indeed, the longer they walked, the more Kit recalled and the more annoyed he became. How could she appear so unaffected when all he wanted to do was to seize her in his arms again and begin where they had left off?

Obviously, despite her momentary lapse, Chloe knew better. And he did, too, Kit thought with a frown. She was a gently bred female, as well as a relative, even if so distant as to make the connection faint. He reminded himself that she was a dependent here, and as such, under his protection. To seize her or anything else would not be honorable. And his honor was one of the few things he had clung to in the last bleak months.

At the thought, fresh guilt assailed him, forcing him to speak. "I regret if our meeting last night caused you any dismay. My behavior was uncalled for," he muttered.

"Apology accepted," Chloe said with that maddening serenity of hers. "However, I do not think that such familiarity should be part of the healing process, nor the proper duties of a companion," she added.

"The healing process? Is that what you think you are doing, healing me?" Kit asked, torn between outrage and amusement at her words. The later won out as he decided he did not want Chloe administering her particular medical skills to any-

one else. Out loud, he said, "Then I might have wished for your presence on the Continent when I could barely walk." For one tantalizing moment, he pictured himself lying abed while Chloe applied kisses and more to his injured body.

"That must have been a difficult time," she said.

Kit frowned as memories flooded back. "Yes, but I didn't have the worst of it, there or upon the field of battle. I was one of the fortunate," he said, though he had not really felt so before. He had long wished to change places with Garrett or his comrades, but now, selfishly, he was glad that he alone, among so many fallen, was here standing beside a beautiful, gentle woman with eyes like warm chocolate and a mouth that would make a man forget all else.

"Tell me," she said.

"What?" Kit asked in some surprise, his mind still upon the tantalizing curve of her lips.

"About the war," she prompted.

"I can't," Kit said. Despite the rustle of leaves overhead and the crunch of grass beneath his feet, he felt tension cord his body, and he turned away.

"You must," Chloe said, drawing his attention back to her. Tucking her cloak beneath her, she sat in a patch of sun, her back against a thick oak, and gazed up at him expectantly.

Kit blew out a long breath. No one had ever asked him seriously about the experiences that he had pushed into a deep, dark place inside him, and he was both horrified and tantalized by Chloe's insistence. Against his will, he felt a pressing need to speak, but it was tempered by a reluctance to sully Chloe's ears with tales no decent female should hear.

Oh, he knew camp followers and wives who had been to battles, sometimes even charging in to save their husbands at a cost of their own limb or life. But that was different. Chloe was as far removed from that world of gunpowder and blood as was humanly possible, and Kit wanted to keep her that way.

And yet, the need to unburden himself suddenly surged through him until he could not control himself, and he began to recount the events that had led up to Waterloo. He spoke slowly at first, and then a torrent of words came, startling him with their intensity. After a time, his leg ached, so he sat down beside her, and after a longer time, he found himself unable to talk anymore.

And Chloe, calm and steady Chloe, did not turn away in horror or revulsion, but reached out and pulled him into her arms until he lay his head against her soft breasts and wept like an infant.

* * *

Kit wasn't sure what had come over him. Somehow he had made it back to the house after breaking down, returning to his rooms to rest. And, miraculously, he had slept. Now he actually felt refreshed, free somehow of a great burden, though nothing had changed. However, despite his comparative well-being, he suspected that he ought to be ashamed of his display, and he was loath to face Chloe again.

What would she think of him? Kit prepared himself for the worst, only to find her seated in the grand salon, looking as calm and steady as always. Although he searched for it, Kit found no condemnation in her face as she smiled up at him, only acceptance and something else. If he hadn't known better, Kit might have thought it admiration. But what woman could find anything to appreciate in a man who cried?

Certainly not his grandmother, Kit thought, for she glared at him with her usual expression of contempt. "And just where have you been?" she demanded. "I've had the entire staff out combing the hillsides for you! Sawyer has arrived and needs to meet with you about those London properties."

"I was resting," Kit said, walking to the tall windows to gaze out at the serene landscape.

"Resting? That's all you've been doing since

you got here! Now its time to *do* something!'' the dowager snapped. ''Someone needs to take the reins or this family will fall to ruin, Hawthorne!''

''I'll meet with Mr. Sawyer.'' The offer, coming as it did from Chloe, made both Kit and his grandmother turn to stare at her. Kit felt his lips curve in silent approval of her fortitude. Nothing frightened Chloe, not horrific war stories or weeping soldiers or even the dowager countess of Hawthorne.

Predictably, his grandmother was unimpressed and showed it by snorting loudly. ''Just what we need, a destitute girl advising our man of business!'' She stood up, giving them one of her sweeping, imperious glances, and then thumped her cane. ''I will go, since you continue to shirk your responsibilities,'' she said, glowering at Kit. Then she turned to Chloe, sending her a hard glance. ''And you have done nothing here to earn your wages,'' she added before storming from the room.

Kit opened his mouth to defend his companion, but the sound of her low voice, tinged with anxiety, stopped him.

''She's getting too old for this, Kit,'' Chloe said. Her words so startled him that for a moment he didn't think he had heard her correctly.

''My grandmother? Too old?'' he asked. ''She'll wrestle the devil himself in her very grave.''

But Chloe didn't smile. "Take a good look at her, Kit, and you'll see that she's about to break."

"Nonsense," Kit scoffed. "She's made of stone."

"Or so she would like us to believe," Chloe said. "Did you ever think that this is her way of coping?"

Kit uttered a low, bitter bark of laughter, but Chloe did not join him.

"Truly," she said, lifting those great dark eyes to his with gentle remonstrance. "I believe that if your grandmother allowed herself to really mourn her husband or her son or your brother or your health or the dynasty in which she has invested her very life, she would crack in two, like a brittle sliver of rock. She takes her strength from her pride of family, and that is what keeps her going, despite age and infirmity and disappointments. And that is why she clings to it so desperately."

Kit blinked in amazement, prepared to argue, but he had learned that Chloe didn't debate. She simply stated her case as reasonably as possible and then waited patiently for him to agree. But in this instance, how could he? And yet, as if against his will, he began to see the wisdom of her words. How often during these past few months had he decried his grandmother's ranting? But did he truly want to see the embodiment of fierceness, the stal-

wart pillar of his youth, the last bastion of his family, crack and crumble?

As if accepting his silence as agreement, Chloe spoke again. "I think, too, that if you consider it, you will find that you and your grandmother are not so very different. You share the same love of the land, the same pride in your heritage, the same fierce loyalty."

Kit sank down onto a carved gilt couch, astonished, as Chloe enumerated the dowager's finer points as well as his own. And, as she did so, she delicately forced him to examine the consequences of his guilt. Not only was he making himself and those who cared for him suffer, but he was letting the estate go, and that affected the tenant farmers and the villagers, as well.

While all of his grandmother's railing had fallen on deaf ears, Kit found himself listening to Chloe. He knew she shared his love of the countryside, and when she spoke of it and the people who were entrusted to him now as earl, he felt a subtle reawakening of his sense of responsibility, a sudden interest in the duties of the earldom.

All because of Chloe. She continued to speak, and Kit watched her, his gaze resting lovingly on the smooth sheen of her dark hair, on her thick lashes, on the curve of her cheek, which sent his attention lower, to other curves, and he took in a

harsh breath at the sudden stirring of his body. He remembered every luscious detail of Chloe's sweet form and suddenly he wanted nothing more than to uncover them, one by one, to his eyes, his hands, his mouth.

"Think about what you're feeling. Be honest with yourself is all I ask," she said softly, and Kit jerked to attention.

He knew what he was feeling all right, and mostly, it was unbridled lust for his companion.

Chapter Five

Chloe sat by the window in the study, ostensibly reading, but more often than not dividing her attention between the rain that pounded against the glass and Kit. He was seated not far away at a massive desk, looking through some papers that Mr. Sawyer had left behind, and Chloe practically held her breath rather than disturb the fragile tenure of his interest.

Despite the dowager's accusation that she was not earning her keep, Chloe knew she was helping and that Kit was getting better. His grandmother was impatient and frustrated, but any kind of healing took time. Why should recovery of the spirit be any different? And Chloe had seen changes in Kit, leading up to today's effort. If she could just restrain the dowager a while longer, she sensed that Kit would eventually assume a role in the house-

hold. The two would still argue, Chloe was certain, but Kit would return to his own.

And then what of herself? Chloe's joy at each step he took out of his guilt and mourning was tempered by a kind of sadness. For she knew that Kit's resumption of his life would put her out of a position, one that she had initially disdained only to come to love. *No.* Love was too strong a word, Chloe thought, shying away from it. Yet there was no denying she had made the ultimate mistake of those who served, whether governess, companion or paid help of any kind: she was becoming far too fond of her charges.

She had come here expecting to be miserable, a useless charity case with naught to do but fetch and carry. Instead she had found a challenge, an opportunity to help someone who desperately needed it. Having lost her father, she had never thought to be part of a family again, but she had created a new one in this household of misfits. She loved the Yorkshire countryside, the immaculate beauty of Hawthorne Park, the spacious rooms and elegant ambience of the house itself, and she had grown fond of its inhabitants, both the fierce old dowager and her difficult grandson.

Glancing at the latter, Chloe felt a curious sensation within her breast, and her heart began a new rhythm. His hair glinted in the pale light from the

window, as if producing its own sunshine, and the golden glow of his skin seemed a testament to it. He was putting on a little weight and losing some of his leanness, though he would never be anything except fit, despite his limp.

Blushing, Chloe looked down at the book in her lap, acknowledging her own weakness. Somehow, Kit had gone from being a beautiful but fatally flawed man into being a beautiful but vulnerable man, with a character that drew her admiration, not her scorn. And her initial dislike had turned into something else entirely.

Even as she tried to tear her attention away, Chloe glanced back at Kit, letting him fill her thoughts, worrying for him, wondering about him, and she knew she cared far too much. And unlike a governess or a normal companion, there was a certain yearning attached to her affection that endangered both her good name and her heart. It was wholly inappropriate, *especially after what had happened in the folly.*

Chloe refused to consider that night, pushing the memory way down deep until it receded into something resembling a dream. She had been determined to ignore it in the hope that Kit would, too, and he did, after a perfunctory apology. Indeed, he seemed to have dismissed the encounter with uncommon ease, and although Chloe told herself she

was grateful, she could not help feeling a tiny twinge of disappointment.

With a frown at her foolishness, Chloe reminded herself to be sensible and to view the incident in the proper perspective. As Kit healed, it was only fitting that he resume his former activities, including a man's natural inclination towards the opposite gender. She simply had been the only female at hand when he had been struck with the reoccurrence of that…interest, and that was the extent of her significance in the matter.

When he was more fully recovered, no doubt Kit would return to the social whirl and choose a suitable countess, just as the dowager wanted, his former companion long forgotten as he made a home at Hawthorne Park, raised a family and reigned as earl. Although that future was certainly what she was working toward and wished for him, for some reason the thought of such success brought a painful lump to her throat, and Chloe cleared it noisily.

"Hmm?" The low sound came from Kit, and Chloe realized that she had diverted him from Mr. Sawyer's documents. She knew a moment's regret even as some selfish, churlish part of her demanded that she steal whatever attention she could get while it lasted.

"What?" Kit asked when she did not respond. He turned his head to gift her with the full power

of his gaze, and Chloe felt like melting into a puddle in her seat.

"I was just wondering about your fiancée," she heard herself say. *Where had that come from?* Chloe thought even as she blushed anew. But hadn't she insisted on discussing other painful things? What made his engagement any different? *Perhaps the fact that she was consumed with curiosity about the woman who had broken it,* she decided.

Kit laid down the paper in his hand, but for a long moment Chloe thought he would not answer. Indeed, she was just going to change the subject when he finally spoke. "Julia was from another world—of frivolous parties, inane conversation and the vagaries of society. It seems a lifetime ago."

As if lost in thought, Kit stared off into the distance. "She was a toast of the ton, a duke's daughter, and a great prize upon the marital market. So, naturally, I was quite pleased when she began to show me marked attention," he noted with a wry expression. "I was only a younger son then, but she claimed to have been smitten by a dashing cavalry officer. Perhaps she admired the uniform."

"More likely the way you wore it," Chloe commented acerbically.

Kit turned to look at her then, as if startled by

her presence, and he laughed, his green eyes aglow with mischief. "Surely, I wasn't the only fellow in the entire army able to fill out a uniform."

Chloe shifted in her seat, suddenly uncomfortable with his perceptive gaze. "Perhaps," she mumbled.

"And maybe you are right, and she only liked the looks of me, for when I returned without the same looks or charm, she was eager to move on to a more robust fellow."

Flooded with mortification at her thoughtless comment, Chloe felt terrible for causing Kit more pain. "No! That's not what I meant at all—" she began, but he cut her off with a lift of his hand.

"It doesn't matter now," he said. Then he paused as if considering the truth of his words, and his lips curved into a smile that rendered Chloe into warm butter. "It doesn't matter at all."

They were spending too much time together, Kit thought with something akin to panic. Over the past week Chloe had, indeed, become a companion of sorts, despite his continued misgivings. Although he sensed that she was a threat to the existence he had made for himself here, she managed to lull him with her quiet manner and reasonable speech.

Just when he swore to put some distance be-

tween them, she would give his arm a gentle touch of reassurance and he would lose his intention in the warm pleasure that flooded him. Or she might fall into a peaceful silence, and instead of driving her away, he would nearly forget her presence, only to look up to find her there, a comforting sight. And if Kit still thought to deny her, he had only to gaze into those great dark eyes of hers, full of compassion, not pity, of sense instead of nonsense, and brimming with the promise of something more, for which he dared not even hope.

So they took long walks or rides together, and when the weather kept them inside, she read out loud or they played cards or she wrote letters while he began to look over the business of the earldom. He could do it, too, if Chloe was nearby. He could forget that he was taking over Garrett's position and startle himself with his abilities.

Chloe was not the least surprised, pointing out that he had led men and planned attacks and strengthened communications in the field, so why couldn't he do the same here? And, so he did, organizing the tenants, promoting the agricultural methods that had been Garrett's passion and taking up correspondence with the managers of the vast family businesses. He even found some of it to be challenging.

But when he was alone in the study, Kit would

sink into the dismals again, feeling as though he was betraying Garrett's memory with his new-found skills. Determined to not forget his brother, he questioned Chloe's efficacy. And that was when the nagging sensation of danger overcame his good sense, and he began to fear her and everything she represented.

Leaning in his chair, Kit put a hand to the back of his neck, pressing against the tight muscle. He should be out walking instead of here in this close room with a pile of written words before him. He needed to breathe fresh air to clear his head, to feel the wind, to eat up the countryside with his strides until he was well away from his grandmother's nagging, from the business of being earl, but most of all from the woman who had taken over his world until it wasn't his own anymore, but some-one else's. *Garrett's.*

Just then the door swung slightly, and Kit opened his mouth, prepared to curse whoever dared disturb his momentary quiet, only to swallow his protest at the sight of Chloe. As always in her presence, his body warmed and elation filled him, driving away the tension—until he jerked it back and hung on to it for dear life. Fixing her with one of the glares that had sent so many of his old friends and family packing, he unleashed the beast.

"I can't do this," he said coldly. And throwing

out an arm, he swept the pile of reports, receipts and correspondence to the floor in one fell swoop.

Anyone else would have been horrified by such a display, but Chloe appeared undisturbed. "Then do something else," she said, stepping forward to perch on the edge of a small divan. She was so beautiful that Kit could not look at her, not without losing what little resolve he had left.

"And just what do you suggest?" he asked with a snarl. In the back of his mind, he thought to insult her, but the words only incited him further. Images of just what he would like to do, here with Chloe, flickered through his mind, stealing his breath.

Seemingly oblivious to that sudden flare of desire, Chloe eyed him calmly. "Did you ever think that you might be alive for a reason?" she asked in a deceptively casual tone.

Kit shot her a hard look that told her such speech was unwelcome, but Chloe ignored it. "Or at least that you might put your own survival to some good use?" she asked.

"Haven't you been listening to my grandmother? I'm here solely for the maintenance of the family enterprises and the propagation of the species," Kit said. And if Chloe pushed him to fulfill the former duty, why shouldn't she assist him with the latter?

"I'm not talking about that," she said. "Al-

though I think you'd enjoy serving as earl, if you let yourself, I certainly don't view the continuation of your line as a matter of life and death or a moral obligation.''

Well, that was entirely too bad, Kit thought.

"Instead of brooding over those who are dead, those you cannot aid, you might do something to help those poor men, thousands of them I daresay, who have been dismissed from the army and navy since Waterloo, with no pensions or provisions or employment," she said.

"Why, I have seen them upon the roadways, doing the meanest of jobs, humiliated and beaten when they should be victorious. You are in a position now to do something for the men who saved your life and our country. You might think upon that," Chloe said.

And before he could argue or comment in any fashion, she rose to her feet, as if what she had just said was of little consequence. But it was, and Kit knew it. He had seen them himself on his way home, in London and on those few times he ventured forth from Hawthorne Park, men who had risked everything and now had nothing. And he found himself deep in thought before he realized just what she had done.

Unlike his grandmother, Chloe never raised her voice or argued. She simply laid out the best

course in the plainest, most reasonable terms with unassailable logic. As for the rest, it was implied. She didn't tell him what to do, she simply expected him to do what was right, and though he resented the hell out of it, Kit knew she had done it again.

Only this time he wasn't in the mood for her manipulations. How often had she played with him since her arrival, twisting and turning his thoughts and emotions until he forgot all about his guilt and his grief? Kit had reached the very limit of his endurance. And instead of mulling over her words, he surged to his feet, angry that she had left the room without his leave, that she didn't seem to care that he wanted her beyond all reason, and, worst of all, that she dared give him a reason to live when he didn't want one.

Kit caught up with her in the grand salon. Or rather, he shouted at her, and she halted, eyeing him with that unperturbable expression that so annoyed him. "Maybe I don't want to think about it," he said. "Maybe I don't want to listen to you or to sit still for your so-called healing. Maybe it's time I paid you off and sent you on your way, Miss Chloe Gibbons."

Kit thought he detected a hint of hurt in her dark eyes, but that didn't stop him. It seemed that this was his last chance, his final opportunity to push her away, drive her from his home and his life

forever, and he grasped at it, throwing the worst things he could think of at her head.

"Who ever heard of a hired companion for a man, anyway?" he demanded. "There's only one thing a man wants from a woman like you, and it isn't companionship! You might remember what it is from the night in the folly when I put my hands and my mouth on you, when I tried to get under your skirts."

Kit watched the blush stain her cheeks, but didn't heed it, and, driven by something he could not name, he continued to lash out at her. "Just in case you've forgotten, Chloe, shall I tell you exactly how you can heal me? Shall I tell you just what I want to do to you?"

Although she shook her head, Kit said it, anyway, using the foulest word possible for the sex act, and, at last, he got a response. She flinched as if he had struck her, and the color drained from her face.

"I know what you're trying to do, but I won't listen to this, Kit," she said, walking away from him with a dignity that he decried. Her calm rejection of his hateful barbs only infuriated him further, and he hurried after her, but she had already reached the stairs.

Kit increased his pace, consumed by the need to finish this now, to end whatever was growing be-

tween them before it was too late. But his limp slowed him down, aggravating his temper. Cursing, he wished he could forget his injury and run up the stairs as he had before the war, catching Chloe easily, though he was not quite sure what to do with her when he caught her, whether to toss her from Hawthorne Park or to keep her forever.

Kit had no chance to do either, for as he took the steps too fast, his cane slipped and he lost his footing. His bad leg went out from under him like a useless prop, and he fell, tumbling down the stairs to lie prone at the bottom. And there he lay for long, dreadful moments, overcome by a gut-wrenching fear so potent, he dared not breathe. In that instant he was back on the field at Waterloo, pinned beneath his beloved mount, watching the animal and all else around him die and knowing he would be next.

"Kit!" A voice called him back to the present, and he lifted his lashes to see Chloe's lovely face hovering over him, anxiety creasing her brow. "Are you all right?" she whispered in that sultry voice of hers that promised sin and gave comfort. *Right now he would take the comfort, though the sin looked pretty good, too.*

For as he lay there on his back, afraid to move lest he discover some new injury, Kit thought of all the men he had known who were paralyzed or

had lost limbs or lives, and suddenly he wanted very much to be right where he was and to not trade places with any of them. For the first time since his return home, he preferred life, not death, and not just any life, but this one, *with this woman.*

All his imagined reasons for driving Chloe away now seemed foolish indeed. She was his salvation. Not only had she pulled him back from the abyss, but she was the best thing that had ever happened to him in all his long, selfish existence, before the war or after. He only hoped that it wasn't too late to take what he wanted, what he so desperately needed, and make a real future for himself.

"What is it? Where are you hurt?" Chloe whispered. She knelt over him, the curve of her breasts nearly touching him, and Kit was delighted to discover that at least one part of his prone body was still functioning properly. Gingerly, he began to move, and he was grateful that nothing seemed amiss, except for his injured leg, which throbbed painfully.

"Shall I call a doctor?" Chloe asked.

"Not unless he's from Bedlam, intent upon putting me there, for its no less than I deserve," Kit muttered.

Chloe looked slightly alarmed by his words, so he forced a smile through gritted teeth as he lifted

himself to his elbows. "Just get me the cane," he said.

One of the footmen, drawn by the noise of his fall, hastened to retrieve the fallen prop, while Chloe helped him to his feet, putting her slender shoulder under his arm as he pushed off the floor with his good leg. Kit's pleasure at her assistance was tempered by the look on her face once he stood upright.

"I'm sorry, Chloe," he said, knowing that she had no right or reason to forgive him. He grasped the cane and waved away the footman with a gesture of thanks even as he clung to her, unwilling to let her go, for fear he had succeeded in driving her away for good.

"You ought to be ashamed of yourself!" she said, confirming his worst fears. "You might have broken your neck!"

When Kid blinked at her in surprise, she scowled. "You have behaved abominably! And I don't know if I should accept your apology," she added. But her first telling thought had been for him, and Kit felt hope enter into his life again, after a long absence.

Nodding in agreement with her words, he attempted to put some weight on the injured limb and groaned as it nearly buckled beneath him. Although such was not his intention, the sound di-

verted Chloe from his misdeeds, for she immediately leaned close, an expression of anxiety back on her beautiful face.

"You had better soak that in a tub of hot water," she said, eyeing his leg in a proprietary fashion that started another part of his body to throbbing.

"No, I'm fine," Kit said. Indeed, he felt better already, better than he had in years.

Chloe ignored his protest. "I know!" she exclaimed, glancing up with bright expectancy. "This is the perfect opportunity for you to try the hot springs. The weather is unusually fine, so I don't think you will catch a chill, and the water there will never grow cold. It should ease you considerably."

Kit groaned again, but not with pain. The last thing he wanted to do right now was to trudge up to the woods and wash with that smelly stuff, but he could see there would be no stopping Chloe, and he hadn't the heart to argue with her. Indeed, that heretofore cold, silent organ was thrumming with a wholly new urgency. Although the sensation was unknown to him, Kit suspected there was a name for it. *Love.* And who was he to deny the woman he loved?

And so he let her help him toward the rear of the house, drawing the line when she suggested

they use a carriage, or worse yet, a cart, to haul him to the glade. Quite sensibly, he told her that any such conveyance would be difficult to maneuver into the trees, and, anyway, he could ride well enough.

"We ought to clear out some of the oaks and underbrush and create a broad approach to the spring if you are going to use it more often, which you very well should," Chloe said, giving Kit a sidelong glance that was meant to chastise, but only warmed him thoroughly instead. Surely no other being on this earth had ever basked in the glow of such concern, undeserved though it might be. "And you should encourage the tenants and neighbors to go there, as well," she added.

"Right," Kit muttered. But he had no intention of inviting everyone in Yorkshire to tramp through his favorite glade and muck about. He might not particularly care for the foul-smelling hole, but he liked the seclusion of the woods and their proximity to the house.

Already, as they rode under the first of the low-hanging branches, Kit could feel the serenity of the spot wash over him. When they reached the glade and dismounted, he tethered the horses, then turned to eye the odiferous water warily. The day was uncommonly warm, so he removed his coat, placing it on the grass to make a comfortable seat for

Chloe, half hoping that she would be diverted by the pleasant surroundings. Or by him.

But even though he unbuttoned his waistcoat and shrugged out of it, Chloe's attention remained firmly fixed upon the lower part of his torso, on one leg in particular, much to his disappointment. Still, a man in love could hope, couldn't he? Kit perched on a rock and tugged off one boot, then made a game effort with the other one, to no avail. The task was difficult on his good days, and having twisted the old wound beneath him in the fall only made it more difficult.

"Here, let me get that," Chloe said in a rather odd, breathless voice, and Kit felt a bit breathless himself as she knelt before him and put her hands on him. Warmth spread through him, from her fingertips to every part of his body, filling him with such sweetness that he seemed buoyant without even entering the water.

But as he gazed down at her dark head, her satin hair, and lower to her beloved face and the gentle curve of her breasts, he was seized by another sort of heat. Suddenly, Kit was reminded of that sin he had been saving for later. *It was already later, so what was he waiting for?* Although momentarily distracted by the pain that came with the removal of his boot, when Kit felt her hands return to his calf, sin was, once again, foremost in his thoughts.

"Let's have a look," Chloe said, and before Kit knew what she was about, she was gently pulling down his stocking. Somehow the unusual gesture felt more intimate than sex, and he stifled a moan as the brush of her fingers against sensitive skin sent a rush of blood to his groin. And then, as if that weren't enough, she started kneading his calf. This time Kit couldn't help it, he leaned back his head and groaned in pure pleasure as the tight muscles gave beneath her ministrations.

She rubbed the lower part of his injured leg for a long time, then removed the stocking from his other foot, and fell into silence. Having sunk into a kind of erotic torpor, Kit lifted his lashes at last to find her still kneeling before him, staring thoughtfully at his groin. He blinked as that part of him jerked to life, but Chloe seemed to take no heed, and he realized she was eyeing his thighs, or more specifically, the thigh that had been shattered.

Frowning, she glanced up at him. "I take it your wound is…higher up?" she asked. At Kit's mute nod, she took on a determined expression. "Then I'm afraid the breeches will have to go."

If Kit had harbored any lingering doubts about the efficacy of his nether regions, his response to that statement set them immediately and permanently to rest. Indeed, he thought he might burst

from the cloth that now constrained him far too tightly.

"Chloe—" he began in a hoarse croak.

But she cut him off with a firm shake of her head. "I discovered that father's gout was much better when he could soak his foot directly in the water. I realize that at Bath and elsewhere, the bathers are fully clothed, but I fear that these breeches of yours are far too constricting."

Although those were his thoughts exactly, Kit didn't think innocent Chloe was referring to quite the same sort of swelling that concerned him at the moment. Apparently she was oblivious to everything except his injury.

"Unfortunately, we don't have the smocks that they provide in Bath, either, but I brought along some towels. And, since we are secure in the privacy of your own property, I see no reason why a towel will not be sufficient," she said, rising to her feet to fetch one from the back of her mount.

Kit stared after her, dumbfounded. Obviously she was in her healing mode and oblivious to the impropriety involved in stripping off his breeches, let alone the danger to herself.

"Do you need some help?" she asked, returning to eye him questioningly.

"Lord, no," Kit muttered. The thought of Chloe unbuttoning the fall of his breeches was more than

he could take at this point. Already the pain his leg was long forgotten, replaced by an insistent throbbing elsewhere. Pushing off from the rock, he rose to his feet, surprised by the sensation of cool grass beneath his toes. Perhaps this wasn't such a bad idea, after all.

He glanced at Chloe, but she was still watching him with a matronly air. Hands on her hips, she looked rather like a governess waiting for her charge to obey, so Kit casually pulled out his shirt and lifted it over his head, tossing it to the ground.

Now he had her attention.

"What are you doing?" she asked in a squeak that little resembled her usual sultry tones.

Biting back a smile, Kit adopted her own reasonable manner. "I'm taking off my shirt."

"But…but your shirt would have offered some…protection. For your privacy," she choked out, her eyes focused unswervingly on the wide expanse of his chest. Having finally flustered her, Kit decided he could be forgiven for feeling supremely good about it. He might have lost a little weight and battered one of his legs, but he still had the basic body that had dazzled more than a few ladies in its time.

"I hardly think it necessary for you to remove *everything!*" Chloe protested. She was staring *and* sputtering, and Kit knew a giddy euphoria. In all

their encounters he had rarely shaken her preternatural poise, but she definitely appeared to be a bit nervous now. He grinned.

"In for a penny, in for a pound," he replied with a shrug. Then he put his hands to the fall of his breeches and looked at her expectantly. He watched the blush stain her cheeks, enjoying every minute of her discomfiture even as her admiration of his chest fueled the heat between them. When she still stared, as if unable to tear her gaze away, Kit very slowly slipped one button loose of its mooring.

It did nothing to ease his own discomfort. If anything, his breeches only seemed tighter, for the unexpectedly erotic act of disrobing before Chloe made his body swell and surge painfully against the doeskin. He paused, savoring each moment of this new experience. Although more than one lady had deliberately removed her clothing for him, Kit had always been on the receiving end of such a display. Now he found himself excited by the reversal of roles, his senses heightened to a fever pitch by his smallest movement, by the audible hitch in Chloe's breathing, by the way her dark eyes widened and fixed upon his body.

He had her full attention now, and he gloried in it. For the first time since Waterloo, Kit felt good, whole, fine even, despite the limp that slowed him,

and he took his time, anticipation stealing his breath as he moved downward to the next button. He fingered it provocatively as he watched Chloe's face. When she wet her lips, Kit felt himself jerk against his own hand, but still he continued slowly, carefully releasing the fastening.

He heard a low sound from Chloe, and his lips curved in delight. Another button slipped free, and the fall finally began to dip. Kit wore no undergarments, so he knew that the patch of his dark blond hair was visible, and excitement shot through him at the thought. If possible, Chloe's dark eyes grew even wider as she stared and made another low sound, louder this time, before abruptly turning 'round.

Kit released a shuddering sigh. He had to admit to some disappointment at the sudden end to his show, but then again, he was becoming pretty hard pressed, so to speak. He paused to take a few deep breaths and regain some composure. Then he yanked down his breeches and stepped to the pool's edge. By now the water's odor was the least of his worries, so he ignored it as he dipped in a foot. It was hot, all right. Gingerly, he stepped against the rocky side and lowered himself in.

Hooking his arm atop one of the smooth stones along the edge, Kit eased deeper into the water that bubbled up through fissures in the rock below,

spilling into the hollow. He didn't know whether the years had carved out the niche or someone had created it, but suddenly it felt very welcome. Although he had never been to Bath or Tunbridge Wells, he began to understand the appreciation for such places.

His family had always complained about the mineral spring with its foul odor, thankful that the water piped into the house was from a different source entirely. But now Kit wondered why no one had made use of this delicious place before. As the heat enveloped him, he felt boneless, his body floating, his mind free, and he laid his head back and groaned out loud with pure pleasure.

"What is it? Are you all right?" Before Kit could respond, his faithful nursemaid was crouched beside him, unabashedly peering into the water, as if she expected to see his leg puffing up like a Montgolfier balloon below. He smiled, with a genuine warmth that he could not recall ever feeling before in his life, even when young and whole and careless.

Indeed, he felt like laughing with pure joy, and though he had been momentarily diverted by the sybaritic pleasure of the spring, Kit returned his attention to his starchy companion, who was once more eyeing his chest rather avidly. His body

roused to life again, even more eagerly than before, egged on by the hot water and his own nakedness.

Maybe he was prompted by the first real ease of his body or the first true lightness of his heart or just some devilment, but whatever the cause, Kit didn't answer Chloe's query. Instead he said the first thing that came into his mind. "Perhaps you should come in."

"Do you need some help?" she asked in a breathy whisper. Her great brown eyes grew darker as they lifted to meet his own, and Kit felt whatever restraint he had possessed upon land slip away in the bubbling waters of the pool.

"Yes," he said.

Kit saw her swallow, saw the flush rise in her cheeks as she removed her slippers and stockings, hurriedly, as if his need for her was great, as well it was. Then she lifted her skirts in a dainty gesture and dipped in a toe.

"It is quite, uh, warm, isn't it?" she asked in that husky voice that was his downfall.

Her foot was small and delicately arched, her toes perfect, and Kit couldn't help himself. He reached out and took hold of it, pressing his mouth to that tempting arch. Chloe trembled at his touch, enflaming him further, and he kissed each of her tiny toes, nipping gently, then took one into his

mouth. He heard her low gasp, felt her legs give way, and reached up to catch her.

Kit's hands slid naturally under her skirts and he tugged the ugly black up higher and higher, even as he lowered her into the spring. She murmured softly as the water engulfed her ankles and calves until she stopped his progress by sitting upon the bank, the material bunched up about her thighs to reveal a glimpse of white, startling against the darkness of the severe garment. *Her shift.* And it was edged in lace. Kit's body shuddered in response to that bit of feminine whimsy on his seemingly prim companion.

"My gown!" she protested.

Kit found a foothold among the rocks and stood. His palms resting upon her hips, he held her gaze with his own. "It has to go," he said, echoing her earlier directive. He wanted to see her, every inch of her, the white and the lace and the skin beneath. And it seemed that nothing else in his life had ever held such importance.

Although Kit expected a maidenly gasp or a protest or an excuse of some kind, he should have known better than to anticipate Chloe, ever a surprise to his jaded senses. He waited a heartbeat as she hesitated, her eyes downcast, and then joy flooded him as she murmured, "All right, but I must keep my shift." She tugged the pale linen

down over her thighs as best she could, dislodging his hands, and he moved back to sink chest-deep into the water as she touched the hem of her gown and lifted.

To the end of his days, Kit knew he would never forget the heart-stopping sensuality of that moment, as, against all odds, his virtuous companion raised her gown over her head, casting off the cold black and becoming for him a forest nymph, clad only in a slip of linen. It seemed as if time itself slowed and the world fell away, leaving nothing except the hot spring, its odor mixing with the sharp scent of the leaves rustling overhead.

A shaft of sunlight broke through, illuminating Chloe as the stiff material slid upward, revealing the delicate undergarment that clung to her thighs and her belly and her breasts. Gracefully and calmly, as she did all else, she pulled the gown over her arms and set it aside. And then Kit looked his fill: at her legs, smooth and shapely as they dipped into the water, at the arms that fell to her sides, and at the pale slope of her breasts that disappeared beneath the lace of the shift.

The darkness of his past faded away, banished by this woman who brought light and beauty and comfort, and the future that had stretched before him as cold and bleak as the tomb he had once wished for, now opened before him, precious and

bright. Investing all that he offered in one movement, Kit held out his hand. For a long moment
their gazes met and held, and then, to his everlast-
ing joy, she put her hand in his, slipping into the
water beside him.

She gasped as she sank into the heat, finding a
foothold on the slippery slope of the hollow. "You
are standing," she said, as if surprised.

"Yes. The pool is not that deep, even in the very
center," Kit replied.

"But, what about your leg. How is it?" she
asked, ever concerned about him. Dearest Chloe,
always giving of herself. She gave and gave to him
and what did he tender her in return? Here, today,
he would gift her with something, pleasure and
wonder, perhaps, and his love, most definitely.

"Good," Kit said. "In fact, I've...never...
been...better." And without giving her a chance
to hesitate or back away, he pulled her into his
arms. With a few simple touches, he unbound her
hair, letting it flow over her shoulders into the pool,
a satin mass of burnished brown. And he kissed
her, long and slowly and so deeply that their
breaths felt as one. And his hands roamed her
body, exploring and caressing, as they half moved,
half floated in the bubbling spring.

It was rather like dancing, but far more wonderful than any turn upon the floor he had made

before his injury. And Chloe responded, slowly at first, but with growing enthusiasm and ingenuity. Her hands traveled up his chest, her fingers running through the hair there, her lips pressing against his wet skin, arousing him effortlessly with her innocent ardor.

Finally, Kit found a slanted outcropping of rock and sat, tugging her onto his lap, the better to see to her pleasure, rather than his own. The shift clung to her breasts, her wide nipples plainly visible, and he stroked and caressed them until her head fell back. He suckled first one, then the other, while he pulled her close, his member rubbing against her, gently at first, then more insistently. She moaned, calling out his name, and he whispered his desire against her breasts.

"Chloe, beautiful Chloe, my love, my only," Kit murmured, dazed by a desire such as he had never known. Had he once thought himself incapable of making love? Now he ground against her with a new fervor as the heat and water and need built between them. He stroked her thighs and her belly and below, his fingers opening and delving and pressing until she lost her perpetual calm and became a writhing, clutching sensualist in his hands, until her arms tightened about his neck and she buried her face against his shoulder, crying out his name.

In the aftermath, Kit held her close, stroking her back, whispering praise into her hair, even as he began again his slow, steady rocking against her, reveling in the feel of her in his arms and upon his lap and between his legs. Eventually, he pressed not just against her, but inside her. Savoring the first inch of entry, he closed his eyes but kept up the gentle pace. Like the water that had carved out the rock, slow and insistent, he took his time to come wholly inside of her, wearing away her body's resistance until she gasped in delight.

And still, Kit did not hurry, cherishing each moment. *Slow. Easy. Hot. Wet.* Every sense was alive and heightened beyond imagining. And when, at last, he took his release with a long, shuddering groan, she was with him, touching him everywhere, body, heart and soul.

Chapter Six

Chloe sat at the dining table, head bent, hands clasped white-knuckled in her lap. She had nearly stayed in her rooms, but she had been loath to cause any more gossip. Already, she suspected the servants were buzzing with the news of her disheveled appearance when she and Kit had returned to the house, her hair a wet, clinging mess and her gown wrinkled beyond recognition.

Thankfully, no one could tell that she wore no undergarment, but she had known. She had been forced to abandon the wet shift that Kit had leisurely stripped from her body after that…first time. Her face flaming, Chloe remembered the sensation of her nakedness, the heat, the water and Kit's touch, as if a fevered dream.

"Chloe! Are you suffering from the sun?" The sound of the dowager's voice roused her to the

present, and she looked up guiltily. Without waiting for an answer, the dowager went on. "You
never wear a proper bonnet! How do you expect
to keep your complexion with such carelessness?
In my day, a lady never went out of doors without
gloves and hat!"

For once the dowager's ranting provided a welcome distraction from Chloe's own tempestuous
thoughts, and she nodded dutifully, though it was
not the sun that had reddened her skin, but the
brush of Kit's shaven face against various parts of
her body, both visible and unseen. Mostly, however, it was shame that caused her to flush.

In the hours since her wanton behavior, Chloe
had tried to justify her actions. She told herself that
she had responded to Kit's need, giving her body
to him because he so desperately craved it, to
prove himself a man once more and to heal himself
with such intimacy. But what of her own needs?
Although Kit and his well-being was never far
from her thoughts, Chloe knew that when she sat
on the edge of that pool, it was her own desire that
had prompted her to take that last step into the
water and into his arms.

And was it any wonder? Chloe had never
dreamed of half of the things they had done, of the
slow, steady build of sensation until she thought
she would die of it only to become more fully alive

than she had ever been before. And it was not only the pleasure that had enthralled her, but the communion between them. How could two people become so close, as if even their very spirits enmeshed? Although Chloe told herself that married couples must achieve something of the sort when they took to their beds, still she remained in awe of something so... She swallowed hard, having no words for it.

Although that wonder threatened to drive away her shame, Chloe clung to it as she tried to recollect who and what she was. She had passed the boundaries of proper behavior once with this man and had sworn never to do so again, yet those few kisses in the folly were as nothing compared to what she had done now. She was a ruined woman! Chloe choked back a sound combining both laughter and despair. She, a spinster who had never felt a hurried pulse for any swain, had fallen from grace, and with a man so unsuitable as to be wholly beyond her reach. *And what was worse, she had fallen in love with him.*

"Well?" A cane thumped, and Chloe, startled, raised her eyes to the dowager's piercing gaze. She had lost all thread of her employer's conversation and could only stare numbly at the noblewoman, trying vainly to compose herself.

And then he walked in.

He was late, and the dowager had insisted that they seat themselves rather than wait for him. His delay had filled Chloe with a mixture of relief and foreboding, and she had wondered if he were locked away in his apartments, unwilling to face her after what had happened between them. But she was wrong.

When she looked up, Chloe saw him sweep into the room with such elegance and dash that she was reminded immediately of the life he had once led. Indeed, she saw little of the wounded, morose man she had first known in this tall, confident figure. And Chloe didn't know whether to weep for his loss or to celebrate it.

Perhaps the light of love colored her perception of him, but Kit even seemed straighter and stronger and more handsome than before: a golden man with a golden future before him. *And no place in it for a drab companion,* Chloe thought, stricken by a sudden constriction in her throat. While she stared, Kit flashed them each a gorgeous, white-toothed smile, which effectively silenced even the dowager, then took his place at the head of the table with new ease. He looked every inch the earl, a powerful lord, and Chloe reached for her wine. Perhaps the liquid would dislodge the lump that had formed in her throat.

"I've been thinking about the hot springs," he

said, and Chloe choked upon her very first sip. Thankfully, neither Kit nor his grandmother, who was staring at him with a fierce expression, seemed to notice. Indeed, Kit appeared wholly focused on whatever he was about to say, so Chloe took a quick swallow while staring at him wide-eyed.

"And I think we should do something with it, not the one close to the house, of course," he said, sending a provocative glance at Chloe that nearly set her to choking again.

"But there is that other outlet to the north of the property," Kit said. "And I think it would make a perfect spot for some kind of resort, like Tunbridge Wells or Bath, but more exclusive since it will be located on noble land. We own most of the area up there, but I'll acquire more, so we don't have a crowd of tawdry shops springing up, encroaching on the countryside."

He paused, his gaze seeking hers, and Chloe stilled, arrested by his somber expression. "As Chloe reminded me, I am in a position to do something for my comrades, the ones who survived and who are too often forced out on the streets. This endeavor will require a host of new employees, and I will make it known that I will turn away no veteran of the war."

As he spoke, Chloe felt her initial dismay turn to pride. Was it any wonder she loved him? Not

only had Kit taken her suggestion to heart, but he had come up with a creative solution she would never have dreamed possible, proving himself above and beyond her wildest hopes. Setting down her glass, Chloe felt a warmth that had nothing to do with the wine and everything to do with the Earl of Hawthorne.

Unfortunately, the other diner at their table did not appear to share her sentiments, for hardly a moment had passed before the dowager thumped her cane loudly on the parquet floor. "I have never heard of such nonsense!" she said.

"Actually, such spas date as far back as the late 1500s," Kit said easily. "They began with the discovery of a mineral springs or waters with curative properties, and in most cases, the owner enclosed his find, usually providing accommodation for visitors, and reaping a profit."

"All well and good for some money-grubbing opportunist, but not for the Hawthorne earldom!" the dowager screeched.

As if his grandmother had not spoken, Kit turned to Chloe. "I realize, of course, that there are quite a few spas in the country already, but I feel that with our unique cachet, we can make this one a success," he said.

"Well, I will not have it!" the dowager said, demanding his attention with another loud thump

of her cane. "There will be no such thing upon any property belonging to my family. Nor will you besmirch the fine heritage of the title with the stain of trade!"

Although the dowager's rant was no less than what Chloe expected, it seemed to her that the older woman's complaints held none of their usual fire. Indeed, the dowager seemed simply to be going through the motions of a token protest. Was she finally becoming too tired to fight? Chloe studied her more carefully, noting sadly that the noblewoman was so thin that she appeared to exist through the force of her own will alone.

"I find that I like the idea of being in trade," Kit answered with equanimity, and Chloe glanced toward the head of the table. To her surprise, Kit neither argued with his grandmother nor ignored her, but replied quite evenly. "You wanted me to assume the earldom, you have pestered me to take over the duties of that position, and I have done so. And now I am using that authority to do some good," he said.

"Good for whom, some wretched riffraff? What about the Hawthorne lands and name?" the dowager snapped.

"Both are now mine to do with as I see fit," Kit answered. "And, if you don't care for it," he added, forestalling a new tirade with a sharp look

at his grandmother. "You have only yourself to blame for dragging me back into the land of the living."

Chloe caught her breath at Kit's cryptic words of gratitude. Would his grandmother recognize them as such? The dowager shuddered, taken aback, and glared at him, as if to dispute his statement, as a matter of course. "I did nothing but hire the gel," she said with a snort.

Kit's beautiful, golden face turned toward Chloe, and the green gaze that met hers shown with a new light. "That was enough," he said softly.

Chloe flushed as a rush of warmth and delight filled her, but the feeling turned bittersweet as she recognized the truth. *He is healed,* she realized with sudden insight. Despite all her misgivings, she had somehow affected a cure of sorts for this man's ailing spirit. *And now she must let him get on with his life.* The thought caused her throat to tighten again, along with a new, far more painful, constriction farther down, in her chest. Was her heart breaking?

Yet, around her, the world continued as usual, for she heard the dowager speak once more. "Be careful, young man, or I shall think you are thanking me," the noblewoman warned.

"Whatever you say, Grandmama," Kit answered.

The dowager cackled loudly. "Ha! I never thought I'd live to hear those words, though little do you mean them."

"I mean to turn my enterprise into a successful one, and you, with your social contacts and formidable forms of persuasion, are going to help me," Kit said without even a glance at his grandmother.

Caught up in the by-play once more, Chloe held her breath. "You young whippersnapper, why I ought to take my cane to you!" the dowager threatened. Then, rising regally from her seat, she stalked out the room, effectively putting an end to perhaps the first argument that she could not win.

Concerned, Chloe hurried after her, only to come upon the noblewoman in the grand salon, leaning hard upon her cane and staring out one of the tall windows. Obviously she had not heard Chloe's approach, for she stood unmoving, her fierce expression belied by the tears that ran down her wrinkled cheeks.

Chloe gasped in alarm. "My lady, are you all right?" she asked, stunned to see the noblewoman weeping. Surely even the dowager didn't value pretense and status so much that she would put it

above her grandson, let alone all those army veterans?

The dowager turned her away with an angry sound. "Can't a woman go a few paces in her own home without being followed and spied upon?" she asked, pulling out a handkerchief.

Chloe ignored the gibe. "Does the thought of Kit's plan distress you so much?" she asked.

"What? What the devil are you yammering on about now, gel?" she snapped, swinging toward Chloe, all traces of her tears gone.

"The hot springs?" Chloe asked. "Don't you—"

The dowager cut her off with a snort. "Stupid gel! As if I could care what you two do with your smelly water!"

"Then what is it?"

For a moment Chloe didn't think the dowager was going to tell her. Then the noblewoman took a rattling breath and looked her in the eye, unflinching. "You did it. You saved him," she said, her voice sinking nearly to a whisper.

Now Chloe was certain that her heart was breaking, but she reached out to take the dowager's hands. "No," she said. "*We* saved him."

Kit was well and truly healed. Chloe was sure of it now. If the look of him, his new attitude, and

his plans for the future had not convinced her, then the rapprochement with his grandmother would have done so. Chloe was so proud and happy for him that she tried to gloss over her pain at the inevitable parting, but as she stood in her rooms, preparing to leave, she found herself more and more reluctant to sever the ties she had formed here.

Yet there was no reason to delay. Chloe had told the dowager as much. Like a governess who had taught all she could, or a doctor who had cured his patient, Chloe had completed her task. Kit was resuming his life, coming into his own as earl, and that meant business trips to London, perhaps even relocating there for the season and reentering society. He had no need for a provincial spinster to serve as his companion any longer.

As for the other aspects of their relationship... Chloe felt her cheeks heat and her breath catch. At one time Kit had accused her of being hired to "service" him. And she could not let it become true. Lifting her hands to her flushed face, Chloe looked in the mirror and swallowed hard as she tried to appear resolute. The woman who stared back at her would not sink to becoming any man's mistress. Not even Kit's.

And Chloe wasn't even sure he wanted that of her. Personally, she suspected that his lovemaking

simply had been a part of the resumption of his life. As if to dispute her theory, memory flashed back, and she heard Kit's deep whisper. *Chloe, beautiful Chloe, my love, my only.* Had he been aware of what he said?

It mattered not, Chloe told herself, for now that he was well, he would want a wife and children to whom he could pass his legacy and his title. Soon he would need to court a suitable woman to provide those heirs the dowager demanded, and perhaps the two could find some common ground in the next generation of Armstrongs, Chloe thought. Yet the image of Kit's babies born by some strange woman was so painful that Chloe's legs gave way, and she sank down upon the edge of the bed with a sob. *Better she leave now, than witness that painful reality.*

Taking in a long, shaky breath, Chloe used that knowledge to shore up her weakening resolve. No one really would miss her here, even the dowager, who had been quite insistent that she stay. Chloe had thought the noblewoman would be happy to be rid of her, for no matter what Kit might say, the matriarch could hardly condone a connection between her grandson and his companion beneath her roof. But, as usual, the dowager had argued, complaining that Chloe hadn't fulfilled her duties, that Kit wasn't cured…and that he needed her.

Just as she needed him. Oh, not to provide her with a position, for that once all-important worry was the least of her concerns now. Kit and his grandmother had given her not only a task but a home, far different from the place she had shared with her father, but just as viable, just as dear. And all the time Chloe thought she was tending Kit, he had been tending her, as well, shaking her from her complacency, challenging her, introducing her to love. And wherever she might go, Chloe would never forget. What had the bard said? *'Tis better to have loved and lost...*

Rising from the bed, Chloe squared her shoulders and dragged her trunk from the dressing room once more. She had spent the night weeping and the morning in a muddle of indecision, and she was well done with both. Determined, she began to replace her meager belongings. Where would she go now, and what was she to do? Chloe had no idea, only that she could not remain.

A knock startled her from her thoughts, and she frowned at the painted wood. Kit had come to that same door earlier, to ask if she was well, but she hadn't the heart to open it, knowing what might pass between them in her private rooms. And so she had sent him away.

But now he was back, for she heard his beloved

voice, a bit impatiently, on the other side. "Chloe? What are you doing?"

"I'm, uh, I'll be down later," she said, hoping to postpone their confrontation and the ensuing farewell until the last possible moment.

"Chloe, open the door or I will break it down," Kit said quite evenly. "Although I don't care about the wood itself, I might hurt my leg and that would call for another session at the hot springs, wouldn't it?" He paused. "On second thought, don't open the door. I'll be happy to destroy it."

Chloe was swinging the panel wide in an instant, and he stepped in, so tall and handsome that her heart raced even as her throat constricted. Like the captain he had once been and the earl he was now, he surveyed the room, his gaze lighting on the trunk.

"What do you think you are doing?" he asked.

"I've finished my assignment here," Chloe answered, as calmly as she could. "You've made a full recovery, I'm satisfied of that, and I must prepare for a new position."

"Well, I'm not satisfied," Kit said in a low drawl. He stepped closer. "Indeed, I doubt that I shall ever be," he murmured. Casually, as if he had the right, he picked up a stray lock of her hair and rubbed it between his fingers in a manner that

threatened, as usual, to melt her into a puddle before him.

"And as for your new position, you have one right here," Kit said.

Chloe shook her head, determined to not be tempted by this golden man or her love for him.

"As my wife."

For a moment Chloe succumbed to the dizzying euphoria that swept over her at his words, but then reason prevailed and she shook her head once more. "I'm no countess, Kit," she managed to say in a voice that threatened to break at any moment. "I'm just a simple girl with simple tastes for home and hearth and family."

"And I must be a simple man, for I want all the same things you do, peace and quiet and rustication," Kit countered. "And children," he added in a whisper that sent her pulse skittering. "I crave them all, but they are nothing without you. You've become more necessary to me than breathing, Chloe, so you cannot refuse me."

Still, Chloe hesitated, uncertain if his offer sprang from simple affection for his companion or something deeper.

Kit put a hand to her chin, lifting it so that she was forced to look into his handsome face, somber now, and the green eyes that glowed from within. "You care for me, don't you?" he asked.

"Well, of course," Chloe sputtered, "*I love you, but*—"

He put a finger to her lips. "That's all I wanted to hear," he said with a devastating smile, both tender and triumphant.

"I love you, Chloe, and if you can love me after all I've put you through, then I have no fears for our future. I can't promise that I'll ever be the cheerful, carefree fellow I was before, but I can vow to do my best by you, to give you this home among the Yorkshire dales we both adore, and to fill it with love and children, a legacy far more enduring than any title."

Chloe felt the tears that had threatened to choke her well up to fill her eyes until Kit's beautiful face was naught but a hazy image. He leaned forward, as if to kiss the drops away, when a loud thump echoed behind them.

"If you don't accept him, you're a bigger fool than I thought, gel!" The unmistakable bang of the dowager's cane resounded again, and Chloe looked up to see the noblewoman standing in the doorway. She wore a grimace that might be interpreted as a smile by one of her forbidding nature.

"I expect some grandchildren, you know, and soon!" she said with a fierce expression, and for once, Kit did not argue with her.

"I'll get right on that. If you'll excuse us?" he

asked, and without waiting for his grandmother's reply, Kit gently closed the door. Then, he took one look at the trunk on the bed and threw it out the window with a flourish.

"You won't be needing that again," he said, stalking Chloe as she stood by the bed, torn between indignation and amusement. But she was beginning to realize that the too often serious Kit had a hidden penchant for outrageous displays, and she secretly wondered just what he would do next.

Anticipation stole Chloe's breath as he approached, and then all else was forgotten as she melted into a puddle at Kit's feet—and he joined her.

Dear Reader,

I was so pleased to contribute to *The Officer's Bride*. I love working within the shorter length of the novella and the challenge of an intriguing theme. And I was more than happy to revisit my favorite time period, the Regency. I also enjoyed the opportunity to research some subjects new to me, the Napoleonic Wars and Survival Guilt, as well as a chance to learn more about the history of England's hot springs and spas. The most fun, of course, was in putting it all together to create the story of Kit and Chloe.

I hope those who liked "The Companion" will look for my next release, *My Lady de Burgh*, in November. The latest in my series on the medieval de Burgh family, *My Lady de Burgh* focuses on Robin, who is convinced that his marriage-minded brothers have fallen under some kind of curse. Although determined to lift it before he becomes the next victim, Robin is sidetracked when he stumbles across a murder at a nearby nunnery. But surely no woman there is a threat to his bachelorhood!

Thank you, as always, for your wonderful support and encouragement. I wish you all the best, and happy reading!

Deborah Simmons

AN HONEST BARGAIN

by Julia Justiss

To my husband Ronnie
and in honor of the magical day
I became an officer's bride

Chapter One

"Bry!" One of the staffers seated at a camp desk called out to Lieutenant Bryan Langford, Dunbar's Dragoons Twentieth Regiment, as he entered the crowded headquarters tent and stomped mud from his boots. "Good to see you back." The aide shuffled some reports on his desk and then stopped, brow creasing. "I say, wasn't Jeremy Saybrooke—lieutenant with the Ninety-fifth—a childhood friend of yours?"

Bryan looked over quizzically. "Yes, we grew up together." He grinned at Lieutenant Marsden. "If it's gaming you seek, you'll have to catch up with him yourself. I haven't seen him since last fall in Lisbon."

Bryan's smile faded as he considered why. Though he was reasonably sure neither Jeremy nor

his wife guessed his feelings for Audra went far beyond friendship, still it was easier to stay away.

"Sad business." Marsden shook his head. "I'm sorry to say he was killed at Talavera yesterday."

Air whooshed from Bryan's lungs as if he'd been punched in the gut. Jer dead? The two words were a contradiction impossible to couple together. Despite the obvious dangers of battle, Jeremy had always been such a lucky, devil-may-care charmer Bryan had been convinced if anyone survived the war intact, it would be Jer.

His second thought—only shock could have made it his second thought—was of Audra. He grimaced, feeling like a blow to his own heart the terrible grief Jer's death must be causing her. Bright shining Audra, his secret joy, who had shimmered, incandescent with happiness the day she wed Jeremy. The day his silent hopes died.

Audra would be distraught. He must go to her.

That decided, he turned his mind to dispatching the details that would make it possible. "When are the services?"

Marsden regarded him with sympathetic eyes. "Tomorrow morning, I believe. Sorry, Bry. I understand he was a fine officer."

"His widow is a childhood friend, as well. I really should be there for her. Marshall can handle

the company for a day. Tell the colonel I'm packing a kit and will return later to apply for leave."

"To inform him you're going, you mean?"

Bryan had the grace to grin. "Yes. Thank you for letting me know, Charles."

Returning the staff lieutenant's salute, Bryan strode back out of the tent. He'd have to see what arrangements had been made, make sure Audra had everything she needed, set up her transport back to Lisbon. And home to England. She would not be staying in the Peninsula now that Jer was dead.

But it was his next thought that ignited his mind, sped his pulse and once more made his breath catch. Despite a very real grief over his friend's death, excitement swept through him. *Audra was free.*

Even as she held vigil over his body laid out before her on rough planks in the narrow room his army mates had commandeered, Audra Mercier Saybrooke still couldn't believe her husband was really dead. If anyone could have cheated death, it would have been Jeremy.

He'd certainly cheated at everything else.

The ugly thought shamed her, and she raised a trembling hand to her cheek. Only bone-deep fatigue and a year of aching hurt could have allowed

such a thought to escape. Despite all Jeremy had done, she'd loved him.

She moved her hand to touch his cold face. The lance thrust to the heart that killed him didn't show, now that she'd bathed his body free of blood and clothed him back in his dress coat. He might almost be lying there asleep.

Except that the still figure in the uniform was only a plaster casting of the man she'd once loved to desperation. The wild spirit that had animated him even in sleep, made him both irresistible and deadly to her happiness, had been loosed from his battered body somewhere on the heights above the Talavera plain and now roamed free of corporal limitations.

Beyond the power to hurt her anymore.

Oh, Jer, she thought, a single tear sliding down her cheek, *that the love I bore you should come down to that.*

The jingle of spurs made her snatch her hand back and swipe away the tear. She turned to see Lieutenant Allensby of the Ninety-fifth's Third Regiment—and Jer's frequent carousing companion—enter the small room. She nodded an acknowledgment to the bow he swept her.

"I'm so sorry, Audra. He was a good soldier and a great friend. I shall miss him sorely."

She nodded again, unable to come up with a

kind response to this man whose encouragement of Jer's gambling excesses had in no small part placed her in the unfortunate position she now occupied. Jer's foul humor the last few nights he'd returned from gaming told her only too eloquently that his luck had been out. How she was to repay whatever Jer had recently lost to Allensby and the others and still buy the provisions necessary for the march back to Lisbon, she hadn't yet figured out.

"Audra, I expect Jer's sudden…passing has left you in somewhat of a bind. To be blunt, he owes a rather large sum to me alone."

"How large?" she asked in alarm. His murmured reply left her speechless. With hard coin in such short supply, how could Jeremy have amassed such a debt?

Allensby shook his head at her obvious shock. "I'm afraid he owes several others nearly as much. You know Jer. He kept on playing, certain his luck was bound to turn sooner or later. It usually did, after all."

Not always, she thought bitterly, thinking of the bills brought from Lisbon that Jeremy had stuffed in the drawer of his lap desk.

"Well, being a friend, I wondered what means you have available to settle them. Debts of honor, you know, must be paid speedily."

"I know," she said sharply. As if she weren't

aware of that stupid corollary in the even more foolish unwritten code of male conduct.

"And...?" He let the question hang. "It may be indelicate of me to inquire at such a time, but how do you propose to repay them?"

"I haven't yet determined that," she replied through tight lips. "As you may imagine, I've been somewhat busy the past few hours."

He walked over to her, his smile sympathetic. "It must have been horrid for you." He patted her shoulder, but unable to stop herself, she wrenched away from his touch. His smile broadened.

"There are a number of us who've always wondered why, with the responsive wife awaiting him, Jer had a tendency to...wander. And given your circumstances, which I might add are widely known, I wanted to be the first to offer a solution to your current financial difficulties. I fear I'm about to be more indelicate still, but you're a taking little thing and an excellent army wife. If you'd be willing to keep me company on the march, I'd be prepared to settle Jer's debts for you."

For a moment she stared at him, uncomprehending. Then fury, so hot she had to clench her hands to keep from striking him, erupted from the swirling miasma of grief, pain, and fear. "Am I to infer," she asked, with supreme effort managing to keep her voice from shaking, "that with my hus-

band lying dead in front of us, you have the consummate gall to stand there and offer me a carte blanche?''

Allensby sketched a bow. ''Don't suppose Jer is in a position to worry about it now.''

''Get out,'' she spat at him. ''Get out before I forget myself and leave claw marks down your insolent face no amount of glib talk will explain away.''

He merely grinned again. ''As I do so *enjoy* a lady of passion, you're welcome to try. But as you wish, I will leave, madam—for the moment. I realize you can hardly consider the matter dispassionately now, but I did want my offer to be the first. Think on it.''

Though she turned her back, giving him not even the courtesy of a goodbye, amusement continued to color his tone. ''Good day, Mrs. Saybrooke. I hope soon to be fulfilling every one of your passionate commands.''

She ignored him, remaining rigid with her back to the door until she heard the soft slam signaling his exit. Then she staggered to her chair, hardly able to breathe for the violence of the emotion constricting her chest.

How dare Allensby—how *dare* he—intrude upon her with his despicable offer at this moment,

when she was so exhausted, heartsick and defense-
less.

She hated Allensby for making her wonder once
more whether it had been weakness or mercy, over
and over again, to give in to Jer's pleas for forgiveness. With equal fervor she hated Jer and the
highly overpraised emotion called love that made
a woman want to believe the unlikely, despite the
protests of her logical mind. That left her vulnerable, bared before the Allensbys of the world as
weak and foolish.

Even more than love, she hated the passion that
melted logic and allowed a man to mold a woman
to his bidding.

Then it struck her, a blinding beacon of hope in
the blackness of her misery. Jer's death had just
freed her from both.

No, she'd not become another camp follower,
passed along from one man to the next. Somehow
she'd scratch together the funds to get back to England, far from the humiliation of the present and
the torments of the past. Home, to the tranquility
of Hampshire. Alone.

Chapter Two

Audra stood at the windy gravesite, outwardly composed but inwardly shaking. Before the service this morning she'd sold Jeremy's horse, rifle, pistols, and all the useful uniform pieces she could muster. The sum from that, added to the amount she'd gotten when she sent Maria to the town goldsmith to sell a few pieces of jewelry, had covered little more than half of the outstanding debts she'd found carelessly tossed in the drawer of Jer's lap desk. She wasn't sure how she'd be able to come up with the funds to pay the rest, much less settle the frighteningly large total it appeared Jer had accumulated back in Lisbon.

With the fingers of her right hand she worried the wedding ring on her left. It rolled around easily now on her too thin fingers. It appeared she'd have to sell Jer's ring, as well—a fitting irony, probably.

She looked up to find Allensby's gaze fixed on her. As if sensing her thoughts, he had the gall to smile.

Impotent fury rattled through the hollow core of her fear and dismay. She'd almost rather service the entire regiment than be forced to accept a carte blanche from him.

Which was only the first of the dishonorable offers she was going to receive, if Allensby's claim could be believed. She scanned the somber faces of the uniformed men gathered around the gravesite. Who else among this group might consider Jeremy Saybrooke's sweet, forgiving widow an easy target?

Humiliation deepened her grief. It had been bad enough before, the pitying looks she'd catch on the faces of the other wives, quickly veiled when she looked their way. The occasional off-color remarks from some of the officers, apparently testing to see if Lt. Saybrooke's poor, neglected wife might be wishful of a little comfort.

How was she to endure who knew how many repetitions of the scene with Lt. Allensby?

Given her dismal finances, how was she to contrive the trip back to Lisbon if she didn't accept someone's offer?

Almost, she wished she could crawl into the pine

box beside Jeremy and be forever free of heart-ache, fear and worry.

Struggling to compose herself, she flinched from the touch to her shoulder, not sure in her present state she'd be able to prevent herself from striking Allensby should he offer her any more double-edged condolence.

"Audra, I'm so very sorry."

Having tried to shut out sound, as well, it took a moment before the familiar deep timbre of the voice registered.

Her eyes snapped open and she looked up in astonishment. "Bryan?" she cried. And launched herself into his arms.

Having one's heart turn over had always been just a cliché to Bryan—until he walked up to his friend's grave and saw Audra, head bowed and eyed closed in grief. He could scarcely wrest words from his constricted throat.

Then, in answer to an invitation he'd not even been conscious of making, she was in his arms, clinging to him as if he were the one rock of sta-bility in the midst of an ocean of turmoil. He hugged her close, his nostrils filling with the sweet violet scent of her, fiercely glad that, despite hav-ing to endure a dressing-down from his colonel, he'd flatly insisted he would come. He savored the

bite of her fingers into his sides, her closeness a long-cherished dream come true, while her slender shoulders trembled with the tears she would not shed.

Vividly he recalled the last—and first—time he'd held her—the summer he and Jer returned from Oxford to find the coltish, half-wild companion of their youth grown into a young lady, flyaway curls tamed into fashionable ringlets, flat figure rounded with alluring new curves. They'd been teasing of beaux and balls, and she'd played at kissing him—shocking them both with the intensity of the response sparked when her soft lips met his.

Her large dark eyes startled, she'd immediately pulled away, even then interested primarily in provoking Jer to jealousy. And though he knew his quiet straightforwardness was no match for Jeremy's golden charm, he also knew in that one quick kiss he'd lost his heart forever.

And so it had proved, despite having endured watching the jesting courtship between Audra and Jer turn real, despite having suffered kissing her the second time chastely on the forehead when he congratulated her as a new bride. He'd kept his distance after, not a hard task since he'd deliberately chosen a commission in a different unit.

And he'd tried, truly he'd tried, to summon

some enthusiasm for the young ladies, English, Portuguese and Spanish, who showed themselves more than ready to express their appreciation of a handsome dark-haired officer in a dashing red coat.

But for him, there was only Audra.

Having learned to his surprise that she had followed Jer to the Peninsula, he hadn't been able to keep from stopping by in Lisbon, to make sure Audra was well and happy. More than happy, he remembered with a pang—she'd been glowing with joy in the child she carried. Though she begged him to visit often, he'd not been able to stomach returning.

She straightened in his arms now, pulling him out of memory. Reluctantly he released her.

"Bryan, I didn't even know you were in the area! But thank you so much for coming. It would have meant a lot to Jeremy to have you here."

Still Jeremy. Bryan cleared his throat. "I'm sorry I wasn't able to stop by earlier, when…when I heard about the babe. You did get my letter?"

She swallowed hard, a shadow passing her face at that other grief. "Yes, thank you. It…helped."

"Corunna was a terrible retreat."

"It wasn't that. My horse fell on me." She laughed, the sound shaky and unconvincing. "The doctor said it was lucky he didn't lose me along with the babe." Her glance wandered off. "Some-

times I wonder whether he meant good luck or bad. But no matter, the service is starting.''

He took her hand and after a startled moment, she let him keep it, even gripping his tightly when Jer's colonel spoke the last words and she was forced to toss the first clump of earth on the coffin. She made no resistance when he led her away immediately after.

She'd rallied by the time they reached the small village inn, offering a smile. ''Can you stay for luncheon? Nothing fancy, but the other wives and I have contrived a simple meal, and the wine hereabouts is exceptional.''

''I'd counted on remaining. But cannot I be of more use to you? You'll want to return to England as soon as possible, I expect. I'd be happy to look into transport and sell off—'' he caught himself before uttering the words and said instead ''—any items for which you no longer have use.''

A harsh look stole over her face. ''Thank you, but I've already sold off Jeremy's equipment. I'm such an *excellent* army wife.'' She laughed, the sound brittle.

She certainly was organized, he noted as he watched her conducting the other mourners into the inn, seeing to the serving of the meal, chatting with the assorted guests. He was still puzzling over the meaning of that odd exchange when he noticed her

take her maid aside and whisper something, then pull a small diamond clasp off her cloak and hand it over.

When the girl curtsied, and speedily exited, all his suspicions roused. His good friend Jeremy, Bryan regretted to admit, had been a hardened gamester. Though he won more often than he lost, if caught at a time when fickle Lady Luck had not been smiling on him, Jer might well have left Audra very short on funds. Anger kindling at the thought, Bryan decided on the spot to follow the maid.

He'd be damned if he let Audra sell off her jewelry to pay for his reckless friend's funeral.

Silently he slipped out the door. With his superior height, he had no trouble keeping the girl in sight as she wove through the streets of the village and stopped, as Bryan had feared, in front of a small shop bearing a goldsmith's sign.

Speeding his steps, he caught up with the maid and halted her with a hand to the shoulder before she could enter. With a squeak of alarm, she turned to him.

"Did your mistress order you to sell her clasp? Let me have it!"

"*Sí, señor*. I was to sell it. I was not stealing it, I swear! Please, *señor!*"

"I believe you," he answered hastily, wishing

to forestall the attack of tears that appeared imminent. He took the clasp the girl thrust toward him. "I'm a friend to your mistress and her late husband, did she tell you?" When the girl nodded, Bryan continued, "Lieutenant Saybrooke would not want his wife selling her jewels. Here, take this instead." Swiftly he pulled out a purse and handed her several coins. "Will that be enough?"

"*Sí, señor,* more than the jeweler would have given."

"Good. Take it to your mistress, but say nothing of how you got it. I'll keep the clasp for now."

"As you wish, *señor.* The Holy Mother's blessing on your kindness!" With a curtsy, the girl hurried back toward the inn.

Bryan followed more slowly, uneasiness growing. Just how desperate was Audra's financial situation? Surely by the time she reached Lisbon, Jer's family would have received the notice of his death and could arrange to transfer funds to his widow. Still, if her husband had left her so poorly circumstanced that she must sell baubles to pay for this meal, how was she to buy the necessities for her trip back to Lisbon?

He would not, he vowed, return to his headquarters until she told him the whole.

He waited until Audra was busy upon some task before easing back into the crowded dining room.

Several bottles into the feast now, the assorted guests had become more merry. While toasts were drunk to the fallen, to the honor of the regiment, to the health of the sovereign and various commanders from Wellington on down, Bryan watched Audra.

She was thinner than he remembered, but then, they all were, the vicissitude of campaigning in a rocky, mostly barren country having taken its toll. A few wisps of dark hair curled out from under her simple cap, and the wanness of her face accentuated the high cheekbones and made her dark eyes appear even larger. Eyes shadowed by, shoulders sagging under, a weary grief he could read with poignant clarity even when she smiled.

As soon as decently possible, he'd get her out of here, insist that she go up to her room and rest.

He was not, Bryan realized with a jolt after observing her for some minutes, the only man watching her. Feet propped on a stool at the corner of the rustic bar, with a glass in his hand he regularly emptied and refilled from a bottle on the table beside him, a tall blond rifleman also followed her every movement.

The half smile of anticipation that kept growing on the man's increasingly bosky face Bryan did not like at all. Though he was too far away to understand what the rifleman said to her each time she

passed him, Bryan liked the tone of the man's words and the wolfish grin with which he said them even less.

When next she carried by another platter of food, Bryan caught Audra's sleeve. "Can you not sit with me?"

"I'm sorry—I don't mean to neglect you so, when you've come all this way. As soon as the guests leave, we shall have a long talk, I promise."

Bryan thought of the maid at the goldsmith's shop. "Yes, we have much to discuss. By the way, who is that rifleman near the bar?"

Audra did not even look in the direction indicated. "Lieutenant Mark Allensby," she said tightly. "A great friend of Jeremy's."

But not of mine, her tone implied.

Jeremy's colonel and his wife walked over to claim her attention. "My dear," the wife said, "we must be going soon. But I would know what you intend. Shall you return to England?"

"All that damp and drizzle," the colonel said with a shudder. "I expect you may eventually pine for the heat of Spain."

"I must admit, I shall miss the campaigning. No, truly," she added, when the wife gave an exclamation of disbelief. "I suppose at heart I'm still the grubby brat with her braids coming undone and her gown torn, happy to ride all day in the sun and

sleep at night under a fortress of stars." With a laugh, she indicated Bryan. "As you may ask Lieutenant Langford. He knew me when Jeremy and I were growing up."

"Absolute truth," Bryan affirmed, smiling, too, at the memory of adventures shared. "A hoyden indeed."

"Hoyden or no, you must find the notion of sleeping in one's own bed, having ample hot water at the ring of a bell pull, and leaving a full staff to worry about one's next meal exceedingly attractive!" the wife said.

Did Audra wince? If so, she recovered quickly. "Yes, they surely are."

"Again…well, you know how sorry we are," the colonel said. "About everything. You know if we could have—"

"Let me see you out," Audra said quickly. After grasping the lady's arm, she glanced back at Bryan. "Later," she promised, and walked the couple off.

Was the colonel aware of a problem, too? Bryan wondered. Since he knew few of the officers present, he took no part in the festivities as the party wound down. After another hour, the group had been reduced to a few hearty drinkers who, Bryan expected, would remain bending elbows throughout the night, and the blond rifleman, whose smile

had gradually turned to a frown when he apparently realized Bryan was also awaiting their hostess.

Returning the man's scowl, Bryan vowed he'd not depart until the green-coated lieutenant was well away.

Finally, Audra came to sink wearily into the chair beside him. "I'm declaring the party officially over," she said. "So, before you ride back, tell me all your news."

Bryan glanced around the room at the drinking patrons, the lingering barman—and the glowering rifleman. "Is there somewhere more private we could talk?"

"Not really. Unless…unless you want to come to our—my room?" She managed a shaky smile. "I must confess, I've been dreading going up there alone."

Bryan pulled a coin from his pocket and left it on the table. "Let's go."

Before they could reach the stairs, the rifleman heaved himself upright and wove his way over to Audra.

"Mrs. Saybrooke, a word with you."

"Not tonight, Lieutenant Allensby."

"Might be good to get—"

"I believe the lady said not now," Bryan interrupted, stepping between Audra and the rifleman.

The soldier looked him up and down. "And who might you be?"

"Lieutenant Bryan Langford," Audra inserted. "Jeremy's childhood friend. And mine." With obvious reluctance, she continued, "Bryan, may I present Lieutenant Mark Allensby of the Ninety-fifth Rifles."

The blond rifleman stared at Bryan assessingly. "Prior claim?" he said to Audra, and laughed. "Tomorrow, then. I'm a patient man." With a surprising steadiness considering the quantity of wine he'd imbibed, the soldier bowed. "Delay if you like, but we will have that chat."

Over my drawn sword, Bryan thought, anger rising at the man's tone and innuendo. "The lady bids you good-night," he said in a clipped tone. Grasping Audra's elbow, without further word, he guided her up the stairs.

The room she led him to was small and bare, furnished only with a trunk, a dressing table, a writing desk and a bed that filled the center of the room. Averting his gaze and forbidding his mind to entertain any thought of the activities that must have been carried out there, he walked to the desk. Indicating for Audra to take the chair, he sat on the smooth, worn surface.

She looked so exhausted and forlorn he wanted to pull her into his arms, carry her to the bed and

lay there with her, holding her through this first long, lonely night. And then had to smile a little at the thought. His mind might want that—but despite the events of the day, should he have her that close in such a location, his body would soon generate other ideas.

He hated to press her when she already looked near collapse, but his impatient colonel had granted him only a day's leave. He must settle this tonight. "What will you do, Audra?"

"Travel to winter quarters with the army, then arrange transport to Lisbon and passage home, I suppose."

"With what?" Before she could answer, he laid her diamond clasp on the table. "Do you have enough jewelry left to fund the trip?"

"You followed Maria?" she said after a moment. She dropped her eyes, avoiding the intensity of his gaze, and exhaled a long sigh.

"Didn't Jeremy leave you any cash? You cannot be very plump in the pocket if you're reduced to selling jewelry to fund his funeral dinner."

She looked up at him and he could see the shame and uncertainty in her face.

"Please, Audra, tell me honestly! Jeremy was my friend—he'd want me to help you. Were the circumstances reversed, you'd both do the same for me, would you not?"

A slight smile warmed her weary face. "Yes. All right, I'll admit that as far as I can ascertain, Jeremy left no cash—and a rather large stack of gambling debts. I've sold his equipment and most of my other jewelry, but...but I've still not paid off the whole of it."

"How do you propose to do that? And purchase supplies on the trip back to Lisbon?"

She closed her eyes and leaned her head against one hand. "I...I don't know. I'll come up with something."

Anger at the improvidence of his feckless friend sharpened his tone. "Come up with what, Audra? You've just told me you've already sold nearly all the assets you possess. Unless you've a stash of gems tucked under the mattress in this room you can turn into the ready, how on earth do you expect to get yourself back to Lisbon?"

"I—I've not sold my horse yet."

"Paltry."

"I've a few more rings and bangles—"

"Not nearly enough."

She lifted her head, eyes wild and already glassy with tears. "I—I don't know. Damn it, Bry, I don't kn-know!"

Her last word ended on a sob. As if she'd finally reached the very end of her resources, she buried her face in her hands and began to weep.

Remorse scalded him. "Damn—dash it, I'm sorry, Audra! I didn't mean—"

But his apology was doubtless lost in the sobs that increased in volume and strength, shaking her slender frame. After an agonized moment, Bryan cast prudence aside. He gathered her weeping body into his arms and carried her to the bed.

Retaining at least a little wisdom, he merely perched at the edge, settling her on his lap and holding her to his chest while she sobbed out her grief. Even anger at Jeremy drained away as he sat there helpless, his heart emptying of any emotion save an aching pain at her anguish.

At last the sobbing slowed. With what must have been supreme effort, Audra straightened. "I—I'm sorry, B-Bry."

"Hush, 'twas nothing." He rubbed her tear-stained cheek, and to his joy she closed her eyes and leaned into his caressing fingers.

After a glorious moment she opened her eyes again and seemed to become fully conscious—of where she was and what she was doing. To his regret, she sprang up, her face pinking. "Oh, dear! I *am* sorry!"

"Sit." He patted the bed beside him. "It's a bit more comfortable than the desk. And we still must decide what's to be done."

She gave him a watery smile. "I suppose it's too late now to stand on ceremony."

"Yes. Besides, when did we ever, you, Jer and I?"

When she'd seated herself and drunk some wine he'd poured her from a pichet by the bed, he continued, "Let me help, Audra. I'll find out what Jer owes, pay off his debts, and lend you enough to get you back to Lisbon. Surely if you write him now Lord Cranmore will advance you passage money home."

"He might rather prefer me to rot in Lisbon, and be well rid of a relation he never wanted."

"Nonsense, he—"

"No, of course, duty would force him to fund me. Nor have I any doubt Jeremy's sister-in-law Amelia will know just the right tasks to set before me once I'm home."

Bryan could well imagine what Jeremy's eldest brother's wife would consider the proper place for the new widow. Scion of a duke's family, Amelia had never bothered to hide her disdain for the daughter of the country parson her brother-in-law had been foolish enough to wed. Especially since the old earl, who'd had the temerity to prefer his youngest son's vivacious, spirited bride to his heir's icy blue blood, was now dead and unable to protect Audra from the new countess's spite.

"Are you sure you wouldn't rather remain here?" he said with an exaggerated shudder.

"I should rather return to live with Papa, though I doubt Amelia will allow it. She'll want my pound of flesh. But still, Bry," she said, returning to the point, "good friends though we be, I can't allow you to advance me the money. I—I can approach the colonel's wife, some of the other wives, see what I can borrow. Surely I can beg or steal enough to get me to Lisbon."

"What wife has that kind of money?" Bryan shook his head. "Especially out here on campaign. I should have to call in some markers myself to come up with any sum, and I've a better chance of raising it than you. I know you'll pay me back, sooner or later."

"It's not that." She paused, looking extremely uncomfortable. "You see, it seems to be general knowledge within the regiment that Jeremy was heavily in debt. Friend or no, Bry, you're entirely unrelated. If it became known—and it would become known—you'd paid off Jer's debts for me, people would assume I'd agreed to accept something more than a loan of cash. Something...much less honorable. My reputation would be ruined." She essayed a smile. "Lord Cranmore might truly leave me to rot in Lisbon then."

A vision of the blond rifleman flashed into his head. "Have you already received such an offer?"

She turned her face away, her silence only too eloquent an answer.

He'd kill the bastard. Until he realized the situation had just handed him the opportunity of his dreams, one he'd vaguely begun to plan toward ever since he'd heard the news of Jeremy's death. Why not seize it right now?

"You're right, Audra. There is only one honorable solution. You must marry me."

Chapter Three

Eyes opened wide, she stared at him. "M-marry you? Bryan, that's ridiculous! I mean no insult, but...it would be an absolute betrayal of our friendship to allow you to sacrifice your whole future, just to help me out of a dilemma for which you bear no responsibility whatsoever!"

"How a sacrifice? I shall have to marry someday. I'm nearly eight-and-twenty, and there is no other lady to whom I could contemplate proposing matrimony with anything approaching the pleasure with which I make that offer to you. Indeed, does it not seem reasonable to suppose that a long-established friendship, shared memories stretching back nearly a decade and a half, aren't at least as good a base on which to build a comfortable marriage than any other?"

"Than love, you mean?" She winced and closed

her eyes, took a shuddering breath, and he could see the pain of that blow against wounds still too fresh. "You may have the right of it indeed."

Better to marry a friend, he read on her stark grim face, than a man whose loss could cause such intensity of suffering. Something twisted in his chest, and for a moment he almost regretted the offer.

Dismissing the unease, he forged ahead. "Were circumstances otherwise, you know I'd never be so callous as to offer for you now. I don't expect you to pledge any affection beyond friendship. You're grieving—but so am I. Perhaps we can help each other. And after, when life seems more like living again, you'll be settled." He offered her a grin. "Just think, you could remain on the Peninsula with me and never have to go back to Amelia."

"Now that is an inducement," she agreed, mustering a slight smile.

"Granted, I can't claim to be an earl's son—"

"As if such a consideration mattered to me!" she interrupted hotly.

"—but Glenwoods is a prosperous estate. You'd have a comfortable income and a respected position in society."

"I do not doubt it! You must not think I do not appreciate your offer, or fail to value the nobleness of character that prompted it. Such a step would

certainly alleviate my current difficulties—but would it not just create more, graver problems in the future? What if you should meet a woman you truly love?''

For a heart-stopping instant, Bryan considered confessing that he'd met such a girl nearly sixteen years ago. That he'd just proposed to her—to the only woman he'd ever loved or wanted to marry.

But fear and caution stilled his tongue. For one, it would be the height of bad taste, with her husband barely cold in his grave, to press on her vows of love she couldn't possibly return. And then, if she guessed the depth of his true feelings, being Audra, she might refuse him, thinking it not honorable to enter a marriage when her feelings did not equal the intensity of his.

Better that she believe this union based on mutual regard alone.

''I know myself rather well, and can with perfect confidence assure you I cannot ever envision meeting a lady I could care for more than I do you now.'' That, at least, was truth. ''Perhaps ladies have a more romantic view.''

''Perhaps so,'' she agreed sadly.

''Then you will marry me.''

''I didn't say so! It still does not seem right.''

''How could it, when for these past few years

you've thought of yourself only as Jeremy's wife?"

Once again she grimaced, and he cursed himself for mentioning the name. Before he could think of something to soften the error, she said, "It's certainly not that. But Bry, I couldn't..." Her face flushed. "Men expect certain...privileges within marriage, and simply could not—"

"Heavens, Audra, give me credit for some sensitivity! Of course I wouldn't press you for that."

She averted her face. "But you would want children someday."

"Yes, I suppose." He didn't add that he wanted no other mother for those children than Audra.

"I'm—I'm not sure when I would ever..." She swallowed again. "Oh, Bry, this is too much, too soon."

He cupped her face in his hands. "I know, Audra. I swear, I'd not insist you decide now were it not absolutely essential to act immediately. If you can think of any other solution that will keep your honor intact and still get you back to Lisbon, I'll withdraw my offer."

She'd closed her eyes again wearily, but a moment later snapped them back open. "There may indeed be a way."

Alarm ricocheted through him, and he primed himself to dismantle any solution she might pro-

pose. The dream of claiming her for his own loomed so close, he simply couldn't let it elude him now. "Tell me."

"Marriage *is* the only honorable option I see. But why not make it an honorable bargain that will preserve the future for us both? If you can obtain leave to accompany me to Lisbon, I will marry you and let you pay Jeremy's debts, but ours must be a marriage in name only. With no false pride, I can state I am a good army wife. I can manage your billets, care for your equipment and supplies on the march. And when we reach Lisbon, we can have the marriage annulled. You will get your freedom, and I will preserve my honor."

Bryan listened to her growing enthusiasm with dismay. A temporary bargain wasn't at all what he envisioned. He scrambled to line up some convincing argument against it. "But, Audra, that will still leave *your* future unsettled."

"I'll have time on the march to consider that. No, Bryan, this solution feels so right, I will not entertain any other option. I will marry you on these terms—or not at all."

Despite her fatigue, he recognized in the set of her small pointed chin the same determination she'd possessed since she was a child of ten, insisting on riding his stallion although her legs were

barely long enough to reach the stirrups. He knew that look in her eye. She would not budge.

What else could he do, then, but agree to her terms, little as he liked them? Leave her to the tender mercies of Lieutenant Allensby and Lady Cranmore?

But as she said, they'd have time on the march to consider the future. Not nearly long enough for her to finish grieving and come to care for him with the fervor he'd want—but if he were gentle, and thoughtful, and cherishing, perhaps by the time they reached Lisbon she'd be able to believe his declaration of love, and agree to give their marriage a real chance.

Far more chance than he was likely to get if he refused her conditions.

Swiftly he went down on one knee. "Mrs. Saybrooke, would you do me the honor of becoming my wife?"

"In an honest bargain, for the duration of the march back?"

"An honest bargain," he agreed reluctantly.

"Then, Lieutenant Langford, I should be privileged to accept your offer."

It was nearly midnight, when by the light of the full moon Bryan made it back to headquarters. As he expected, lamps were still lit in the staff tent,

while, taking advantage of the moonlight and the mild evening, several knots of men sat up talking or playing at cards. He was relieved to find Charles Marsden among them.

"Welcome back, Bry. Again, my regrets. Did you help settle the widow's affairs?"

"In a manner of speaking. Which reminds me, sorry to be so precipitate with this, but I'm going to need that money I lent you back in Roiça. If you would, let Henry and Richardson know I'm calling in their debts, as well. And can you tell me where the chaplain is tonight?"

"I believe he's still down with the wounded. In need of some comfort? Not surprising."

Bryan smiled wryly. "Not exactly. I need him to perform a service. I'm getting married tomorrow."

Marsden burst out laughing—until he noticed Bryan hadn't joined in the mirth. "M-married?" he gasped in mid-chuckle. "Surely you're not serious!"

"Can you have a runner take a message to him? I've a number of other preparations to make."

"You *are* serious. Marrying who?" Then he seemed to puzzle out the rest, his eyes widening. "Lord, Bryan, you can't be telling me you mean to marry Saybrooke's widow!"

"I do indeed."

"But why? And in such haste?"

In a few terse sentences, Bryan detailed the precarious situation in which Audra Saybrooke now found herself.

"I appreciate nobility and all, Bry, but isn't this taking friendship a bit far? I mean—marriage! 'Tis a rather permanent solution."

"I devoutly hope so. But perhaps it will reassure you my sanity is intact if I explain that I've loved Audra Saybrooke for sixteen years. I've never wanted any other woman."

Marsden paused a minute, considering. "Viewed in that light, it does make more sense. Does...does the lady know the nature of your sentiments?"

"You'd have me tell her now? When? Should I have made love to her over her husband's coffin?"

"I can see that would have been rather gauche. Still, what if later you should find out the lady cannot...reciprocate the intensity of your feelings?"

"I shall just have to hope that she does." Not even to Charles, the closest thing to a best friend he possessed at headquarters, did Bryan want to confess the temporary nature of the union Audra had agreed to. "Besides, given the circumstances, what else would you have me do?"

Charles sighed. "Nothing else in honor you

could do, I suppose. When is the event to transpire?''

''I'll bring Audra back with me tomorrow and arrange the ceremony for immediately after.''

''Then there's nothing else to do but wish you happy.''

Bryan reached out to clasp the hand his friend extended. ''Thank you. I intend to be.'' And prayed with all his heart good intentions would be enough.

Bryan had not previously imagined the circumstances of his wedding night, but if he had, never would he have envisioned himself hunched over a well-scuffed desk in the small upper room of a village inn, tallying up bills, while his bride sat in uneasy silence behind him, brushing the dust from his dress jacket.

The total of those bills, he had to admit, shocked him. He knew Jer had gambled—all the officers did—but that his friend, with a wife to care for, would have been imprudent enough to continue play when dipped this badly, he found almost unbelievable. No wonder Audra had been so distraught.

Anger at his dead friend's recklessness stirred in his chest, to join the uneasy mix of longing, desire, and shyness that had kept them both nearly tongue-

tied since Bryan's fellow officers had ushered them back here after their brief exchange of vows and a short, impromptu reception.

A celebration as unlike the daylong, flower-family-and-food-filled frolic of her wedding to Jeremy as could be imagined.

In an attempt to lighten the tension, he held out a bill that bore the elaborate crest of a Lisbon jeweler. "Really, Audra, sometimes Jer was outside of enough! He's had me pay twice for this bauble—once for its purchase, and then again to buy it back from Sanchez."

Audra stopped her brushing and glanced at the embossed velum. For a moment she looked almost...stricken. Then she turned back to her work, her hand trembling slightly.

"Bry," she said softly, dry irony in her tone, "did you notice diamond ear bobs among the trumpery stuff Maria sold to Sanchez for me?"

He looked up, frowning. "Now that you mention it, I—"

"Bryan, those ear bobs weren't for me."

It took him an instant to understand the implication. "You mean...there was another woman?" he asked, astounded.

Her hand stilled on the brush. Then she laughed, a sharp sound utterly devoid of humor. "'Woman'? Make that 'women.' Spanish women,

Portuguese women, chamber maids, laundresses—
I believe there was a condessa, as well, back in
Lisbon. Did you truly not know?'' She took a
harsh, uneven breath. "Everyone else in the army
did.''

He sat stupidly with his mouth open, shocked to
the core. "I—I don't know what to say.''

She shrugged, as if to imply there was nothing
to be said, and began to ply the brush once more.
"Jer never intended to bring me to the Peninsula.
I begged to come. I was three months gone with
child when we married, you see, and I couldn't
bear to face alone what would happen back home
when the babe came so early. My father's disappointment and shame. Old Lord Cranmore's censure, and Jer's brother's wife, Amelia, whispering
that she'd always known there was something
havey-cavey about a mere vicar's daughter catching herself the son of an earl.''

She laughed again, another failed attempt. "I
thought it would be a grand adventure. And I loved
him so—'' Her voice caught and she took a shuddering breath. "I loved him so much. I thought it
would be enough. It wasn't.''

Bryan couldn't yet comprehend the enormity of
it—Jer betraying Audra, the heartache and embarrassment she must have endured—but with every
atom of his being he longed to give her comfort.

"Audra, I can't explain why…Jer would have done something like that. But I know he loved you."

She wiped at her eyes and looked back at him, her serene mask in place. "Did he? He claimed as much. Every time I'd discover a new…lapse, he'd beg my forgiveness, promise it would never happen again."

She smiled, her eyes gazing into the distance, a world of aching sadness in them. "But you know Jer—so gay, and handsome, and charming. Men liked him immediately, and women adored him. Perhaps he thought it ungentlemanly not to respond in kind." Her soft voice took a bitter twist. "Or perhaps 'love' is only the sweet word a man uses to persuade a woman into his bed."

From the faraway look in her eyes Bryan knew she wasn't referring to Jer's recent inamoratas, but to a laughing sprite of an English girl two years ago. Rage shook him, and if his friend were not already dead, at that moment he could cheerfully have put a bullet through him.

Before he could dredge from his rattled mind something, anything of solace to offer, Audra shook her head, as if to break the spell of the past, and her expression turned matter-of-fact.

"Now you know why I was so reluctant to pledge myself again to a man who didn't want

me," she said briskly. "Thank heavens we've always been friends—best of friends, haven't we, Bry? This situation is awkward, but we'll brush through it. And I thank you again for your kindness. Now, let me see if the innkeeper can contrive us some tea."

Gritting his teeth, Bryan watched her walk away. With an urgency he could almost taste he wanted to pull her into his arms, cradle her against his chest as he had when she'd broken down yesterday, promise to show her that a man's love could be so much more. But she'd thrown up that brittle wall of friendship between them again. He had the oddest sense that if he tried to breach it, she'd shatter.

He picked up another voucher before the stark, unwelcome realization seized him. By trying to show consideration for her grief, hiding his true feelings behind a brotherly solicitude yesterday when he asked for her hand, had he made a grievous mistake? True, Audra might have considered it inconsiderate, even shameful of him to express to her vows of love, with her husband newly laid in his grave, but at least she might have thought them genuine.

Rumor said Soult was marching to join the French Marshals arrayed against the English. Despite his victory at Talavera, Wellington would

have to abandon his plans to advance on Madrid and fall back to the border fortress of Badajoz to protect his supply lifeline to Portugal.

From Badajoz it would take only a fortnight to reach Lisbon. Having begun under a false banner of friendship, and with Audra still bleeding from the pain Jer's infidelity had inflicted, how in that short time was he to convince the only woman he'd ever loved to make their temporary bargain permanent?

Chapter Four

In the common room downstairs, Audra arranged the tea things on the tray, fatigue only partially responsible for the shaking in her hands.

Certainly she was exhausted after the shocks and strain of three nearly sleepless nights. She knew the surface calm she'd managed to maintain throughout this endless day, a calm she'd constructed by so mentally removing herself that events unrolled around her as if in a distant dream, could not last much longer.

She desperately needed rest.

At first she'd felt a detached relief to be gone from the Ninety-fifth's encampment, away from the pitying or leering faces of those who'd known the reality of her life with Jeremy—away from his room, his things, and all the memories.

But now that she'd journeyed to the headquar-

ters of Bryan's unit, the room to which she'd be bringing tea was Bryan's room. If she wished to sleep, the bed she must lie in was Bryan's.

How in heaven's name had she muddled into this?

In the tiny logical part of her brain not snuffed out by fatigue she realized she was no longer reacting rationally. Still, as the enormity of what she'd pledged before the chaplain this morning fully registered, fear and worry seemed to seep from the corners of the shadowed room to attack her vulnerable mind.

She touched the engraved seal on his signet, which had been pressed into duty as a wedding ring. She'd really married him. Despite the restrictions stipulated in their wholly nonbinding verbal agreement, she now belonged to Bryan Langford. Who could dispose of what little property she still possessed, beat her—take her body whenever and however he liked, with the full blessing of the law.

But he'd promised he would not touch her—hadn't he? The Bryan she'd grown up with had never lied—not once, not ever. He'd even joked before leaving for the army that he'd chosen Dunbar's Dragoons in part for the regimental motto: *Veritas et Virtus*—Truth and Valor.

If he'd sworn not to take her, he wouldn't. But had he actually promised that—or had he only

pledged to seek an annulment once they reached Lisbon?

She simply couldn't remember.

Uneasily she recalled the hard tall strength of him, whipcord-lean. Bigger, stronger than Jeremy. Should he decide to exercise his marital rights, there'd be little she could do to prevent it. She had no allies—Maria, her maid, had begged to remain with her friends in the Ninety-fifth. Physically, Audra was no match for him, and as she knew only too well, when had a wife's refusal ever stopped a man?

No, she was being ridiculous. Bryan would never force her. He was her rescuer, wasn't he? He'd salvaged her reputation, saved her honor. She was much better off here. After all, she had no illusions whatsoever about the uses to which Lieutenant Allensby had been eager to put her.

Bryan was no casual acquaintance of her husband's, but one of her oldest friends, a man she knew well. And yet...she'd seen almost nothing of him in the two years before he'd turned up at Jer's grave. War could change a man. And a woman.

Before their marriage she'd thought she knew Jeremy.

Enough! she nearly cried out loud. She recalled a time in childhood when, playing without permission with her grandmother's shawl, she'd been dis-

covered by her tattle-tale younger sister. When her sibling tried to wrest the knitted garment out of her hands, Audra had clung to one trailing strand—and watched in dismay as the whole end began swiftly unraveling.

Which was what the little sense she had left was doing now. She simply must get some sleep. Whatever fate had in store, she could do nothing now but face it. Taking a deep breath, she picked up the tray and mounted the stairs.

Still seated at the desk, frowning at the sheaves of bills, Bryan scarcely looked up as she entered. She hesitated, uncertain. Perhaps it had been a mistake to admit Jer's philandering. Would Bryan now think her weak, pitiful, for not leaving a husband who could not even offer a pretense of fidelity? A woman who, despite brave words to the contrary, would tolerate anything?

Longingly she glanced at the bed. She could endure whatever she must. The past two years had proven that.

''T-tea is ready,'' she said, breaking the silence.

Bryan looked over, his face lightening when he saw her, and a bit of her anxiety lessened. ''Put it here. There's not much other place.'' He cleared a spot.

She set the tea down, trying to avoid watching him watch her as she fixed the cups. She scooted

away from the table, waving off Bryan's offer of
the desk chair, preferring to stand by the window
rather than sit on the bed—an action that might be
construed as an invitation.

Bryan kept up a flow of conversation during tea,
though Audra was scarcely aware of what she replied. Finally he put down his cup.

"You must be exhausted. Why don't you go to
bed?"

She moistened her lips. "I—I believe I shall."

"Don't worry about the tea things—I'll take
them downstairs later."

So much for the hope that he might not be sleeping here. Keeping his well-muscled body in sight,
Audra backed toward the bed, sitting down
abruptly when it caught her behind the knees, and
bent to shakily remove her shoes. Heartbeat echoing in her ears, she lay back.

"You *must* be exhausted!" Bryan said with a
smile. "Don't you wish to remove your gown, take
down your hair? Let me help you."

"No!" she cried, or at least she thought she did,
though it was quite possible no sound exited her
panicked lips. And then he was beside her, sitting
on the edge of the bed, tugging at the pins in her
hair.

"No!" she cried again, a tear squeezing out the
corner of her eye as she grabbed at his hands.

He looked down at her, and all the teasing warmth drained from his face. "Audra!" he exclaimed, shocked disbelief in his tone. "You can't be...afraid, not of me! Surely you didn't imagine I might..."

As if scalded, he jumped up and stood motionless, reading in her expression Lord knew what combination of misery and dread. Then while she watched, frozen, in two strides he reached the side table, snatched one pistol from its holster, and marched back, holding the weapon out.

"Take this. Sleep with it beside you. I cannot deny I think you beautiful, that I desire you, but I gave you my word of honor to leave you untouched. If I ever put a finger on you against your will, shoot me."

For a fraught moment Audra could see only the pistol in Bryan's outstretched hand. Then, tension in her overwrought nerves nearly unbearable, she snapped, "All very well, that! I could be hung for murder, whereas a man violating his wife isn't even a crime."

His affronted, faintly incredulous look faded. After carefully setting the pistol on the bed, he began to laugh.

His mirth seemed to spark her own, though hers had a hysterical edge. "I—I'm s-sorry, Bry," she said, catching her breath on a gasp. "For the tears

I can't seem to stop, the bills, everything. I didn't mean to insult your honor. I'm not myself.''

He gestured to the bed, and when she nodded, sat beside her. Gently he took her hand, and this time she did not flinch away.

''Audra, in rapid succession you've seen your husband's lifeless body carried in, buried him, left the friends with whom you've traveled for nearly two years and entered a new encampment. Of course you're not yourself. If you could suffer all that without weeping, I should think you cast from stone.''

She managed a smile and patted the hand that held hers. Only then did she notice his knuckles were scraped raw. Frowning, she caught his other hand before he could pull it away and saw the skin on that fist was also broken.

He tugged his hands free and shrugged at the unspoken question in her eyes. ''Had a minor disagreement with your Lieutenant Allensby. He didn't, when I paid him off, offer quite the respectful thanks I felt the occasion required.''

''Did you mill him down? Oh, I'm glad!''

Bryan chuckled. ''Bloodthirsty chit. As it happens, you're lucky you didn't have to meet your bridegroom at the provost marshal's prison tent. Had some of his company mates not pulled me

away, I should probably have kicked his insolent face in.''

His expression sobered. "You're my wife now, Audra, and I mean to keep you safe. From everyone—me included," he added, tapping the pistol's grip. "If it comes to that."

The trickle of tears began again. "Thank you, B-Bryan. I should n-never have doubted—"

"It's all right. 'Friends forever?'"

"'Friends forever,'" she repeated, and grasped his out thrust hand in the thumbs-up gesture that had always accompanied their childhood oath.

But then, despite her best efforts, from the aching void within her chest a sob broke free, and another. When gently, so gently, Bryan gathered her to him, without fear this time, she laid her head against his chest.

She wept for the Jeremy she'd loved as a girl, wept for the loss of innocence, the death of that love and all her childhood hopes. And she wept with gratitude for the friend who'd found her in this darkest episode of her life. A man in whose trust and honor, just maybe, she could truly believe.

When at last the aching eased, she pulled away. "I seem to be doing a good job keeping your jacket soaked. I shall have to make sure it is scrubbed and brushed at least as well."

"The jacket has seen far worse. And the shoulder is yours, whenever you need it. But you'll be wanting your rest." He leaned to kiss her forehead. "Sleep now."

"You...won't be staying here?"

"No. Once we go on the march, you'll have little enough privacy. After all that's transpired, I thought you would appreciate some tonight. My equipment is in good order, my dutiful wife, so you may sleep as long as you wish. I'll be just downstairs if you need anything. Rest well, Audra."

Gratitude swelled her throat. "How can I thank you?"

He stood up, smiling, and waved away her words. "'Friends forever.' Good night."

"Good night, Bry," she echoed, and watched him walk out. Leaving her blessedly alone.

Sleep. Rest. Undisturbed rest.

Heaven.

With quick, jerky movements she stripped to her chemise and ripped the pins from her hair. Groaning with pure pleasure, she slid between the crisp linen sheets.

One last thought crystallized before consciousness faded to black. For the period of their bargain, she must do everything within her power to be a friend—and a wife—worthy of Bryan Langford.

* * *

As pale dawn painted the eastern sky, Bryan crept up the stairs to his room. He'd slept well enough on a cot in the headquarters tent—after a year of campaigning he could sleep nearly anywhere—and awakened with a deep sense of elation. It took several minutes for his groggy mind to discover the source.

Audra. Audra was now his wife. The sheer wonder of it swept through him anew, and he nearly laughed out loud.

He'd sprung up immediately, compelled to silently steal to his room. Not that he wished to rouse her—she needed rest, for one, and after that episode last night he'd have to be doubly careful not to alarm her. He simply wished to gaze upon her and be reassured the incredible notion that they'd married was fact, not an illusion generated by some dream from which he'd just awakened.

He eased the door open and his breath caught in a surge of gladness. Audra lay against the pillows, one hand to her cheek, slow even breathing proof of how deeply she slept. A long fringe of lashes rested against cheeks dusted with faint brown freckles, and her hair—ah, her glorious, curly tangle of hair—fanned out over the pillowcase and down across the blankets.

Audra asleep in his bed. The only thing better

would be to wake and find himself lying there beside her. But he'd take one miracle at a time.

A short-lived miracle, unless he were very careful and very lucky.

He frowned at the memory of her fear last night, a fear that still disturbed him. He'd have thought she had a better opinion of him than that. But then, the ways of an army at war were often not pretty. Since arriving in Portugal she'd doubtless witnessed scenes that might shake the faith of any woman in men's potential for honor.

Surely it hadn't been lust seen in his own eyes that sparked it.

Of course he wanted her, as he'd honestly admitted—what man with blood still flowing in his loins would not? Wanted her despite the shattering events she'd lived through the previous three days, though of course he would never have acted upon that need.

He froze as she stirred, sighing, then turned to her side, leaving one bare shoulder exposed in a beam of sunlight.

His mouth went dry and his heartbeat sped as desire, thick and hot and urgent, pounded through his veins.

Backing a step away, he had to further admit that, once the memory of Jer's death receded, keeping his hands off his beautiful wife might

prove a problem. Perhaps giving her that pistol had been wiser than he thought.

Because he couldn't afford to make a mistake. He absolutely had to change her mind about the duration of their marriage, and he was willing to use just about any means within his command to make that happen. Having taken her to wife, union consummated or not, promises given or not, he knew he could never compel himself to give her up.

Chapter Five

Late one afternoon several days later, Audra paused on the heights above the small town, watching as the Dragoons, along with the rest of Wellington's army, staged baggage carts to move out at dawn. Like a vast, majestic, multicolored caterpillar, the long line of men, horses, and wagons would crawl for miles through the dry canyons and rocky hills toward the distant fortress of Badajoz.

By now, Audra was acquainted with several of the wives traveling with the regiment. As Bryan's tackle, harness and uniform were in as good order as he'd claimed, aside from securing a few loose buttons and tidying up his linen, Audra had little to do for her new husband. She fell back into what had become a familiar post-battle pattern in the Peninsula, heading off once Bryan left for drill to

assist the other wives and the doctors tending the wounded.

She'd grown comfortable as well with Bryan's fellow officers, with whom they often took their meals and shared their evenings. Though she observed them gaming, no one appeared to call for high stakes, putting that niggle of worry to rest.

Her temporary husband was not likely to land her in dun territory again.

Nor, at least for the moment, did he appear to catch the eye or pinch the bottom of every serving girl who attended them.

With her, he displayed the easy camaraderie she remembered from their years growing up together. Sometimes she could almost believe them still childhood compatriots embarked on a shared adventure. A large part of the tense foreboding that had troubled her on their wedding night had dissipated like morning mist on the sunny hillsides. Would that their relationship could remain so simple.

However, beneath the friendly banter there remained a simmer of most unchildlike attraction. Sometimes, at table or among his friends, she would turn to catch Bryan watching her, fondness—and something more—in his eyes. Something that made her tongue dry and her stomach quiver.

Had it always been there, that—pull—between them, and she too preoccupied by Jeremy to take heed? Though not by the slightest word or action did he indicate more than a brotherly regard, she was glad that he continued to sleep in the head-quarters tent.

Well, perhaps she could admit just a tiny bit of pique. Not that she thought Bryan should be driven mad with desire for a thin, sunburned widow he considered merely a friend, but she could have handled without alarm a little more indication of interest in her as a woman.

Idiot, she chastised herself as she turned to walk down to the river. Was that not precisely what she'd begged him *not* to indicate?

Clutching towel and soap, she picked her steps through the scrub by the bank down to the swift-flowing stream. She'd take advantage of the warm afternoon sun and give her hair one last good wash before having to embark tomorrow.

She heard footsteps behind her, and turned to see Bryan following. Slowing her pace to allow him to catch up, she watched him as he approached.

He was a man to catch any woman's eye, she realized with sudden appreciation. More than a head taller than Audra, aside from the muscled width of his shoulders—acquired after a year of

wielding a dragoon's heavy sword—he remained lance-slim, even given the bulk of cord and braiding that ornamented an officer's uniform. Dark straight hair and peaked brows, laughing dark eyes, a determined chin and a mouth fashioned for humor as much as command made a most attractive face. He was quite handsome, her noble rescuer.

Suddenly shy, she glanced away when he reached her. "I looked for you at the hospital tent, but Mrs. Carlyle said you'd headed for the river. I thought I'd join you. After loading tackle, I could use a good bath."

A bath. Oh, my. "I planned just to wash my hair," she said a little breathlessly, trying not to envision what he'd look like out of that uniform.

"Bathe, too, if you like. I'll stand guard and warn off any who approach."

The idea of him hovering at a distance, perhaps secretly watching as the cold water slid over her naked skin made her tingle in a number of places she'd wanted never to feel again. "Thank you, no," she replied a little too sharply. "I—I shall have enough trouble untangling my wretched curls."

He merely nodded, seeming much less moved by the idea of his seeing her naked than she was. "As you wish. I'll go just out of sight, then."

And so, whistling cheerfully, he disappeared be-

yond the bend where the rushing stream took a sharp left curve.

Well, brotherly solicitude was what she'd wanted, wasn't it? Irritated for no good reason, Audra threw down her shawl, unfastened and pushed down the top of her gown to keep her wet hair from dripping on it, and caught up a length toweling. Before shedding her shoes, she kicked a small rock viciously out of her path.

But as she immersed her head in the water, the cool, silken flow through her hair soon soothed away her irritation. She pulled the bodice lower still, baring her shoulders and the tops of her breasts, wishing she'd taken Bryan up on his offer and could shed the rest of the restricting garment and sink her whole body into the stream's liquid embrace.

Having at last rinsed the soap from her long riot of curls, she threw the toweling over her shoulders and trudged out of the stream. Choosing a large, flat rock, she sat, leaning her head back into the sun to dry her tresses while she struggled to pull a comb through the tangled lengths.

So pleasant were the golden rays on her forehead, she closed her eyes. Bryan's voice behind her startled them open.

She barely stifled a gasp. He stood just behind her, clad only in his breeches, head still dripping,

a king's ransom of tiny water droplets bejeweling the dark hair of his bare chest.

"I'll do that," he said, his voice husky. "Comb through the tangles." He reached out.

As if enchanted, she gave over the comb. Then tingled at the cool touch of his hand as he laid it on her naked shoulder, his fingers grazing the top swell of her breast.

He positioned himself behind her and, bracing her with his hand, began to comb with long, sure strokes, gently worrying free the snarled ends. After a moment her eyes drifted shut again and she leaned into the pull.

She'd always loved having her hair brushed. Mesmerized by the slow, even strokes, she scarcely noticed when he dropped the comb and began using his fingers instead, burying both hands in the damp tresses, massaging her scalp, then pulling his fingers inch by delicious inch through the strands.

He sat down, straddling her, and she let her head loll back against his bare chest. He plunged his fingers into her hair again, massaging her temples, the tips of her ears, down her neck to her shoulders, then sliding his hands to cup her shoulders, his fingers once again tantalizingly close to the aching fullness of her breasts.

She drifted in sensual lassitude, nearly dozing, all feeling reduced to the seductive stroke of his

fingers against her skin. The shudder of a sigh escaped her lips.

She felt his warm breath at her ear, his lips against the back of her neck, the nip of his teeth at her shoulder.

"Beautiful," he murmured, his voice a ragged whisper.

Hot, brandied breath behind her, against her ear. The stench of cheap perfume. "You make me crazy, sweeting," he whispered, dragging her from sleep, pulling her back against his hardening length. Though she tried to roll away, an arm like an iron band bound her against him while his fingers teased at her nipple, his mouth nipped her neck, her shoulder.

Her eyes flew open. "No!" she cried, trying to sit upright.

Despite her struggles, he held her trapped, so tightly she could scarcely breathe. "See how hard your sweet bottom makes me," he whispered, rubbing against her. "If I'd taken a thousand women, you could still make me hard again." His other hand pushed up under her shift, despite her attempts to bat it away, moved inexorably up to cup her mound, mold her against him, one finger seeking through the right curls to find her cleft...

Gathering her strength, she wrenched away from Bryan, nearly falling when she met no resistance

and belatedly realized he'd let her go. Her heart pounding in her chest, gasping, she whirled to face him.

"No, I won't let you do it to me! Not you, too!"

The flood of pain and humiliation robbed her of breath to say more. Nearly ready to come out of her skin with remembered loathing, she turned and ran, leaving towel, soap, shoes, shawl behind.

Tears blinding her, rocks biting into her bare feet, she stumbled up the slope, but she couldn't outrun the hurting, shameful memories.

"Yes, struggle, sweeting. I love how you move against me. And you love it, too. See how your sweet nipple peaks between my fingers. And here— you're already wet against my hand. I'll make you wetter, my darling. I'll make it so good for you…"

She tripped, caught the slap of a branch on her face, reached out blindly to push it away. But the sting of memory could not be avoided—how her body betrayed her, always, eventually responding to Jer's touch, her resistance softening until his hand between her thighs had free play, until she sagged, shattering against him.

And even that was not enough, no—he must move over her, while she lay limp and helpless, thrust in slowly at first, then faster and faster, not allowing himself to reach his own peak until once again he drove her to climax.

Only then, in triumphant satiation, would he roll away from her, fall deeply into slumber. While she lay sleepless beside him, weeping with humiliation and self-loathing. Jeremy Saybrooke's favorite whore.

Who, even when he came to her from another woman's arms, could no more resist the wiles of her husband than the countless other women he beguiled and bedded.

She felt hands at her shoulders and lashed out blindly, but they held on, jerked her upright, set her on her feet. She swung her arms, fingers splayed into claws, but met only air, and then she was shaken hard, once, twice.

"Audra! Audra, get hold of yourself!"

Bryan's voice. Bryan's voice, not Jer's. She froze, her breathing erratic, her pulse drumming in her ears.

Hands parted her tumbled hair and she saw Bryan's face, grim and worried. Trembling all over, she tried to pull herself back into the present.

The river. She'd been washing her hair. Bryan sat behind her to brush out the tangles. That was all. Nothing else. He'd meant nothing else.

Very slowly, as if not to startle her, he reached out to touch her face.

She forced herself to remain motionless, though every still-alarmed nerve urged her to flee.

"You've cut your cheek," he said, his voice unsteady. "Merciful God, Audra, what did Jer do to you?"

She shook her head, lacking words to describe the gaping wounds.

"He hurt you, forced you—"

"No! No, I could have borne that. He never f-forced me." She swallowed hard. "It was w-worse. Even when he came back to me after whoring, he made me want—" Her voice broke. "Please, I cannot speak of it. But I vowed upon Jeremy's grave I'd never let passion rule me again, and I won't."

He stared at her for a long moment, then cleared his throat, his voice still rough. "Your foot. It's…it's bleeding, as well. Let me carry you to—"

"No! Thank you, I can walk. I'm calm now. After all, 'tis my own foolish fault." She made herself offer him an apologetic smile, a rather good attempt. "Seeing what a Bedlamite you've stumbled into marrying, you're no doubt imploring Heaven that the march back be swift."

Giving him no chance to reply, she set off down the hill. She picked her way to the jumble of belongings, wincing on her cut feet, embarrassed and ashamed now of her outburst. What if someone else had approached the river?

Bryan, who'd followed silently behind her, helped gather up the soap and towel. He said nothing when, despite herself, she stiffened as he pulled tight the loosened lacings of her gown. But after she'd replaced her shoes, thanked him and turned to walk back up the hill, Bryan stayed her with a touch to her shoulder.

He took his hand back immediately, as if to reassure her. "Audra, I can't pretend to understand what happened between you and Jeremy. I'm not sure I even want to. But anything I could do to make it easier, to help you heal, please tell me. 'Friends forever,' remember?"

Once again he left her humbled. "'Friends forever.' I shall try my utmost not to embarrass you by creating any more wretched scenes."

Since it was impossible for her to explain the whole, to him or even to herself, there seemed nothing further to say. Squaring her shoulders and ignoring the pain in her feet, Audra set off for the village.

The next morning before dawn Bryan loaded up his borrowed cot into the headquarters wagon, then returned to help Charles Marsden pack up the remainder.

"Suppose you'll be pitching your own tent on the route, Bry?" Marsden asked.

"Yes." Audra would need it, of course.

"And…will you continue to use our cot? Not that I mind, you understand, but it might be a tad crowded with all of us. I must confess, I shall miss the opportunity of being quartered in a real bed."

"I'm…not sure yet." He'd hoped, once they went on the march, to sleep at least in the same tent as Audra, but after yesterday…

"Your wife is a lovely little thing. I imagine you're looking forward to—"

"Forcing myself on a woman who lost her husband a bare fortnight ago?" he said savagely.

"Damn it, Bry, that's not what I meant!" Charles slammed the last pack into the wagon bed. "All I was going to say was I figured you'd be anxious to reach winter quarters. Perhaps by then, Audra's grief will have lessened and you can both get on with your lives." He gave Bryan an aggrieved look. "Then maybe you won't be so blasted testy."

Bryan had the grace to feel guilty. "Sorry, Charles. I expect I've not been as congenial of late as I might."

"You'll get no complaints here. You've probably been without a woman longer than any of us. If I had a lady as lovely as Audra, and couldn't take her, I'd be testy myself."

When Bryan merely nodded, Charles continued,

"Don't think I don't admire you for it. You've shown incredible restraint. Which, of course, she entirely deserves. But given that she is one's legal wife, other men might not have been so...considerate."

Like one he could mention. Unable to comment on that, Bryan turned to help Charles fasten down the wagon flap.

"That's the last of it," Charles said, tying it off. "You're welcome to the cot tonight, if you want it. I'd best get my ill-tempered beast saddled."

With a casual salute, Charles walked off toward the stable enclosure.

Bryan needed to saddle his roan and Audra's mare, as well, but first he would stop by the inn. As organized as she'd been about everything else, he was certain she'd be already up and packed.

He set off in that direction, a little nervous about how she'd receive him.

They'd been awkward around each other last night after returning from the river. He still harbored vestiges of the sickness, acute as if someone had kicked him in the gut, that had struck him when Audra wrenched herself out of his arms and looked at him, loathing in her face.

Sickness that she'd run from him—from *him.* And even learning that her fear had been of what

Jer had done, her loathing for how she had reacted to it, didn't make him feel much better.

Jeremy's prenuptial seduction had already robbed him of the chance to make her believe in his love—especially after yesterday, when his desire for her had, he was sure, been only too nakedly obvious.

A desire she had shared, at least at first, thrilling him when she went soft and pliant in his arms.

But the very fact that she could, she had responded, he knew now to be not an advantage but an impediment. Perhaps an insurmountable one. Whatever Jeremy had done to her—and he didn't want to pursue that dark thought—his childhood companion had somehow made Audra hate the responses of her own passionate body.

So much for the possibility of seducing her into abandoning their bargain.

Had he made a terrible mistake, pushing her so precipitously into wedlock? Entirely unaware of the dark undercurrents in her marriage, so naively sure their past affection and his deep love would prove enough to win her, had he blindly rushed into a situation that would prove not opportunity but torture? Like the greenest of new officers, charging his troops forward without adequate preparation or reinforcement.

Halting outside the entrance to the inn, with a

weary sigh he closed his eyes, girding himself back into his role as platonic friend.

A role sometimes nearly impossible to play, as when he saw the anguish in her face on the hillside yesterday. Every instinct screamed at him to pull her into his arms, cradle her wounded body against his strength. To shield her, like some mythic knight of yore, and slay every dragon and demon who'd ever oppressed her.

Except the worst of those demons, his former friend Jeremy, was already slain.

Stripped of love and love-play as weapons, how was he to reach his princess, rescue her from the dark prison in which Jer had cast her?

Enough gloomy thought. He'd fought desperate battles before, their outcome uncertain, even been several times convinced he'd seen his last day. He'd continue to fight this one, mile by mile on the road to Lisbon, using care and concern and gentleness, if those be the only weapons granted him.

The journey would be short, so impossibly short. Hardly enough time to heal wounds far deeper than mere grief, wounds so grave Audra preferred the tender mercies of life with Amelia to the hazards of becoming once again a wife.

But despite the dismal odds of convincing her to do so in the handful of days allowed him, he

would never give up. Like a good officer fought to a standstill, he'd regroup. One way or another, he was going to persuade Audra safety lay not in a ship waiting to take her to England, but in his arms.

to the relief as well. Take a mind of one. Just as he
is somehow held to me up. One way is quicker. It
was going to have made to the maybe beaten as
sleep without Whether her her black and, but it his
spun.

Chapter Six

Hearing Bryan's footsteps in the hallway, Audra
braced herself for his entry. He'd been so kind, so
understanding after her lapse yesterday, she was
still embarrassed around him. She'd slept badly
and risen almost two hours ago to assemble her
baggage, then waited in growing apprehension.

She hadn't considered until this morning that he
might be the subject of scorn among his compatriots for having a wife with whom he didn't even
share a bed.

Jeremy had considered it a point of pride that it
be known Audra did continue to share his, no matter how flagrant his lapses. Little wonder, then,
men of Allensby's ilk had sought her out, even
before Jer's death.

No, she wouldn't think of that now. She would
put it behind her. Bryan deserved far better from

their bargain than she'd given so far. Not only had she subjected him to the possibility of ribald gibes, but selfishly lost in her own turmoil, she'd robbed him of his last opportunity to sleep in a real bed, perhaps until they reached Lisbon.

She would do better from now on, she vowed. She'd be the wife she'd promised, attentive to his comfort, arranging billets with his batman, making sure he received fresh tea and hot meals.

Insisting he sleep in his own tent during the march.

A skitter of unease skipped through her at that resolve. Lingering discomfort notwithstanding, after his forbearance yesterday, she owed him that much.

His voice pulled her from her musings. "Good morning, Audra."

She looked over to study his face and found no trace of reproach or irritation. Not until that moment did she realize she'd been preparing herself for both—and deservedly. His unexpected compassion inspired her with the oddest desire to run over and kiss him.

Instead she indicated the neatly roped baggage. "I've got everything ready. All my things, and such supplies as you left in the room."

"Very good. My most efficient wife."

His praise deepened her guilt. "Would you like

tea? I've kept some hot. I considered bringing it over to headquarters, but I—I didn't want to get in the way.''

''You wouldn't have. Thank you, but I believe at this hour we'd best stow the rest of the baggage and saddle our horses.''

She picked up a portmanteau and followed him as he hefted the trunk and led the way downstairs, offered farewell thanks to the innkeeper, and headed down the street toward the stables.

''Where should you like to ride?'' he asked after they'd saddled their mounts.

''I thought to stay by the baggage wagons. I can help Mrs. O'Malley tend the convalescents who are fit enough to make the march.''

''You'll be safe there,'' he agreed. ''By the way, word has already filtered back to headquarters that you are an excellent nurse.''

She flushed a little. ''I've had much practice.'' She didn't add that, with Jeremy often gaming and carousing, nursing had filled the long empty days and nights.

''Mrs. O'Malley tells me you're the best she's ever seen for skill in treating wounds and for soothing the men—and the wounded of the Dragoons are not even familiar.''

She shrugged. ''All fought in the same cause— and all wounded suffer alike, whether I know them

or not. Besides, it makes me feel I serve some useful purpose.'' That perhaps despite the wreckage of her marriage to Jeremy, her time in the Peninsula had accomplished something of value.

"Few other wives work as diligently, or do as much good, Mrs. O'Malley told me. I'm proud of you, Audra.'' He gave her a salute before handing her up in the saddle.

Absurdly pleased she'd finally done something that reflected well on him, she could think of nothing further to say. Bryan guided their mounts past the clumps of troopers and carts to the place at the rear allotted to the wagons.

"I'll turn you over to Mrs. O'Malley,'' he said, indicating the tall Irishwoman, his sergeant major's wife and the Dragoon's chief nurse. "I must ride with my company, but I'll stop back later to check on you.''

"Please do, and send your batman, as well,'' she said as they dismounted and secured her mare to a lead line. "We'll contrive dinner and see to disposing your kit and setting up the tent.'' She smiled deprecatingly. "I intend to do better, you see. I've been a rather sorry bargain of a wife thus far.''

He reached up to touch her cheek with one gloved finger. "I could never think so.''

"And...and tonight, you take the cot. I'm quite accustomed to a bedroll."

She waited nervously for the import of her words to sink in. When they did, Bryan studied her intently.

"Are you sure? I can continue to sleep—"

"No, you should have your own things." She squared her shoulders. "It's time I began conquering my weaknesses, instead of burdening you with them."

She was rewarded with a smile so brilliant it almost stole her breath. "Although in a large column with sentries posted, the chance of attack is slim, I must own I'd feel better being close. To protect you, if necessary. However, I must insist you take the cot."

"No, I've had the luxury of a bed for several nights."

"Perhaps, but I've much more experience bedding down on open ground."

She chuckled. "We can argue about this later."

His expression softened. "You have a lovely laugh, Audra. I hope in the days ahead to hear much more of it." He grinned. "As you know, to retain any sanity whatsoever, one must meet the trials of an army on the march with humor. Now I should muster my men. Until later."

He saluted her again and turned his mount. She watched, still smiling, as he rode off.

The affection she'd always cherished for Bryan, strengthened by gratitude at his kindness, tightened her chest. Bryan, who overlooked her lapses, dedicated himself to her protection—and wanted her to laugh. For the first time since Jeremy's death and her hasty marriage, she felt herself relax.

What would it be like to have a husband like that, not just for this journey, but for always?

The idea startled her. It was impossible, as she'd told Bryan from the first. Nothing good lasted for always. Besides, though her initial anxiety was slowly fading, marriage involved much more than camaraderie, and that scene at the river yesterday amply demonstrated she was far from healed enough for intimacy. She wasn't sure she'd ever be. No man deserved a wife whose mind and body were still possessed by ghosts from the past, who met his touch torn between wanting and revulsion.

A wife waiting with secret dread for even so manifestly honorable a man as Bryan to make a false step.

But despite that unconquerable sense of dread, after barely two weeks of marriage, she was beginning to sense how wrenching it was going to be to let him go.

She looked up to find Mrs. O'Malley grinning at her.

"'Tis a handsome devil of a husband you've got yourself, Mrs. Langford. No wonder you stand and watch him ride away. But he'll be back 'ere long. Such a care he takes of ye!"

"He is kindness itself."

"A good man, and that's the Lord's truth. I've known the lieutenant all the time me Andy's been with the regiment, and always aloof he's kept himself, never rousting about like the other men, even the officers. Almost as if he was waitin' fer something."

"Waiting?"

"Aye. I always thought he'd a sweetheart back home, or lost one. But now I see 'twas you he'd been pining for, sure as the Irish hills are green. 'Tis all there in his face when he looks at ye."

Bryan—pining for *her?* Audra opened her mouth to deny the claim, then realized she'd best say nothing.

"Now, don't ye be blushin'—I'll leave ye be." The older woman chuckled. "But ye're a lucky woman, Mrs. Langford, and don't ye forget it! Now come along, we've work to do."

Bryan cherishing a tendre—*for her?* Shocked by the notion, Audra docilely followed the sergeant major's wife.

Surely Mrs. O'Malley was mistaken. But for a giddy moment, a fierce gladness filled Audra's heart at the thought of being loved by such a man.

It might also explain his insistence on marrying her barely a day after Jer's burial.

No, he'd wed her because that appeared the only honorable solution. He couldn't love her—or else, why had he always hung back when Jeremy came courting, never putting himself forward or attempting to press any claims of his own? He had a fondness, that was all.

If Mrs. O'Malley were indeed correct about a sweetheart, it certainly wasn't her.

Audra felt a piercing, unexpected jealousy.

She couldn't imagine that a woman Bryan Langford admired would not return his regard. Since he claimed to now have no particular sweetheart, perhaps the girl Mrs. O'Malley believed he'd been pining for had died.

Bryan, having lost someone he loved. Perhaps they shared more than she'd imagined. Perhaps, were she not so weak and weary, they might have been able to comfort each other.

Somehow, being widowed and safely home in England, alone, no longer seemed quite so appealing.

By the time Bryan joined her that evening, she had even less cause to laugh.

As men become hardened to the horrors of battle, so Audra had armored herself against the horrors of its aftermath. When she arrived at the Peninsula, she'd left the hospital tents on her first visit after less than half an hour, rushing out to vomit helplessly in the privacy of a nearby copse of trees, sickened and revolted by the smells of torn and bloody flesh, the sight of moaning men with gaping wounds, shattered or mangled stumps of limbs.

Now she scarcely noticed the odors, and her practiced eyes saw the injuries only to make professional assessment of the soldier's chances for survival.

But her heart still bled for their suffering. And perhaps the never-ending work of tending those in greater need helped put her own suffering with Jeremy in clearer perspective. She, at least, had survived with limbs, if not soul, intact.

Unlike one of the young officers she'd been watching today. His doubtful future still clouded her mind as she worked with Hastings, Bryan's batman, to set up camp and prepare a frugal dinner, then kept her mostly silent through the meal. So preoccupied was she it wasn't until afterwards, when Hastings bid them good-evening, that she realized Bryan had fallen silent, as well.

After his batman departed, Bryan turned to her. "You seem...distressed tonight. I had Hastings

pitch his cot just behind this one, so you should be safe enough. Perhaps I should bed down in the headquarters tent."

She stood confused a moment, until the reason for his sudden decision occurred to her. "No, please stay! You mustn't think I've been concerned over that. It's one of the wounded men who worries me."

Bryan exhaled, tension seeming to leave his body. "You're certain it won't—"

"No. I should feel better, having you here."

His dark eyes lit. "Thank you, Audra," he said quietly. "For trusting me. Now, who is this young fellow who's troubling you? Shall I mill him down?"

Tears pricked her eyes even as she smiled at his attempt at humor. If only she could bring herself to truly trust him. Thankful he couldn't read the fear under her calm invitation, she moved over to give him room beside her on the fallen log that served her as a bench.

"I expect he'd be thrilled to be hale enough to be milled down, even if he didn't deserve it. Oh, Bry, he's so young! Barely eighteen. He took lance blows to his arm and chest, and though he's scarcely begun to heal, he refused to be left behind in hospital. He's determined to take convalescent

leave back in England. I don't think he's going to make it to Lisbon.''

Bryan reached over to clasp her hand. ''I'm sorry, Audra. We lose too many—friends, comrades, valiant men.''

''He had me write to his mother—and to the young lady he'd hoped to marry. It...was all I could do not to weep.''

Bryan frowned. ''Where was Mrs. O'Malley? Given your recent loss, surely they could have gotten someone else—''

''Oh, I didn't mind about that, and everyone else was busy. But the purity of the emotions he expressed—his devotion, his cherishing of the lady, and his regret that he would likely never see her again...'' She took a ragged breath. ''It almost makes me believe that such love is possible.''

Bryan rubbed his thumb over the hand he still held. ''Audra, you mustn't judge the quality of all men's love by your experiences with Jeremy.''

That struck too deep a chord. The aching place within where she locked up all the pain, disappointment and grief swelled again, and she knew she'd soon be helpless to contain it. She rose unsteadily, her vision already blurring with tears.

''E-excuse me, but I fear I'm about to w-weep again.''

He caught her arm, lifted her tear-streaked face. "Sweet Audra. Of course you must weep."

With the barest pressure, so she could easily pull away at any moment, he gathered her once again into his arms. Once again, he lifted her and carried her to the cot, sat with her in his lap and whispered soothing nonsense into her hair as she wept against his chest.

Exhausted from grief and the tasks of the march, she leaned into his strength until she had no more tears, until she felt herself, drained and cleansed, drifting to sleep in his arms.

Sometime later she seemed to sense him easing her onto the cot. And though it might have been only a dream, she thought she'd felt the brush of his mouth against her lips.

Though he'd slept a little, the following day Bryan went through his duties in a cloud of hope so buoyant none of the usual petty irritations of the march—squabbling among the troopers, a misplaced tent, a horse pulling up lame—could put a dent in his good humor.

Audra had asked him to stay near. She'd even come back into his arms.

He'd wanted to carry her to his own bedroll, sleep with her cradled close. But though when she turned to him in distress, he couldn't think of any-

thing but easing her sorrow, if he woke to find her snuggled beside him, relaxed and rosy with sleep, he knew his thoughts—and his body—would soon urge action beyond comfort.

Even that brotherly kiss on the lips, whisper-light that it not disturb her rest, had fired his blood. Though he considered himself master of his appetites, there was no sense courting disaster. As it was, on an evening when Audra retired with smiles instead of tears, he might best offer her the pistol again.

Tonight—tonight when he'd once again sleep—or at least attempt it—with her but a few feet away. So close, so very close to all he desired.

Spirits vibrant at the idea of seeing her again, he'd almost reached the spot near the riverbank where the baggage wagons had halted for lunch when he noticed something wrong. Audra and Mrs. O'Malley stood by the stream, and from their impassioned gestures, he could tell they were arguing.

"'Tis sorry I am and all for the lad, but ye know the orders well enough. We canna allow a wagon to fall behind the column. If 'tisn't the blinkin' scavengers that follow every army train lyin' in wait for whatever scraps be left, there's *bandidos* all over these hills that would cut yer pretty throat for the ring ye wear, and think nobbit of it!''

"What's amiss?" Bryan asked as he dismounted.

"Yer missus has a kind heart, for which I do praise the dear Lord daily, but ye must tell her if the lad can no longer ride, there's naught to be done!"

Audra came over to seize Bryan's hand. "It's the soldier I told you about. His wounds have festered, his fever's high and the pain so great he can't possibly stay in the saddle. We cannot simply abandon him by the road like...refuse!"

Audra turned back to the sergeant major's wife. "He won't last more than a few hours—not with the infection raging and him already so weak. Could you rest easy tossing him out to die alone if it were your own husband in such torment?"

The Irishwoman shook her head, tears in her eyes. "Ah, lass, ye know I hate it. But he's hardly the first. We must go on."

"Then...then let's make a pallet. I'll stay behind. The end won't take long. At least he can die peacefully in the shade of these trees—not fallen out of the saddle onto the roadside somewhere in the blazing sun."

"Blessed saints be praised, woman, no more can I leave you here with him! For the very same reasons."

Bryan barely listened to the arguments, his at-

tention captured by the anguish on Audra's face. Audra who had seen too many wounded men left behind, unable to keep up the pace of the march. Audra who grieved for her own loss and the pure love of a dying young man.

To help her believe once more in the reality of love like that, he was prepared to do almost anything.

"I'll stay with her," Bryan interrupted.

Mrs. O'Malley looked at him, astounded. "But, Lieutenant—"

"Yes, Mrs. O'Malley, you've stated all the dangers quite accurately. But I think my pistol will be sufficient to keep the scavengers at bay, and if what you both say is true, the unfortunate soldier will be dead soon. I can fashion a grave for him while Mrs. Langford keeps watch and we'll both be back to the train before dark."

The look of gratitude in Audra's eyes was worth everything—the very real risks inherent in the hasty scheme, the outrage his colonel would doubtless express once he heard of it, the strain on his nerves of maintaining a four-direction watch for however long it took the boy to die. "Thank you, Bryan," she whispered.

"I'm naught to tell ye nay, if ye be fixed on it, Lieutenant. But idiocy it is," Mrs. O'Malley muttered. "Pure bloomin' idiocy, and if harm comes

to either of ye, I'll send my shade back to worry
ye both in the hereafter.''

"Thank you, too, Mrs. O'Malley. You'll be able
to manage without me—''

"Tsk, and it's not me who'll be needin' assistance. Ye just finish this quick as possible and get
back.''

While Audra fashioned a bed of fallen leaves
and blankets, Bryan tethered their horses, pulled
out a few extra rounds and checked his weapons.
Together they helped the barely conscious ensign
onto the pallet. Then, as the army resumed its
march, Bryan made a quick reconnoiter of the surrounding area.

When he returned, Audra had scooped a bowl
of water from the river and sat beside the soldier,
crooning to him as she mopped his fevered forehead.

His chest ached with love for her. Fierce, passionate Audra, who was willing to risk her life that
one wounded soldier might die more at ease.

His life, too, when it came down to it. But, as
he'd assured Mrs. O'Malley, he didn't really worry
that they'd be attacked now. Scavengers and *bandidos,* though as fearsome as described, generally
operated at night, by which time he intended for
them both to be safely back in with the army train.

But his disquiet increased as the afternoon wore

on. Though the young soldier weakened by the hour, his rapid, gasping breaths continued. Finally, when the sun set behind the hills in a nebula of rose, gold and flame, Bryan had to face the very real, and very troubling, fact that they would be spending the night here.

A dying man, an unarmed nurse, and one overzealous Dragoon alone in the blackness under a brilliant star-swept sky, waiting for whatever—or whomever—crept down the Badajoz road.

Chapter Seven

Bryan rose from his lookout on the rocky spur above the stream. He couldn't let Audra and Ensign Wetherford remain on that exposed site by the river. He'd better set up some sort of crude camp here in the bolder-strewn heights above.

He walked down to where Audra was keeping vigil, and saw by the look on her face that, veteran campaigner that she was, she'd already realized what he'd been about to tell her.

"I'm sorry, Bry. I didn't think he'd last this long." She laughed wryly. "Were we in London, I could spare myself the necessity of conversing with you, simply by ordering up calling cards with 'I'm sorry' engraved upon them and pinning one to my bodice."

He could hardly be angry with her, not when he was probably more responsible than she for land-

ing them in a situation that grew more dangerous with every moment of gradually dimming daylight. "I hope your soldier appreciates this."

She sighed. "I'm afraid not. He's been unconscious this past hour."

He had to laugh. "Let's hope virtue is its own reward, then. I'm going to find us a safer place to camp for the night, then come back for you. See if you can gather up everything and erase all the traces that might show we've been here."

Bryan worked rapidly, hiding and hobbling the horses, putting down blankets in a high narrow gorge that allowed no hidden approaches save up a sheer rock cliff even a goat couldn't navigate. Then they managed the difficult climb, Audra bringing their knapsacks and two full canteens of water, Bryan hefting the soldier's fevered body. Mercifully the unconscious man made no sound.

Muscles screaming, Bryan was sweating from exertion and worry when they finally reached the hideaway. Full dark was nearly upon them now. How many eyes might have spotted them while he struggled to carry the wounded man, unable to keep watch?

Thankfully he laid the ensign down, only to have Audra whisper a moment later, "He's dead, Bry."

The soldier could have had the grace to die be-

fore he lugged him up that cliff, Bryan thought with a flash of morbid humor. But he couldn't have left a dead comrade for the vultures to find. And he'd already prepared a resting place for the man up here among the rocks.

"Let's bury him before the light fails entirely," he whispered back.

And so, quietly reciting the burial service they'd both heard too many times, they consigned the body of another young Englishman to a barren Spanish hillside far from the home and the lady he'd loved.

Afterward, Bryan led Audra back to the enclosure and dropped down onto the makeshift pallet. For a moment both sat silently, too weary and battered by the day's events for speech. Finally an owl's distant hoot broke the silence.

An owl—or a signal? The hair at the back of his neck rising, Bryan tensed, peering into the now-black landscape.

Audra touched his hand. "Should we try to ride back?"

"Not in the dark. I don't know the road, and we'd be an easy target for…anyone out there."

He heard her take a deep breath. "Is someone out there?"

He couldn't lie to her, not even now. "Probably. The army's departure was common knowledge. At

the very least, scavengers will be following to see what they can find. Which likely means *bandidos,* too, to relieve the scavengers of anything truly valuable.''

Good move, Langford, he thought, wincing inwardly at his own words. *Fine way to win the love of your wife—take her away from the protection of the army, terrify her with the prospect of attack or possibly murder. If we get back unscathed, she's going to bolt for Lisbon as fast as her horse can carry her.*

He felt her tremble, and regretted even more his rashness and incurable honesty—until he realized she was softly laughing. ''Oh, Bry, you couldn't ever tell a convenient lie, could you?'' She squeezed his hand.

Despite the direness of their situation, his spirits soared. ''I'm afraid not. But we're better off here than trying to move out. This position is defensible, if it comes to it.''

''As long as there aren't too many attackers.''

Damn, she had been with the army too long. ''As long as there aren't too many,'' he reluctantly agreed.

''Give me a pistol, then.''

''Can you shoot it accurately?''

''How do you think I filled the dinner pot on campaign?''

Without further ado he carefully fingered in the dark for the holster and handed her a pistol—the same one he'd given her just a few nights ago to protect herself from him. "Don't shoot unless I tell you. And keep my other pistol, as well. I'll use my rifle, draw fire and see if I can beat back any attack. I won't let anyone by me. But if…if it appears I've failed, save one shot for yourself."

Neither of them needed to voice what would happen to her if *bandidos* captured her alive.

"I'll keep watch as long as I can. Mercifully, no one can approach without our hearing them."

Audra shivered, from cold this time, for the dry air turned frigid after the sun's warmth left it. Bryan eased a blanket over her shoulders, settled her behind him, and propping his loaded rifle on a rock, stared out into the blackness.

His hypersensitive nerves sparked at every sound—the hoot of an owl, the cry of a wildcat, the small scufflings of various nocturnal creatures going about their business. Once, Audra scared him silly by jumping forward with a muffled gasp, then explaining in a shaky whisper she'd felt something scurry behind her back. Without even thinking he gave her a hug and a fierce kiss before turning back to resume watch.

After a seemingly endless night, Bryan was about to congratulate himself—and offer up a fer-

vent prayer of thanks—for their good luck when he heard it. As the inky blackness of night ever so slightly lightened with the approach of dawn, a jingle of harness and the low tones of men were clearly audible in the stillness.

Audra had been dozing, her head against his shoulder, but the sound of voices roused her, as well. Abruptly she sat up, clutched his arm with one hand. He squeezed her fingers briefly, then pointed to the narrow gap in the rock that was an attacker's only point of entry. Careful not to dislodge any pebbles whose rattle might give them away, he moved slowly toward it.

He reached the edge, able to make out through the lightening dark the moving shapes of several men. If their luck continued to hold, the marauders might comb the area and leave without discovering their presence.

But then one figure froze, gesturing to the others. Stealthily they began to pick their way up the hill toward Bryan's position. Had they found the tracks of his staggering journey up the slope with the ensign's body?

His mind coldly logical now, he focused entirely on the coming confrontation. Rifle leveled and sighted, ball primed, he waited, still hoping it might be avoided, but ready to fire.

Then he heard a man call out near where he'd

hidden the horses and knew stealth was no longer possible. If they lost their mounts, they were as good as dead anyway. They'd never manage to catch up to the army train on foot.

How many marauders were there? Two, three, maybe four? He'd have to take them out quickly, before they could find and capture or unhobble the beasts. Taking a deep breath to steady his aim, Bryan sighted the man closest to the hidden paddock and fired.

With a shriek, the man went down. Two others who'd been approaching his position scrambled backward down the rocky slope. Another, near the fallen man, leveled a weapon and fired.

He heard the ping of a ricochet on the rocks nearby and squeezed off another round. The shooter yelped and fell back, but several men ran into view from beyond the bend in the stream. One of them headed in the direction of the hobbled horses.

Audra appeared behind him, pistols in hand. "Don't mind the men on the slope—must protect our horses!" Bryan cried as he frantically reloaded.

She nodded, and before he could think to order her away, leaned over the outcropping, aimed her pistol and fired at the man scrabbling toward the makeshift corral, increasingly visible now as dawn

grew nearer. The intruder clutched his chest and fell.

Bryan scarcely had time for surprise or jubilation, for another shot rang out, and another. He jerked Audra below the level of the rock and fired again.

One of the attackers screamed and grabbed at his knee. The two remaining men, firing as they went, dragged their comrade away and retreated down the hill.

Methodically, Bryan fired and reloaded. But without bothering to retrieve the other two wounded men, the remainder of the group mounted horses tethered by the stream and rode off.

The whole encounter had lasted barely a few minutes.

Breathing hard, Bryan kept his loaded rifle trained on the two downed desperadoes, but when after several minutes neither stirred, he lowered his weapon. He'd approach them carefully to be sure, but it appeared they'd pose no further threat.

Only then did he look back at Audra. "Sweetheart, you're an incredible shot."

Part of her hair had come down and rock dust powdered her chin and cheek. "I know," she said, and grinned. "So are you."

And suddenly the mere fact of being alive was so sweet, so precious, he laughed out loud. Laying

down the rifle, he pulled Audra into his arms and kissed her.

She kissed him back, holding his head close, opening her mouth to his assault, startling him by nibbling at his lips while her tongue sought his.

At its first liquid touch he lost all track of time or place. Existence narrowed to the glorious taste of her wickedly ravenous mouth, the feel of her warm pliant body.

Groaning, he leaned her back against the rock, his hands tracing her sides, cupping her shoulders, seeking to fit her more closely against him. So intent was he on kissing her harder, deeper, it took him a moment to realize she was no longer encouraging—but resisting him, her fisted hands pushing against his chest.

Heart thundering, his inflamed body screaming a protest, he made himself release her.

She stumbled backward, away from him, one hand at her mouth. "I'm s-sorry, Bry. I can't. I just c-can't."

He shook his head, trying to clear his mind of the fog of passion and teeth-gnashing frustration.

Attack. They'd been attacked. He must make sure the remaining marauders were dead, the horses safe. They must get away before any other miscreants, having heard shots, came to investigate.

"Never mind," he told her roughly. "Get the blankets and canteens. I'll make sure our uninvited guests give us no more trouble and get the horses saddled. We're lucky—they probably were scavengers. *Bandidos* wouldn't have given up so easily. Regardless, we must make for the army train with all speed."

She nodded, then bent to gather up the pistols. Hands still shaking, he picked up ammunition and rifle, and sidestepping cautiously, made his way toward the fallen attackers.

Who were both safely dead. With a sigh of relief he trotted to the hobbled horses, soothing them and quickly getting them saddled. By the time he had them ready, Audra approached, all their remaining gear stowed and ready.

Wordlessly he gave her a hand up, then leaped onto his own horse. Together they eased their mounts down the hill to the stream, watered them, and spurred them on the road toward the army train.

They rode without speaking, both knowing it imperative that they distance themselves from the scene of the attack and reach the safety of reinforcements as quickly as possible. Bryan tried to empty his mind of all but the ride back.

He didn't want—couldn't allow himself to think of that aborted kiss, the sickening feel of Audra's

fists at his chest, struggling to push him away. The sickening thought that in an unguarded moment of desire he might have destroyed the trust he'd been working so hard to build.

The army train moved slowly and had only half a day's march on them. With Bryan driving their mounts as hard as he dared, just after noon they spotted the dust cloud in the distance that announced the army's passage.

Bryan signaled Audra to rein in. Immense relief eased the sharp anxiety that had dogged him since the sun set the millennium ago that was last night. They would make it. Audra would be safe.

"We've done it," she said, echoing his thoughts. "We're safe now, thank God. And you, Bryan. I apologize—"

"No need," he interrupted, knowing he could not stand it if she regretted that kiss. "Let's get back before Mrs. O'Malley worries herself into a decline."

Tacitly she accepted the rebuff. They urged their tired horses onward, and twenty minutes later rode in to the exclamations and excited hollos of the rear guard.

There was little chance for any private word once they'd caught up with the wagons. "I shall have to go take my tongue-lashing from the colonel," Bryan told Audra after Mrs. O'Malley had

fussed, scolded and gone off to procure tea. "Rest if you can. I'll see you tonight."

He endured Colonel Richardson's scathing reprimand with such unaccustomed meekness that, when his commander had at last finished shredding Bryan's character and judgment, the colonel was moved to drop the disciplinary action he'd threatened and restore Bryan's permission to accompany his wife to Lisbon. Abjuring Bryan to take his worthless carcass off and get some sleep, the colonel dismissed him.

Exhausted though he was, there'd be no rest for him until the army made camp tonight. How would Audra greet him then? With understanding and forgiveness—or with cold, distant wariness in her eyes?

Uttering a fervent prayer that it be the former and not the latter, he grimly hung on in the saddle and waited for evening.

At Mrs. O'Malley's insistence, Audra slept for a short time in one of the wagons. She'd need the rest to summon enough energy to get Bryan's gear stowed and the dinner prepared after the column halted for the night.

He'd be exhausted, for though she'd caught at least a few snatches of sleep, she was reasonably

sure he'd had none. He'd give her, she imagined, no argument about who took the cot tonight.

She was still too tired herself to puzzle out what had happened between them on that rock ledge after the attack. Whatever it had been, one thing she knew clearly—only at her invitation had Bryan turned what had been a euphoria of deliverance into something more.

An inseparable jumble of emotions—pride, anguish, terror, pleasure—overcame her whenever she remembered the short fierce battle and the kiss she'd welcomed, deepened and fled from.

Would he think her a tease, a wanton, to promise yes with her body and then say no? A ''no'' he was then not bound to respect, as Jer always claimed?

Whatever he thought, she owed him an apology—again. As for the rest, she suspected they were both too tired to deal with it tonight.

And in truth, by the time Bryan reached their billet he was so stumbling with fatigue he could scarcely walk. After a minimum of conversation he took the dinner offered, wolfed it down, and without argument fell into the cot, asleep almost before his body met the blankets.

Scarcely less tired, Audra bedded down soon after. But hours later, as the dark sky lightened to dawn, something woke her. She glanced over—and

saw Bryan's cot was empty. Sitting up, she noticed his tall figure hunched by the embers of the campfire.

Drawn by a need to see him too strong to explain or deny, quietly she rose, threw a cloak around her and went to join him.

He looked up at her approach, reached out a hand. She took it and sat on the camp stool beside him.

"Are you still angry with me?" she asked softly.

He lifted her hand and kissed it. "Angry? When was I angry with you?"

"When I...turned you away. Then, on the ride back you were so distant and silent I thought..."

"We set limits before we ever began this bargain. I...exceeded those, rather flagrantly. How could I be angry with you for enforcing them?"

"I did—rather encourage you at first. Which was very bad of me, since I... Oh, Bry, I wish I could respond, but I can't."

"Too many hurtful memories?"

She shuddered, unable to stop herself. "Yes."

"Is that what Jer did?" Bryan said unexpectedly. "Went cold and distant if you chastised him for his infidelities or tried to withhold yourself from him?"

"Y-yes. But I wasn't often able to withstand

his…persuasion. He always sounded so sincere when he apologized! I suppose at first, I blamed it on my being with child, and then afterward on my long recovery. By then the pattern was established, but I kept hoping…hoping he might really change, as he claimed he would." She laughed, a bitter sound with little humor. "I was a fool, I suppose."

"No, Audra. You honored your vows. Even growing up, Jer had always to take the lead, be the one in charge. I suppose he felt he must control you in marriage, too. That was very wrong of him—but it wasn't your fault. You shouldn't blame yourself for offering forgiveness."

"Except that it was my…weakness that spurred him on. Once, when he was deep enough in his cups to be truthful, he told me that it was my fault he strayed—if I were coolly indifferent or ignored it, he might stop. But the idea of having to overcome my repugnance, make me accept him again was a game too delicious to resist."

Bryan snorted. "And that, my dear, sounds like a rationalization offered by a man too selfish to exercise self-control. No, Audra, Jer was the only one responsible for his acts. That he somehow twisted them to make you feel ashamed of the honest reactions of your own body was despicable."

Bryan's exoneration could make no difference—

and yet somehow it lightened the burden of guilt and pain she carried. "Thank you for that."

"If I seemed angry earlier, it was only because I was furious with myself for allowing us into a position where I could not keep you safe."

"But you did! If I'd gone alone as I'd intended, I should never have survived."

"I should have insisted you remain here, as Mrs. O'Malley wished. She was right. It was idiocy to do what we did."

"Perhaps, though I don't think Ensign Wetherford would agree. But we made a good team, did we not?"

He smiled. "That we did. Stay with me after the army, and perhaps we can hire ourselves out as a sharpshooting act at Astley's."

"Pegging the aces out of cards at thirty paces while galloping on horseback?"

"Something like."

"Ah, but Astley's can't offer a sky like this. Or the warmth of the sun on your back, the wind tearing through your hair as you gallop across a wild arroyo. Nights around a campfire, troopers singing in the distance and a glory of stars overhead. Despite the real horrors of this war, when I remember my time here it will be those things I recall, and the bonds of friendship with men and women of courage and endurance, like Mrs. O'Malley and

Ensign Wetherford. Experiences I shall always treasure.

He laughed softly. "That's exactly how I feel about it. Please, Audra, won't you stay here and share it with me? I know things happened with Jer that will take you time to forget—much more time than we'll have before Lisbon. But the bond between us is strong enough that together, we can move beyond the past. Build from affection something beautiful and lasting. I'm willing to work toward that—and wait for the other, as long as it takes."

A terrible desire possessed her to say yes, to accept the comfort he continued to offer and remain in this stark, harsh, beautiful land she'd come to love.

But that would be cheating him—and setting herself up once again for misery. The anguish of lying near him, craving and avoiding his touch with almost equal fervor. Of always watching and wondering how many days or weeks or months of harmony they'd share before the lapses would begin—the missed meals explained by facile excuses, the nights when he came in near dawn, soap not quite covering the scent of another woman.

She took a shuddering breath. "I'm sorry—there, I have need of my cards again. But I cannot.

Please, do not ask it of me. Now I—I think I shall try to get some more sleep.''

A wishful part of her yearned to accept what he offered—the possibility of a full, lasting marriage with a man who seemed a better candidate for remaining honorable over a lifetime than any other man she could think of. But the wiser part, the bruised, experienced part, demanded she refuse. Once she'd joyously given her heart and hand to a man she thought she knew. Falling after another such reckless leap of faith would surely destroy what little strength and self-respect she still possessed.

Especially since, incredible though it seemed in such a short time, she was now certain she'd fallen in love with Bryan Langford.

Chapter Eight

A few days later they left the army encamped around Badajoz and set out with a small party of convalescents and officers on furlough. And this morning, some ten days after their departure, the excited shouts of the advance guard announced they'd sighted the distant walls of Lisbon.

Bryan looked ahead and sighed, feeling as if he were caught in a noose that slowly tightened day by day. Although Audra had relaxed around him again, brightening his evenings with her wit and laughter, she also kept her distance.

And by every nonverbal means possible told him she would not again discuss the subject of their marriage.

Short of the declaration she wouldn't believe, he'd done everything he could think of to demonstrate how much he cherished her. But time was

running out. By night's end they would be billeted within the city walls. Tomorrow he'd have to see about passage home for her, as promised.

And find a chaplain to begin annulment proceedings.

Only one thing could prevent that now. He'd vowed upon their wedding morn he'd use any means within his power to keep her. Was he prepared to take her, by force if necessary, to make sure annulment was no longer possible?

He knew with a conviction that resonated to the core of him that Audra, given sufficient time, could be the wife he wanted, their marriage complete in every way. Every day together pushed the trauma of her past farther away, strengthened the trust he was nurturing. She cared deeply for him—of that he was also convinced. He was all but an iota short of certain he could and would make her happy.

If only he could get her to stay long enough to figure that out for herself.

If she left for England, the annulment in train, he might never have that opportunity again. Despite any pledge he might extract from her to wait for him, as a woman with no fortune of her own she'd be entirely at the bidding of her late husband's family. Knowing the icily efficient Amelia, by the time the war ended and he returned, she'd have managed to marry Audra off to some de-

pendent Amelia considered more worthy of her despised sister-in-law's proper station.

If he seduced—or forced—her into consummating their union, he might destroy any chance to finally win her trust. Even though by doing so, he was preserving for her a future he was certain, once free of the demons of the past, she would surely choose herself.

But by robbing her of choice, would he not become just as venal as the husband whose twisted manipulations still haunted her uneasy dreams?

And so his tortured thoughts vacillated between the mistake of holding her and the mistake of letting her go.

Wearily he shook his head. For another few days he would have her with him. He must make that time as unforgettable as possible.

After a day in the city, Bryan had all prepared. He'd bribed the hotel manager to evict another customer and give them his best suite, where, among their several rooms, Audra was persuaded to stay. He'd ordered a sumptuous dinner for tonight. He'd even, with heartbreak in every nerve, procured tickets for Audra on the next packet home and arranged an appointment with the resident Anglican priest for tomorrow morning.

An appointment he prayed they would not have to keep.

Audra had spent the day visiting the convalescents in the hospital at Bellam. Ever conscious of the clock ticking down in his head, his pulse accelerated with anticipation and dread when she arrived back at their hotel.

"I told Señor Lilva you'd want a bath," he told her as she walked in. "Just ring when you're ready."

"How kind, Bry. I should love one." As she walked by him, she wrinkled her nose appreciatively. "Mmm, nice. I see you've already availed yourself of the opportunity."

How he wished he'd dared chance bathing with her—or following her into her chamber, offering to help now.

Later, he promised himself.

"I've ordered dinner sent up when you're ready."

"We shall not have to go out? Ah, heaven! Thank you, Bry. Have them send the water now, please?" With a smile she disappeared into her room.

"I left you a present," he called after her. "I thought you might wear it for dinner tonight. I expect you're rather tired of the gowns from the march."

She emerged a moment later, holding out a dinner gown of peach satin. "It's beautiful, Bryan! The loveliest thing I've owned in years. I should be delighted to wear it tonight."

While she bathed, he supervised the laying out of the table—hothouse roses, fine tallow candles, a glimmer of plate and crystal, the side table loaded with chafing dishes boasting paella and curried lamb, vegetables, sweetmeats and a fine local rioja.

Fortunately he'd finished pouring her wine when she emerged, for he'd surely have missed the glass. The peach satin accented her pale skin and dark hair, its low cut emphasizing the breath-catching swell of her breasts. Though he'd been ravenous at the smell of the waiting feast, after one look at Audra he was ready to dispense with that meal.

He'd worn his best uniform, as well, gold polished, his cravat freshly starched. He made her a deep bow.

"Oh, Bry, how lovely it all looks."

"Not half so lovely as my wife."

He seated her and took his own chair, then raised his glass. "To the prettiest sharpshooter in Portugal."

Throughout the meal, he amused her with anecdotes of campaigning and kept her wineglass

filled. Audra relaxed, adding her own stories, her laughter as sparkling as the crystal glasses.

Later, as he peeled oranges for her, below their window street musicians paused to serenade them. While the mandolin played a plaintive ballad, he fed her the oranges, pausing to trace his finger over her lips. When juice spurted down her chin, with the napkin he slowly wiped it away, caressing her skin with the soft linen.

When the minstrels left, after an exchange of coins and one final love song, he rose from the table.

"Time for bed, sweet wife." Catching up a branch of candles, he offered her his arm.

She took it, sighing. "Bryan, that was wonderful."

The wine flowed molten in his blood, already fired by her nearness and beauty. His pulse throbbed in his ears, every sense acutely alert. *Now,* the voice urged him. *Now.*

He walked her into her chamber, allowing his hip, his shoulder, to brush against hers as they passed through the doorway, then set the candles on the bedside table.

Dark eyes soft and hazy, she smiled at him, her lips full and wine-red. She would taste of oranges and rioja and the innocent sweetness that was Audra.

Gently he placed his hands on her shoulders, worshiping their bareness with his fingertips before he lowered his mouth over hers.

At first he merely brushed her lips, as he'd done that night in their tent, outlining her mouth with his own. Not until she put a hand on his shoulder, parted her lips on a sigh, did he move the kiss deeper.

And even then, at first he only circled his open mouth around hers, letting his top lip snag against her teeth, until with a groan she moved her tongue to touch it.

His hands clenched on her shoulders but he fought for control, wanting to entice, bedevil, seduce her into making the next move. He felt sweat break out on his forehead, between his shoulder blades, instincts driving him to push her down on the bed, take more, now, but he kept himself rigidly upright.

Not until her tongue grew more insistent, actively searching its evasive mate, did he slide his into her mouth and twine them together.

She moaned deep in her throat, her fingers moving from his shoulder to his head, winding themselves in his dark hair, and she shifted her body closer.

Then, finally, he took her mouth hard, a full-out sensual assault of teeth, lips and tongue as he

lifted her and leaned her back against the pillows, laying the tortured hardness straining at his breeches against the softness of her satin-clad thighs. Still plumbing the sweetness of her mouth, he moved one hand beneath her skirt, smoothing it up the silk of her stocking to tease the bare skin above.

Peel down the stockings, coax up her skirts, strip open the buttons of his breeches, all while soothing her with drugging kisses, and in a few glorious minutes she could be his, his for all time.

But even as his body screamed for completion, his mouth hungered to explore the taste of her breasts, her belly, the marvels between her gently parted thighs, he pulled back. Groaning, desire beyond keen and into pain, he forced himself to release her mouth and move away.

He couldn't take her. Desperately as he wanted her, hopelessly as he loved her, he couldn't rob her of that choice. He had given his word.

Knowing in the morning he would damn himself as fourteen kinds of a fool, he staggered to his feet. "G-good night, Audra," he gasped, made her a ragged salute, and stumbled to the door.

The cold air left behind after Bryan's abrupt departure pulled Audra from her wine-induced haze.

Her senses, fired by his teasing advances, clamored for more.

She sat up abruptly, aghast. Had Bryan not pulled away from her, she would have let him do whatever he wished—and the hard bulge he'd nudged against her thighs left no doubt what that was.

Thank heavens he'd come to his senses before old memories rose up to choke her and revolt her, spoil what had been the most beautiful evening of her life.

But she wasn't revolted now—she was hungry, starved for the touch of the man she now admitted she loved. Who deserved far better than she, and whom she intended to honor by restoring to him his freedom to choose a worthier bride.

But before she did so, could she not steal this one perfect evening? Let him wash away with his sure and gentle touch the ugliness that had come to taint the very notion of physical love, and leave her with one shining memory of how beautiful, pure and selfless the act of joining could and should be.

She sat up abruptly, still wine-dizzy. If she truly wanted this, she would have to lure him to it.

Part of her argued caution—what if she went in to him, enticed him—and the demons overcame her again?

But no, Bryan's honest passion would keep them at bay, make what had become tawdry and cruel new again.

She sprang out of bed, hastily stripped off the lovely gown, the silken stockings, pulled the pins from her hair. Clad only in the translucent silk chemise, before she lost her nerve or changed her mind, she hurried to find Bryan.

He was standing before the window in a pool of moonlight, the wineglass dangling between his fingers. He turned when he heard her approach, and caught his breath.

"Audra? Is...is something wrong?"

Marshaling her courage, she walked over, laid her hands against his shoulders and leaned up to kiss him. "Love me, Bryan," she whispered. "Help me blot out the ugly memories. Make it beautiful for me again."

He swallowed hard. "Are you sure, Audra?"

"Please, Bryan."

He moved a hand to tilt up her chin. "Tell me what you want, Audra. Anything. Everything."

"Touch me—" she took his hand and moved it to her breast "—here—" then slid his palm to cup the slight swell of her belly "—and here." She moved his fingers lower still, to rub slowly back and forth over her mound and between her parted thighs. "And ah, yes, *here*."

She dropped her hand away. With both of his he repeated the pattern, slower, fingers lifting her breasts into the stroke of his thumbs across her nipples, then tracing the lengths of each individual rib, the outline of hipbone, the crevasse of belly button, the roundness of thigh from outside to in, and moving in little swirling eddies across the tight curls between.

While his hands played there, she feverishly worked at the buttons of his jacket, the knot of his cravat. "I want to feel your bare chest, like I did at the river."

He stopped in his explorations long enough to shed jacket, shirt, and cravat. "What now, my princess?"

"Touch me. Without the chemise."

He gathered the hem and pulled the garment slowly, slowly from her ankles upward, catching it against her knees, twisting and pulling the silk against her thighs and belly, winding it taut under her breasts so that her peaked nipples showed in sharp relief, then barely brushing the tip of his finger against them. Finally he took pity and pulled it free, leaving her body naked to his gaze, damp with desire and painted with moonlight.

She was trembling now as he repeated the journey of his hands, this time against bare skin. While his slight, glancing touch set the nerves aflame in

each morsel of skin they passed, her seeking fingers found warm hard muscle and flat taut nipples of his chest, twined in the thick soft hair.

And when his hands reached her thighs, traced the lines and angles of her body to their natural center, she cried out, legs suddenly so boneless she nearly fell. "Take me...to bed now," she gasped.

"As you command, my lady," he said hoarsely, and lifted her in his arms.

He laid her on the bed. "And now?"

"Love...me completely. Show me loving... without regret."

Her hands worked the buttons of his breeches, yanked them down. His breathing labored, he stripped them off and knelt beside her on the bed, letting her accustom herself to the sight and size of him.

"Anything you want, tell me. Anything I do you do not like, stop me."

"I want it all."

She lay back, pulling him forward, but evading her urgent touch, he gently stilled her while his mouth and tongue and teeth retraced the same journey as his hands, driving her gasping to the peak and over, then holding her until the shattered pieces came back together and she was ready to begin the march again. This time, as she lay under him begging for completion, he let her stroke and

taste his length, before sheathing himself deep and making them one.

The cry of a gull in the early dawn woke Bryan to the wonder of Audra in his arms. Naked, greedy, passionate Audra whom he'd made his wife in every sense, several times over in the glory of that night.

His wife now, for always.

Surely after last night, when she had turned to a shimmering iridescence of pleasure in his arms, surely she meant to make their union permanent.

Silently he slipped from the bed and went to order coffee. In spite of the deep relaxation of sated senses, a nagging unease kept his joy in check.

He thought to find her still abed, but when he returned she was already up, sitting at the dressing table combing out her tangled curls.

"Sweeting," he murmured, and bent to kiss her neck.

Dread slammed into his stomach when she ducked away. "Bryan," she said, her voice expressionless. Her back still to him, she pulled the comb through her hair with quick, jerky movements.

And ache of despair settled over him. He was losing her, after all.

"You are up early," he said, unable to think of anything clever.

"We have much to do. Passage to arrange, and that chaplain to visit."

The chaplain's call—a death knell to his hopes.

Like a bloody masochist, he had to make it clear. "You...won't be staying, then?"

He thought her hand on the comb trembled, but she kept her back to him. "I thought we'd settled that long since."

Trying to ignore the knife blades slicing a pattern inside his gut, Bryan straightened. If even now she was still resolved, there was nothing left to say, no reason to delay longer. Wordlessly he walked to the desk, pulled a folded sheet of paper from the drawer, and held it out.

Audra took precise, measured breaths, afraid if she did not control every motion, every thought, the devastation of knowing she must soon lose Bryan would undermine her resolve.

So achingly beautiful had last night been, she knew she must not stay. No matter how much leaving Bryan would hurt, bitter experience had already taught her how much worse it would be to watch the pure love they'd shared gradually weaken, be chipped away over time, indiscretion

by indiscretion, and finally tarnished with the dross of humiliation and pain.

Bryan handed her a paper. Careful to keep her expression neutral, she looked up. "What is it?"

"Read it."

She took and scanned it quickly. "The *Merry Alice,* sailing tomorrow at 10:00 a.m. You've bought passage for me? When? I thought the captain told you the vessel would be too full."

"The day we arrived in Lisbon." He sighed. "I wanted the passage arranged and paid for, as stipulated in our bargain. I had hoped to persuade you not to use it."

She chanced a swift look at him, and was surprised by how infinitely sad and weary he looked. Would he truly miss her? She must not think like that, or her resolve would weaken.

After all, he'd managed without a wife for years before she'd agreed to perform those functions for him. Most of them, anyway.

All of them last night.

She wouldn't think of that—she couldn't. But neither could she regret the magic that had happened between them.

"Thank you, that was most kind," she managed to say through her tight throat.

He smiled. "It is rather lowering to my self-

esteem to think you prefer being Amelia's drudge to remaining here as my wife."

"Perhaps. But when I lay in my narrow bed staring at the ceiling after a day spent running at her beck and call, at least I will not have to wonder in whose arms you are sleeping that night."

He slammed his fist down on the bedside table, startling her. "Damn it, Audra, will you never believe it? I am not Jer!"

He ran a hand through his sleep-tousled hair, disordering it further. "Just once, before you leave me, I'm going to say it. You probably won't believe me, and you may not think it matters, but I love you, Audra. I've always loved you. Since we've lain together now, you can't think I say it just to seduce you. I'm not a man like Jer, who's clever with words. Even if I were, if all that we shared on the road to Lisbon, all we shared last night, failed to convince you we belong together, then no fancy words of mine ever could."

"You love me?" Despite the hints of Mrs. O'Malley and the evidence of caring she'd observed with her own eyes, the notion still seemed too fantastic to be true. "But if you loved me back then, why did you never say anything?"

"What was the point? When from the time you grew up, you never had eyes for anyone but Jer-

emy. Would you even have noticed if I'd tried to pay you court?''

''I—I don't know.''

''I thought it would only make you feel you had to choose between Jer and me, and destroy the friendship we'd all shared.'' He gave her a wry smile. ''Though I suppose if I'd truly thought you'd choose me, I would have done it.'' His smile faded. ''As we now know, his friendship wouldn't have been so great a loss.''

''He changed, Bry. The war and…everything.''

She bit her lip, trying to sort out the swirl of thoughts that flurried in her mind with the speed and turbulence of a whirlwind. As friends and comrades they had done so well on the journey to Lisbon. As lovers…ah, she dare not even think how well matched they'd been. But later, when the shiny luster of newness had worn off, might he be faithful to her?

Had Jeremy been so attentive at first? She simply couldn't remember. No, much as she loved Bryan—because she loved him so much—she couldn't risk it. He deserved a wife not already flawed and broken, who might, with her doubts and recrimination, bring about the very destruction she feared.

But—if Bryan loved her, truly loved her— would her leaving pain him? She'd never even

considered it might cause him more than a mild disappointment.

"Will...will my going be difficult for you?"

"Difficult! What do you want me to say? That time heals all wounds, that I will pick up my life and go on? I could recite you a hundred clichés, I suppose. But the truth?" He took a deep breath. "When you board that ship, my heart goes with you. But then, you've carried it everywhere since the summer you turned sixteen."

She felt dizzy, struggling to take it all in. Bryan, loving her. Aching to have her depart. Doomed, as she was, to loneliness. Two separate beings who were both so much more complete together.

When she remained silent, Bryan walked over and pulled his uniform coat off the chair. "I suppose there's nothing left, then, but to go perjure my soul and swear to the priest that the marriage was never consummated."

His bleak words startled her. "Must we do that?" She didn't relish the idea of prevaricating to a priest.

"My dear soon-to-be-former wife, though your remarriage was hasty, it was entirely legal. The only way to obtain the annulment you require is to attest to non-consummation. Were you not a

widow, I suspect you'd be subjected to a physical examination, as well.''

It suddenly struck her how difficult that would have to be for Bryan, who truly exemplified the motto of his regiment—*Veritus et Virtus*.

''Bryan, do you remember when I was eight, newly come to the neighborhood, and we had that battle in the squire's apple orchard?''

Pausing in fastening up his tunic, he looked at her curiously. ''Yes. You told the squire I'd taunted you, so it was really my fault when you started throwing apples.''

''I'd thought you would deny it, that it would be your word against mine, and we'd probably both get off with a scolding.''

''Instead, the squire said it was most ungentlemanly to abuse a lady. Father caned me, I remember.''

''I know, and I felt awful about it. But you would not lie, not even to escape a caning. I've never known you to lie about anything. Ever.''

He smiled wryly, hands once again plying the loops at his tunic. ''Not even about the likelihood of being attacked by *bandidos*.''

''But you would stand before one of God's own priests and swear our marriage was never consummated? You would do that for me?''

Hands stilling on the loops, Bryan turned to gaze at her. "I would do anything for you."

The words sank into her, soaking into every pore and crevice. From deep within her a surge of emotion welled up that she was powerless to stop, desperately as her logical, careful mind tried to resist it.

She couldn't leave. Couldn't go knowing he loved her and her leaving would cause him suffering perhaps as intense as her own. Couldn't leave with him offering her one last, golden chance for a future so much more brilliant than the one to which she'd resigned herself, if only she had the courage to embrace it and believe in it.

Just the same, she was petrified, so terrified of all she was risking that though her lips opened she couldn't seem to form words.

Bryan finished buttoning his jacket. "You'll want to get some provisions for the journey." He didn't look at her. "And, Audra..." His voice trailed off and he cleared his throat. "When this war is over, when we've beaten Boney and Wellington sends us home, if I make it through intact, I'd like to stop by and see how you're getting on. Will that be all right?"

Bryan had been so competent, equal to every threat even when outnumbered and battling ma-

rauders, the idea of his being wounded or killed had never before penetrated. "No!" she cried out in alarm.

He looked back, hurt in his eyes. "I thought, whatever else happened, we'd always be friends. Do you hate me that much for last night?"

She shook her head and forced herself to speak now, despite the shaking in her legs and the terror that had her pulse beating in her ears so hard she feared she might faint. "Oh, B-Bryan, I am so afraid to ask, but d-do you think you might be able to love me, only me, for the rest of your life?"

His fingers hooking the belt at his waist faltered. His gaze leaped to hers, his expression searching.

She swallowed, sure he could hear the frantic beat of her heart halfway across the room.

His eyes never leaving her face, he walked over, took her hand, and kissed it. "Until my last breath."

Giddy from lack of air, she remembered to inhale.

"Let me be sure I understand you, Audra. Do you mean to continue being my wife, in every sense of the word? Campaigning companions, friends, lovers whenever I can seduce you into it, night or day, indoors or out?"

"Especially that. And since I'm vastly in need

of comfort, and suppose we no longer need an appointment with the chaplain, now would be a good time to start.''

The curve of his lips into a smile was joy in motion. ''Now and always, I am yours to command.''

* * * * *

Dear Reader,

After growing up near the U.S. Naval Academy, having a grandfather who built submarines and a cousin who commanded them, I've always had a special affection for men in uniform—in fact, I married one! In a world which often focuses on "me," military men and women live the old-fashioned beliefs of duty, honor and country. Often far from home, they serve knowing they might be called upon to sacrifice their lives at their nation's call. So I'm delighted my wonderful editors, Margaret Marbury and Tracy Farrell, allowed me to contribute a story celebrating a military hero and his bride.

The only thing Lt. Bryan Langford prizes as highly as honor is his childhood friend Audra, whom he's secretly loved for years. When she's tragically widowed, Bryan is delighted to assist her, unaware of the dark secrets that will make winning his lady a Herculean task.

Audra Saybrooke's bitter marriage destroyed her faith in love and honor. After her husband's death, she longs for the peace and safety of England. Her old friend Bryan's kindness in helping her reach that haven inspires gratitude, but she's convinced her shattered heart could never trust again.

I hope you'll enjoy their story. And be sure to look for my next historical, *The Proper Wife*, on sale in July 2001.

Julia Justiss

*Please turn the page for
an exciting preview of Julia's
upcoming Harlequin Historical,*

THE PROPER WIFE,

on sale July 2001.

Chapter One

Gloved hands gripping the windward rail, Colonel Lord St. John Sandiford—Sinjin—braced himself against a gust that threatened to rip the shako from his head and gazed into the gray curtain of wind-whipped fog. Through a momentary cleft in the drizzle, he spotted the faint outline of the approaching shore. England. *The conquering hero, home from the wars at last....*

In the early morning chill a week later, Sinjin rode his last remaining horse from the offices of his solicitor in the city back to Westminster. As if compelled, he drew rein for a moment on the street before Horse Guards, as unobtrusive now in his nondescript brown jacket and worn riding breeches as the uniformed guards outside army headquarters were resplendent in scarlet coats and gold lace.

None of the pickets glancing casually toward him, in the faded garments he'd worn while riding as an intelligence-gatherer for Colcoquin Grant, would suspect his shabby apparel concealed an officer of the Tenth Hussars.

Former officer, he amended. A poignant regret stabbed him, as it had yesterday when, after resigning his commission, for the last time he removed the blue tunic and furred pelisse and packed them away. An outsider now, no longer part of the army that had been his life this last six years.

After the unpalatable news delivered by his solicitor an hour ago, 'twas a good thing he had determined to sell out—even that relatively small bit of cash would be welcome. Jeffers's laconic letters had not overstated his dire financial condition; if anything, matters were worse than his batman imagined.

He'd already, with a sense of grief nearly akin to the losing of a friend, turned his other horses over to the staff at Tattersall's for the next sale, keeping only Valiant, the sure-footed companion of many a hard march. Unless he took the exceedingly stringent measures outlined in prosaic detail by his man of business, he'd very soon not be able to afford him.

The last of his solicitor's recommendations was

hardly unexpected: find a rich bride. Mr. Walters had even added, with a small smile, the same compliment offered by Alex on the ship last week— that for a man of his birth and address, the procuring of a suitable heiress should prove no very difficult task.

To that end, his man concluded, running a pained eye over Sinjin's shabby coat and breeches, he believed the beleaguered estate could stand a small advance of funds to allow his lordship to procure suitable garments for the upcoming season.

Trussed up like a prize trout, he thought grimly, and realized that despite all his ruminations on the subject, not until this morning had the stark reality struck home. He must marry an heiress, and soon.

True, at odd intervals in the six years since his father's death revealed the catastrophic total of the late Lord Sandiford's debts, he'd considered the notion. But each time he'd advanced on the idea only to retreat in distaste, vaguely trusting at some future date he would discover an alternate attack on his pecuniary difficulties that might allow him to outflank the prospect.

Time for such an alternative had run out, Mr. Walters had just demonstrated with chilling clarity. Unless he wished to see the remaining lands and possessions of his ancestors put on the block, Vis-

count St. John Michael Peter Sandiford must now rig himself out to enter unholy assemblage of social events known as the Marriage Mart, there to hawk his looks and lineage as shamelessly as a harlot strutting her wares outside a Haymarket theater.

He took a deep breath and swallowed, the bitter taste of bile in his mouth. No wonder he'd been so reluctant to return to England.

Enough, he told himself. Time to stop bleating like a raw recruit at the first cannonade and get on with the sorry business.

He could drop by the establishments in St. James on his way back to his modest rented rooms at North Audley Street, or perhaps pop in to the Albany and visit Alex. His young lieutenant, plump in the pocket and eager for the beginning of the season, could doubtless advise him which of the gentlemen's shops he should patronize to bring his wardrobe up to snuff. Even to his own admittedly non-discriminating eye, in his current attire, the only civilian clothes he possessed, he looked like a groom.

Not exactly husband material for one of the overdressed, overcoiffed and over-bejeweled damsels over whose perfumed hands he would soon be bowing. He allowed himself a sardonic smile at the thought of the probable expression on one of those

hothouse flowers were he to present himself at her feet in his current garb.

By now he'd reached Picadilly, but his mood was still too uncertain for company. Perhaps a hard gallop would settle him. At least the air and the bridle path of Hyde Park were still free. Turning his mount, he headed west.

Instead of continuing along Picadilly, however, he entered the hubbub of traders going to Shepherd's Market, picking his path north until he reached the relative calm of Curzon Street. As he neared the handsome Georgian house set back from the roadway, he pulled the horse to a halt, his heartbeat accelerating.

'Twas the disorienting changes of the past few days—his life once again turned upside down—that had brought on this fit of black melancholy, he told himself. He'd indulge it but a moment longer and then ride on.

As if in a dream he dismounted, looped Valiant's reins around a post, and silently approached the quiet dwelling.

Though it was early enough for most of the aristocracy to be still abed, somewhere within those stately walls he knew Sarah would be working. Not his Sarah anymore, the girl who'd grown up his neighbor, friend, and confidante, companion or instigator of dozens of childhood adventures. The

girl who'd metamorphosed from boyish hoyden to young lady and taken his heart with her. The lady who for the past three years and three months had been wife to the Marquess of Englemere.

What little was left of that organ he believed long since shattered seemed to convulse, sending a shudder marrow-deep. *Ah, sweet Sarah, my one and only love.*

She was well, he knew. Though after he rejoined his regiment three years ago he'd resisted opening her first two letters, intending to destroy them unread, in the end he'd succumbed to the need to preserve at least the feeble link of friendship. Reception of a new letter, full of the most interesting of the events taking place back in London, had rapidly become a high point in the mostly dull routine of his days. He'd kept them all, including the latest received just three weeks ago, tied in a neat package that now resided on the bedside table in his North Audley Street rooms. All but one.

A slight noise at the front door riveted his attention. He'd best be moving along, before someone came out and discovered him standing like a beggar at her gate.

Before he could retrieve his grazing mount, a horse rounded the corner and galloped toward him at a reckless pace. A peddler scurried out of range,

his display of pans clanging to the pavement, several housemaids squealed and abandoned their feather dusters on the roadway, and he himself had to step back as the rider pulled the huge black brute of a stallion to a clattering halt.

A rider on a sidesaddle. He looked up at a feminine profile whose classic perfection of shape and smoothness of skin doubtless inspired slavish adoration in men and envy in less-favored damsels. Long curling lashes shielded the beauty's eyes, which were turned toward the horse whose neck she patted with one expensively gloved hand.

His lip curling with distaste, he noted other accoutrements that, given his experience in discharging the bills incurred for his mama's finery, he knew represented equally lavish expenditures. The wool superfine of her habit, Italian by the look of it, and a sovereign an ell at the least; the dashing bonnet of velvet and ostrich plumes, the finely-tooled leather of the riding boot in the chased silver stirrup. The price of the gold lace lavishly embellishing the bodice in, he realized, pale imitation of a Hussar's uniform coat could have fed his unit of skirmishers for a year.

And the stallion— Having just undergone the painful business of having his own cattle evaluated for auction, he judged that prime bit of blood pawing an impatient hoof before him would fetch up-

ward of five hundred pounds. In addition to being totally unsuitable for a lady's mount, a fact that precipitous bolt through the London streets had just demonstrated.

Behind the rider, the peddler stoically regathered his pans. Sinjin felt irrational anger flare. What could her lackwit of a papa been thinking, to purchase such a horse for his daughter? And the chit herself—how dare that pampered, protected, frivolous creature usurp a uniform he had just put away with such pride and regret, a uniform worn by so many in valiant struggle through the sweat and blood and filth of countless battles? He thought of Uxbridge losing a leg and Alastair his arm, of the decimated ranks of the charging Seventh, of the Twenty-Seventh Foot who had stood, and died, to a man in their square atop the bluff at St. Jean's wood.

While she, no doubt, had spent her mornings asleep in her boudoir, her afternoons primping at her mirror, and her evenings dancing until dawn.

Had his brain not been fogged with fury, even one as scornful of beauty as he might have been impressed with the brilliance of the emerald eyes now turning in his direction, or the perfection of the full soft lips opening to speak.

"You, sirrah! Hand me down, if you please, and take my horse to the mews."

His attention distracted to the butler now opening the door of Sarah's town house, a long, incredulous moment passed before he realized the beauty was addressing *him.*

"Take him yourself, Miss," he spat back.

Still too angry to think, he turned on the heel of his worn boot and strode away. With one motion he snatched up Valiant's reins and flung himself in the saddle, then spurred his mount toward the park.

Her lips parted in an "O" of surprise, Clarissa Beaumont watched the tall blond man ride off without a backward glance. Clerk or farmer or— gentleman? At any rate, *not* the servant she'd taken him to be. Though in that garb, and in front of Sarah's house where a groom usually awaited her after her morning ride, she could hardly be faulted for the mistake.

With an experienced horsewoman's eye she noted the quality of his mount and the effortless grace with which he controlled it. Quite possibly a gentleman, she concluded. Though if he were, he was the rudest and most deplorably dressed she'd ever encountered.

And, she concluded with a wry grin, the most

unimpressionable. Her oft-praised beauty had elicited from him none of the awe, astonishment or reverence she'd come to expect after four seasons as the ton's reigning Belle.

A flicker of feminine interest stirred. If he *were* a gentleman, and she *were* to meet him again, it might be quite interesting....

Harlequin Romance®

Delightful
Affectionate
Romantic
Emotional

Tender
Original

Daring
Riveting
Enchanting
Adventurous
Moving

Harlequin Romance®—
capturing the world you dream of...

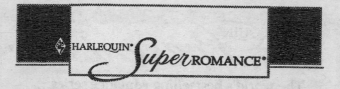

HARLEQUIN *Super*ROMANCE®

...there's more to the story!

Superromance.
A *big* satisfying read about unforgettable characters. Each month we offer *six* very different stories that range from family drama to adventure and mystery, from highly emotional stories to romantic comedies—and much more! Stories about people you'll believe in and care about. Stories too compelling to put down....

Our authors are among today's *best* romance writers. You'll find familiar names and talented newcomers. Many of them are award winners— and you'll see why!

If you want the biggest and best in romance fiction, you'll get it from Superromance!

Emotional, Exciting, Unexpected...

HARLEQUIN®
Makes any time special ®

Visit us at www.eHarlequin.com

HSDIR1

HARLEQUIN Presents

**The world's bestselling romance series...
The series that brings you your favorite authors,
month after month:**

Helen Bianchin...Emma Darcy
Lynne Graham...Penny Jordan
Miranda Lee...Sandra Marton
Anne Mather...Carole Mortimer
Susan Napier...Michelle Reid

and many more uniquely talented authors!

Wealthy, powerful, gorgeous men...
Women who have feelings just like your own...
The stories you love, set in exotic, glamorous locations...

HARLEQUIN Presents

Seduction and passion guaranteed!

HARLEQUIN®
INTRIGUE

WE'LL LEAVE YOU BREATHLESS!

If you've been looking for thrilling tales of
contemporary passion and sensuous love stories
with taut, edge-of-the-seat suspense—then
you'll love Harlequin Intrigue!

Every month, you'll meet four new heroes
who are guaranteed to make your spine tingle
and your pulse pound. With them you'll enter
into the exciting world of Harlequin Intrigue—
where your life is on the line
and so is your heart!

THAT'S INTRIGUE—
ROMANTIC SUSPENSE
AT ITS BEST!

HARLEQUIN®

Makes any time special ®

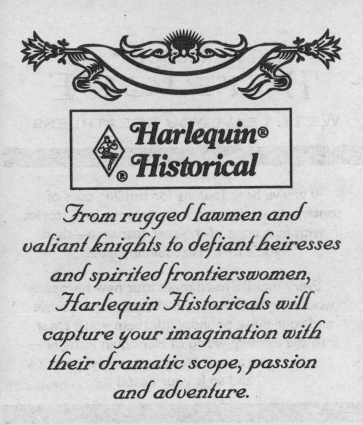

Harlequin® Historical

From rugged lawmen and valiant knights to defiant heiresses and spirited frontierswomen, Harlequin Historicals will capture your imagination with their dramatic scope, passion and adventure.

Harlequin Historicals...
they're too good to miss!

HARLEQUIN®

makes any time special—online...

eHARLEQUIN.com

your romantic life

●—Romance 101————————
♥ Guides to romance, dating and flirting.

●—Dr. Romance ————————
♥ Get romance advice and tips from
our expert, Dr. Romance.

●—Recipes for Romance ——
♥ How to plan romantic meals for you
and your sweetie.

●—Daily Love Dose————————
♥ Tips on how to keep the romance
alive every day.

●—Tales from the Heart————
♥ Discuss romantic dilemmas with other
members in our Tales from the Heart
message board.